SAVING CECI

SAVING CECI

a Kingfisher Key Story of Suspense

EMILY WYNNE STEWART

SKYE'S THE LIMIT
Publishing and Public Relations
stlpublishing.com • Galena, Ohio, USA

Published by Skye's The Limit Publishing and Public Relations
Cover design by Skye's The Limit Publishing and Public Relations
Cover art by Romolo Tavani/stock.adobe.com

Books published by Skye's The Limit Publishing and Public Relations may be available at special discounts for bulk purchases in the United States by corporations, institutions, and other organizations. For more information, please contact the Marketing Department at Skye's The Limit Publishing & Public Relations, P.O. Box 133, Galena, Ohio 43021, (740) 913-1439, or via email at info@stlpublishing.com.

Skye's The Limit Publishing and Public Relations
P.O. Box 133, Galena, Ohio 43021 • (740) 913-1439
www.STLpublishing.com

Published in the United States of America.

Paperback ISBN-13: 978-1-939044-65-5
Hardbound ISBN-13: 978-1-939044-64-8
Kindle eBook ASIN: B0BMW514TB

Library of Congress Control Number: 2022949599

DEDICATION

This book is dedicated to the memory of my son Stew, who died far too young and left a hole in my heart that will never close, but whose spirit will illuminate the rest of my life.

Also my deepest thanks to Susanne Jaffe, editor par excellence and peerless friend.

This story takes place on an imaginary barrier island on the Gulf Coast of Florida. It was written before Hurricane Ian. As a former snowbird resident of the area, I watched in horror as so much of this beauty was destroyed by wind and water. My heart is with the residents who were displaced, those who died, and the families whose lives were so cruelly disrupted. I keep you in my thoughts as you work to rebuild your homes and restore this magnificent part of the country.

ACKNOWLEDGMENTS

Thanks to the unnamed Upper Arlington firefighter I met in the produce section of the grocery who took the time to answer a bunch of questions for a woman he'd never met (and no, I wasn't trying to pick up him up).

Additional thanks to Paul Jenks, for help of every kind; Tobey and Scott Huntley, for being the best kids ever; Salt and Anne Brown, for their exceptional kindness and friendship; the ladies of the '60 girls; and my nieces, Cindy Lynn and Karen Zabalaoui.

And, of course, my most grateful thanks to the team at Skye's the Limit Publishing for their wonderful work and their patience when I said, "Can you add one more thing?" And they did.

CHAPTER **ONE**

S ilence. Not even a cry for help.

On a crystalline early morning two days before Thanksgiving, Ceci Myers sat on Kingfisher Key—Florida's widest, whitest beach—staring at the azure, teal, and aquamarine swirls that characterize the Gulf of Mexico. The air was still and the water flat and shiny as a mirror. A heron strutted while the sandpipers skittered, and the pelicans rode the ground effect air currents. A cormorant dipped his head for food, but in a sort of desultory, world-weary way, as if his heart really wasn't in it.

At that hour, there were few people on the beach, but the snowbirds were out, desperate for sun after their long treks from the dark gray clouds and temperatures already careening into the twenties up north. The males of the species were often identifiable by their plumage: shorts, ill-fitting graphic tees, and sandals, often set off by socks, sometimes black, that accentuated their pale, bony legs. Usually they made her smile, but that morning she barely noticed them.

Those very same men probably noticed her, though. It was hard not to. The perfect figure accentuated by the skimpy red bikini. A tumble of silky chestnut hair that behaved even in the Florida humidity. High, chiseled cheekbones and a full, generous mouth. Gray eyes and lashes that didn't need mascara to be noticed. They might have mistaken her for a model or the trophy wife of a Key millionaire. A person for whom good luck and happiness seemed a given. They would have been wrong. The healing that always soothed her when she came to the Key hadn't materialized. Although she was exhausted by yet another sleepless night, she was too jumpy to relax.

She decided to burn off some of her twitchiness by walking. Usually when she strolled along the beach, she searched for unusual shells, but this time, after only a few steps, something else grabbed her attention. A face. A child's face, bobbing up and down in the water. With her arms stretched out at her sides and her long blonde hair splayed around her head, the little girl appeared to be standing, but Ceci could see she was beyond the sandbar off the beach, where there was a deep drop-off. She rose to her tiptoes to get a better view, and when she saw the child's gaping mouth dip into the water, she took off, dashing down the sand, her long legs carrying her into the Gulf.

Splashing through the shallows, she yelled, "Are you all right?" but there was no answer from the youngster, who floated about two yards away. Ceci sped to the edge of the sandbar, dived in, and snatched the girl, scooping her up in her arms and racing back toward the beach. Semi-conscious at most, the child was floppy and limp in Ceci's arms, and her lips were blue-white.

Startled by Ceci's dash to the Gulf, the few people wading along the water line gathered quickly. "Call 9-1-1," she shouted. "Now!"

Ceci heard a shriek. "Mandy! No!" But the voice faded as Ceci focused on the task before her. For a second or two, her mind reeled with questions. *Is she breathing? No. What do I do? Mouth to mouth? Nobody does that now unless it's for a child. Okay, she is a child. What about a neck injury? Should I tilt her head or lift her jaw? Should I cover her up to keep her warm? Or is hypothermia better? What about the salt in the water? Oh, God, I don't remember anything!*

Terrified but determined to do something, she stabilized the girl's head as best she could, gave two quick rescue breaths, and began immediate chest compressions—hard and fast. After the first thirty, she put her cheek next to the girl's face, but she felt no breath. Out of nowhere came the formula for CPR on a child: 30-2. Thirty compressions to two breaths, so she repeated the rescue breathing and returned to compressions.

Falling into the rhythm of compressions and breathing and concentrating on the little body in front of her, Ceci was barely aware of the mother's continuing cries. Thirty more. And again. She was on the seventh set of rapid compressions when she looked up and saw three medics—two men and a woman—running toward the knot of people surrounding her and the girl.

At the same time, Ceci peripherally noted at least half the people in the scrum circling the rescue attempt were recording video on their cell phones. They'll probably try to sell it to local news or hope it goes viral on YouTube, she thought. Vultures. Bottom feeders. Apparently getting their video means more to them than this child's life. Maybe they'll show it at parties. ("I wasn't three feet from that little girl! I just knew she was going to die right in front of me.") It doesn't even occur to them to offer any help.

Anger fueled her. She kept pulsing the little girl's chest until the shorter medic slid his hands under hers and took up the compressions.

Ceci fell back from her knees, gasping from exertion. As the medics began their work, she could once again hear the woman who had screamed. "I only looked away for a few seconds," she wept. "Mandy's a good swimmer. How could this happen?" She leaned over her daughter, her hands clenched one around the other and her features contorted with terror.

The rescue operation continued. Ceci watched for any sign of life. As she stared at the motionless form, she noticed the child's chest begin a shallow rise and fall. Then deeper. Suddenly the girl coughed and vomited a bit of water. After another few minutes, the second male paramedic broke out in a smile so brilliant it penetrated Ceci's foggy fatigue. "She's breathing on her own," he said, "and pinking up." He turned to the mother. "We'll transport her, Devon. She'll need to be watched for a while at the hospital. We don't know how much water she took in."

"Oh, Brian, thank you," the mom said. "Can I go along?"

"Sure," the medic answered. "It'll be good for her to see you when she comes around fully."

Obviously, the guy with the spellbinding smile knew this child and her mother, and he looked relieved to see the girl's apparent recovery. "Let's get her out of here," he said quietly to the other medics. The three positioned the child on the backboard and lifted her onto the stretcher. The little girl's green eyes popped open, and a look of fear swept across her delicate features. Her mother hovered over her, still sobbing.

The take-charge medic leaned in to speak to the child. "Hi, Mandy, it's Brian, and this is Peggy and Matt. You got into some trouble in the water, but you'll be fine. That thing in your nose is giving you oxygen."

He leaned in close to stroke the girl's forehead. "You won't be able to turn your head right now because we have a collar on you— probably not for very long. We're going to take you to the hospital to be checked out. Your mom's coming along in the ambulance, and I'll be with you, too."

As the two male medics moved the stretcher rapidly, but without apparent haste, toward the ambulance, Ceci could see Brian continuing to chat with Mandy, who seemed to be answering him. Peggy and the mother walked alongside the stretcher, the latter still shuddering and weeping.

With the crowd dispersing, Ceci rose to her feet and immediately thudded back onto the beach, yelping in pain. The medics' heads swiveled, and Peggy trotted back through the soft sand, her short, curly brunette hair bouncing with each step, to where Ceci lay, groaning and pointing to her left leg. The medic dropped to the sand next to her. "Whoa, missy," she said, "that's one nasty-looking ankle." She waved the other medics on toward the road. "I got this," she called.

"I don't know what could have happened," Ceci said. "I didn't feel anything."

"You probably hurt it while you were pulling the kid out of the water and didn't notice," Peggy said. "Your adrenaline would have been pumping, and that can block a lot of a pain." She gingerly rotated Ceci's ankle with her strong, capable hands while Ceci whimpered. "I don't think anything's broken, but you need to have it x-rayed to be sure. There's a lot of swelling. I'll call for another truck." She spoke quietly into her shoulder-mounted walkie-talkie.

"Thanks, Peggy."

"Ah, you know my name, but I don't know yours."

"I heard the other medic say it. I'm Ceci Myers."

Peggy extracted a small notebook from her back pocket. "What's your address?"

"I'm staying at La Casa de las Olas. Unit 6A."

"Date of birth?"

"September 30, 1991."

"Any medications?"

"A multivitamin. Birth control pills. Aleve sometimes. Allergy pills in the spring."

Ceci felt a sudden tremor, and a wave of nausea churned at the bottom of her throat. "Peggy, something's wrong," she said, alarmed at the abrupt onset of sickness. "I'm freezing and I feel like I'm going to throw up. I'm so dizzy."

Peggy checked Ceci's pulse. Ceci couldn't see the medic's eyes behind the dark shades, but she felt reassured by Peggy's serene expression and calm demeanor. "Remember I said you were pumping a lot of adrenaline? That rush is over now, and the chills and nausea are a reaction. Is your ankle starting to hurt?"

Ceci nodded. "Your pulse is up, but not dangerous. I'd expect to see that with as much pain as you're having and the stress you just experienced. I want you to take a couple of deep breaths, roll over on your side and relax as much as you can. I'll stay right here with you, and we'll get you a blanket from the warmer when the truck arrives." Peggy looked up. "Which is now. Here they are." Ceci closed her eyes and let herself be taken care of for the first time in weeks.

•

From near the road, he'd watched it all. Claire Cooper. Still in Florida. In the tiny red bikini he remembered so well—the one that showed off all her assets. She looked as good as she had a couple of months ago. Her hair was longer and tousled, not smooth, the way it had been the last time he saw her. But her legs were just the way he remembered them—slender and perfect for wrapping around him as they made love. A man could spend hours exploring every curve of her body. Imagining it aroused him. His eyes narrowed, and his mouth turned up in a wolfish half-smile. She'd want him, too. As much as he wanted her. He was sure of it. He considered following the ambulance to the hospital, but changed his mind. There was no rush. He had time. He'd have her soon.

CHAPTER **TWO**

At St. Luke's on the Key Hospital, Ceci could see people moving purposefully out of Mandy's cubicle in the emergency department. No one seemed alarmed or rushed, and no technology other than a portable x-ray had been carried in, so she surmised the little girl was doing well. Ceci, too, had been x-rayed. No fracture. A multicolored sprain, but not as bad as the doctor had originally thought. Her ankle wrapped, she'd been discharged, but was waiting for paperwork and the crutches she'd use for the next three days. The damp red bikini, which had been replaced by a hospital gown, lay slantwise on the bedside chair, and she'd finally stopped shivering enough to toss the warmed blankets aside and cover herself with only a sheet. Exhausted, she drowsed while she waited, not even turning on the television mounted on the wall.

Feeling movement near the E.R. cot, Ceci awakened to find the tall, handsome medic standing next to her. His azure eyes were unexpected given his black hair, a mix of features Ceci always had found irresistible. A small scar bisecting his left eyebrow was the only thing that kept him from perfection, at least as she saw it. Even when she was depleted and wrung out on the beach, it had been impossible for Ceci not to notice his beautifully muscled body, which she estimated at about six-two; his commanding presence; his quiet assurance as he handled the emergency; and his tenderness with Mandy when she came to on the backboard. And now he was only inches away.

"Hi," he said, barely this side of a whisper. "Wasn't sure you were awake. How are you doing?"

"I'm fine. Wiped out, though." Her voice, too, was quiet and tinged with fatigue.

"I'm sure you are," he said. "You worked hard out there. We haven't met. I'm Brian Walker."

"I'm Ceci..."

"Myers. I know. I got your name from Peggy. I wanted to tell you what a super job you did. Mandy looks good." He smiled at her and she noticed the right side of his mouth lifted about an eighth of an inch higher than the left; the slightly lopsided result was captivating, she thought. He probably smiled that way as child, and it was no less endearing in the man.

"You haven't been here all this time, have you, Brian?" Ceci said.

"Nah. We picked up a woman in labor a few minutes ago. Fifth child. She's in delivery now. We've brought her in before in the same condition. She's kind of a two-push gal. After Baby Three, the doc should have installed a zipper."

Ceci smiled. "Very graphic," she said.

"And very unprofessional," Brian answered, embarrassed color flooding his face. "I usually talk like this with colleagues, not civilians. I'm sorry."

"Okay by me. I won't tell anyone."

"Anyhow, I decided to check on Mandy while Matt restocks the truck. I have somebody with me who'd like to see you if you're up to it."

"I don't look so spiffy," Ceci said, "but sure." She scooted her backside farther up the cot and raised the head higher.

Brian stifled a laugh. "You look fine. You look like a hero." He motioned to someone in the hall. "Come on in and meet Ceci," he said.

A petite, curvy woman with a riot of white-blonde curls usually found only on children under the age of five; pink-and-white skin that appeared never to have seen the sun; small, even features; and huge hazel eyes stepped into the cubicle, taking a place next to Brian, who put his arm around her. "I'm Devon Carter, Mandy's mom," she said. "There aren't enough words to tell you how grateful I am to you." She seemed to be on the verge of tears again.

"Thanks, but I didn't do anything anyone else wouldn't have. Brian says she's coming along okay."

Devon's face registered surprise at Ceci's first-name familiarity with Brian. It was wiped away almost immediately by a smile as she continued the conversation.

"They tell me she'll go home tonight. You moved so fast she barely got any water in her lungs. It was so sudden! I thought drowning people yelled for help and waved their arms. How did you know what was happening?"

"When I lived in Indianapolis, a six-year-old boy drowned in a swimming pool. I covered the story. There were ten adults standing around on the pool deck and not one of them noticed the kid was in trouble. My news director and a couple of producers decided it would be good to do a story on what drowning really looks like," Ceci said, shifting the position of her injured ankle.

"You're in TV?"

"I was. I lost my job a few weeks ago. I haven't been able to find anything yet, so I came here to lick my wounds."

"Well, I'm sorry about the job," Devon said, "but I'm so glad you were on the beach today, whatever the reason." She managed a wan smile.

"I'm glad I was, too."

"I'd better get back to Mandy, but I wanted to see you. Where do you live? I'd love to bring Mandy by to let her say thank you, too."

"I'm staying at La Casa. 6A."

"I'll hope to see you soon, then. You, too, Brian," she said, touching his hand. Her eyes lost their haunted look and glistened as she gazed at him.

"Friend of yours?" Ceci said after Devon was out of earshot.

"Dev? Yeah. We grew up together. She's been gone from the Key for several years, but after she got divorced, she came back here to live. She's the assistant city manager, so we see each other a lot."

I didn't ask for her biography, Ceci thought, immediately ashamed of her flash of inappropriate jealousy about a man and woman she'd met only five minutes before.

Brian leaned in toward the cot. "You have seaweed in your hair," he said, gently disentangling it from her long curls, which had grown out from the straight, chin-length bob—the "anchor hair" required at her most recent TV job. His hand brushed her cheek and she felt an electric shimmer that ran from her face straight to the center of her body. She was certain his hand had trembled as he touched her.

She hadn't experienced a physical jolt like that in a long time. Don't do this, she thought. You're here for only a little while and who knows where later. He probably doesn't have a coherent thought in his pretty little head, and you've kissed enough of those frogs in TV. And besides, it's clear Devon's in love with him. Back off and leave well enough alone.

•

Brian was waiting in the ambulance as Matt swung up into the shotgun seat.

"Did you see her?" Matt asked.

"Oh, yeah."

"And she's okay?"

"She's fine."

"Beautiful, too, right?"

"Yep," Brian said. "She's got a weird accent, though. I can't figure it out."

"Going to try?" Matt grinned.

"No way. Anybody who looks like her has to be high maintenance. Probably spends all day staring at herself in a mirror. I'll be leaving her alone."

But he knew he wouldn't, and he wondered if she'd someday break his heart.

CHAPTER **THREE**

L urching into the kitchen on her crutches in the evening, Ceci grabbed another bag of frozen peas for her ankle and straggled back to the living room couch. She swigged down the last painkiller from the hospital, elevated her leg on the arm of the couch, adjusted the makeshift ice pack, and closed her eyes.

I saved somebody's life today, she thought, her mind muzzy and her ideas rising and falling like blobs in a lava lamp. I kept a family from having to bury their child. That was all because of me. Well, not really, I guess. Mr. Wonderful, on whose incomparable body Devon Carter seems to have planted her flag, had a lot to do with it. But I was important to the rescue. A shard of pride pierced the sadness and anger plaguing her since the implosion of her hopes and expectations a few weeks before.

She shook her head, trying to regain a semblance of clear thinking. Ever since I was a little kid, I've been the dutiful, responsible older sister. The one who crossed the T's, turned in the homework on time, and followed the rules. But there I was six weeks ago, Responsible Girl being escorted to the parking lot by station security. Humiliating.

She covered her eyes with her forearm and slipped back into a gossamer reverie. I climbed the ladder market to market, she thought. The perfect success story...until Orlando and Psycho Boss. People warned me. They said he was irrational and a heavy drinker. They said the newsroom was chaos because he had tantrums like a two-year-old. They said he swore and threw things at reporters, photogs, assignment managers, and whoever else happened to be in the line of fire. They were right. But I needed to get out of Indianapolis.

The idiot in Orlando wanted me to toss my hair and show just a tad more cleavage. To make you more accessible, he said. To make people like you. What a jerk. "Accessibility" invited exactly what I was running from. And viewers did like me. It wasn't like he was getting millions of letters a week telling him to fire the bitch. Still, the chemistry was off. Jake and I were not a great on-air marriage. Even I have to admit the truth.

Marriage. There's another sticking point, she mused, as she sought a more comfortable position for her ankle. Alex. Alex, who loved me. Who put a ring on it. And who I saw two weeks later parked in his car with Nicolette Graeme, my former close friend, on whom he appeared to be performing a tonsillectomy with his tongue.

Ceci giggled a little as she followed her medication-addled train of thought. Alex was apparently a very thorough surgeon. It was clear he had assessed Nicolette's heart health prior to the throat surgery because her blouse was open, and her new off-the-shelf breasts spilled over the top of her expensive lacy bra. Apparently he was performing a comprehensive examination below the waist as well, given all the moaning. All this in a public park, for Pete's sake, and he never came home that night.

The next day I was...what did they call it at the station? Deselected. God, what a bunch of crap. They kicked my butt to the curb. Now it seems like the rules don't work anymore. Nothing works anymore.

Images washed through Ceci's mind as the pill grabbed hold and she wavered close to the twilight zone at the edge of awareness. She envisioned a zebra in a field of bright flowers. Exactly, she thought. I'm the zebra. My life is black and white in a world where everybody else lives in color. Even here on this Key, with all its lush beauty, all I see is gray.

But today I made a difference. To a child and her mom and probably lots more people, too. I didn't report the news. I *was* the news at noon and five, five-thirty, six, and even at eleven, even though my fifteen minutes of fame came from one of the idiots' cell phones.

And at the hospital, someone touched me, I trembled, and then stared into a face that made Alex look like Shrek. Maybe the future can be brighter than I imagine, she decided, as she dropped like a rock into a quiet, dreamless, restorative sleep.

CHAPTER **FOUR**

As Ceci contemplated the dismal state of the condo's refrigerated offerings and wilted at the thought of trying to navigate the grocery on crutches on Thanksgiving morning, she heard a knock. Tap-tapping through the living room, she maneuvered around the couch to the foyer and opened the door.

"Brian," she said. "I'm stunned to see you. Obviously. I'm kind of a wreck. I was just thinking about a bath."

"You look fine to me," Brian replied with a wide grin and lying only slightly. She looked like someone who'd been sleeping on a couch for a while, with her hair askew and her face a shade too pale.

"I'm off-duty today," he continued, "and I just wanted to drop by and tell you again what a great job you did helping Mandy. I've known her since she was a little girl, and she's the sweetest kid, so thanks for being there."

"Glad to help," Ceci said, mystified. Since when did paramedics make house calls? "Come on in. Leave the door open so we can get some cross-breeze. It's hot for this time of the morning." It wasn't, but she felt uneasy about being alone with this man—gorgeous though he was—who had showed up on her doorstep unannounced when she was alone. What was that about?

"Will do. I think you should sit down. That ankle has to hurt."

"It's much better now, but that's probably not a bad idea." Ceci sank back against the arm of the couch. Brian took the chair opposite her, the one not piled with clothes and a knitted throw, and the two of them engaged in the idle talk of people who don't know one another well.

Out of the blue came a question she didn't expect. "So how come you got fired?" Brian asked.

"Are you always this direct?" Ceci replied, surprised he'd touched on such a sensitive issue with no preamble. Nonetheless, she found herself answering. "I was working in Orlando, and your guess is as good as mine. My contract was for a year and at the end, the news director told me it wasn't working out. Something about my Q score."

"What's a Q score?" Brian asked, as he moved her ankle to test the bandage.

"It's a rating of likeability. If a lot people have heard of you, but they don't rate you highly, you have a low Q. Advertisers use it to make buying decisions. And apparently a news director can use it to fire you," Ceci said with some bitterness, "although my boss also said I didn't have enough personality to match my co-anchor. My score last year was actually pretty high, which I thought was good since the station had taken a real dive in viewership."

"Why?"

"They fired the six and eleven anchor who'd been with them for twenty years. Then they enforced her non-compete clause—for a year. She couldn't work in that market at all, and she didn't want to relocate her family. It didn't go over well with the public."

"I didn't realize people got attached to newscasters."

"Sometimes they do, and I came in right at the height of the storm. The people who stuck with the station barely had a chance to figure out who I was. It takes time for viewers to know and like you, and you have to learn about the town, too, so you don't mispronounce street names or landmarks."

She waved her hand as if to dismiss the whole subject. "It's the name of the game, though. I'm thirty and I've been in four stations already, mostly in the Midwest and South."

Brian looked as if he was ready to ask more questions when he and Ceci heard a voice at the door. "Can we come in?"

"I can't see who it is. Can you?" Ceci whispered.

"It's Devon and Mandy. I think it's safe," he whispered back.

"Come on in," Brian hollered before Ceci had a chance to speak.

"Hi," Devon said, looking as baffled as Ceci had only a few minutes earlier. "I didn't expect to see you here, Brian. Mandy and I came by to invite Ceci for Thanksgiving dinner at our house. I'm having a few folks in. We have so much to be thankful for, and since Ceci's a big part of that, I wanted to share the day with her, too. "

"I don't know how I could refuse such a wonderful invitation," Ceci said. "Please forgive the way the place looks. I've been camped out on the couch for the last couple of days, so things are a bit of a mess. Mandy, you certainly look perkier than the last time I saw you."

Mandy, a replica of her mother except for the curvaceous figure that probably would come later, broke from Devon and hugged Ceci tightly around the shoulders, almost as if she were drowning again. "Thank you," she whispered.

"You're welcome," Ceci said, returning Mandy's hug and resting her hand on the child's head. Her hair was soft as goose down. Ceci sensed some need in Mandy she couldn't identify, especially when the girl immediately ran to Brian and clung to him, too.

"It was so weird," Mandy said, turning back to Ceci, Brian's arm still around her. "I was standing on the sandbar and I stepped off and it was so deep, and there was a whole school of sting rays all around me. I sort of forgot what to do, and then I started swallowing water. I could see my mom, but I couldn't make her hear me. I saw you running toward me, but I don't remember anything else."

"I'm going to go," Brian said, "and let you all talk. I'm glad to see you coming around so well, Ceci." He gently disengaged himself from Mandy and faced Devon. "I'll see you later," he said to her.

"Okay," Devon said, patting his arm and, Ceci noted, smiling at him as if to once again stake her claim.

Ceci hobbled to the door with Brian. "Thanks for checking on me. Above and beyond the call of duty, I'd say. I appreciate it."

"See ya," Brian said, lifting his hand and barely touching her cheek.

I think I made a mistake about him, Ceci thought, as she watched Brian head toward the beach. He's not a frog at all.

•

As Brian walked away, he asked himself what he was doing there. I said I was going stay away from her, he thought, and here I am, making up an excuse to see her. A bad excuse, too. I probably shouldn't have touched her, though. What a dumbass move. It's good I wasn't on duty.

He struggled with his thoughts. It's enough she has those gray eyes, and the legs that go on forever. And I'm beginning to think she's not what I thought. She seems like a genuinely nice person who's a little mixed up.

It was the kind of combination Brian was attracted to.

CHAPTER **FIVE**

"Can I get you anything?" Ceci asked, turning back from the door to Devon, her hostess mode coming to the fore. "No, thanks," Devon said, looking around the condo. "This is a gorgeous apartment."

"Shabby chic," Ceci said. "Less chic, more shabby right now. My folks usually come down during the summer to paint and touch up, but my mom blew out her knee training for a half-marathon and had to have surgery. They said I could have the place if I'd do the cleanup. It was too good a deal to pass up since I'm jobless and trying to conserve cash. I have to find work pretty quick."

Glancing around the condo, Devon didn't make eye contact as Ceci spoke. She seemed to have little interest in Ceci's plight or even to acknowledge it. "I'll bet it's easy to rent."

"It is. Three bedrooms right on the beach is rare," returning to Devon's preferred topic. "The snowbirds do beat it up, though, so I have my work cut out for me. It's such a beautiful morning. Why don't we go out on the lanai?"

"Mom, I'd rather stay inside for a while and watch the parade."

"Okay with you, Ceci?" Devon said.

"Of course. Do you want the TV or are you going to use the iPad I see tucked in your mom's beach bag?"

Mandy giggled. "iPad, please," she said, flopping down and snuggling into the couch Ceci had vacated.

•

Outside, the two women stretched out on blue-and-green striped padded chaises and watched the waves. The surf was much more active now. Ceci wondered if she would have seen Mandy if the Gulf had been rougher on Tuesday. The thought made her light-headed.

"Mandy's gun-shy about the beach right now," Devon said, turning her upper body toward Ceci. "She wants to stay inside. She's having bad dreams, too."

"I suppose that's not surprising," Ceci answered, mirroring Devon's turn. "It's only been two days."

"She wants to talk about it all the time, too. She tells *everybody*, from the mail carrier to a stranger she met at the library yesterday afternoon. It worries me."

Ceci thought back to the night she was robbed in her apartment in Dayton—waking up and finding the guy standing right next to her bed. She lay stiff and silent as a corpse as he pawed through all her jewelry, shoved her grandmother's ruby ring and cameo into his jeans pocket, and eventually left the room. She told the cops, of course, but when she went to the gym the next morning, she found herself telling the guy on the treadmill next to her, too, and the box boy at the grocery and the receptionist at the dentist. And, of course, everyone at work.

"I think it was healthy," she said, explaining the incident to Devon, "because the more I talked it out, the less it bothered me. Until a year later. One night I woke up choking and sweating, and then I realized it was the anniversary. I hadn't even remembered it, at least consciously. She might be frightened for a while."

Staring out to sea, Devon once again appeared not to have heard anything Ceci said. "Mandy's dad will use it against me," she burst out.

"Why?" Ceci asked, once again wondering about Devon's lack of attention. "It was an accident."

"I know," Devon said, rising from the chaise and adjusting her short magenta tank dress, "but Patton has been trying to get custody from the moment we split up. This will be one more indication I'm an unfit mother."

"Do you have sole custody now?"

"No, it's joint, but he wants to take her from me, and I'm panicked that one of these days he'll win. He's not a bad father. He's a good one, in fact, but he produces major events all over the country, which means he travels and works insane hours. Who'd be there for her? Just his hideous parents."

"He hasn't married again?"

"Nope. Not much stability in his life right now. There was the woman he left me for, but they broke up. Now it's a long line of girlfriends he throws away like paper towels. Mandy doesn't need that."

"Is Mandy short for Amanda?" Ceci said, deciding to direct the conversation away from so much personal information coming from someone she didn't know beyond a five-minute chat at St. Luke's. She wondered if Devon had any girlfriends because she seemed to be making Ceci an immediate confidant, which felt peculiar.

"No, her name is Mary Andrea for her two grandmothers. But Patton thought if we called her Mary, which is my mother's name, his mother, Andrea, the mother-in-law from hell, by the way, would be upset. So we decided on Mandy, a combination of both. It suits her, I think."

"It does. She's sweet little girl."

"Not so little anymore. She'll be ten in February."

"Really? I would have guessed a couple of years younger."

Devon shook her head and smiled. "I looked younger, too, when I was her age. It caught up with me."

I'm not getting into the guess-my-age discussion, Ceci thought. It's a loser no matter what I say. "Well, you look fabulous. I wish I could wear that color, and I wish I had your skin."

"It's a deal if I can have your hair," Devon responded. Ceci had to admit to herself her hair was, if not her best feature, among the top two—hair so thick, luxuriant and glossy it should have had its own zip code.

She wondered fleetingly why she had responded to Devon's obvious request for validation about her still-youthful appearance by offering up a sampling of her own physical shortcomings and why Devon had responded in kind. Why did women so often deprecate themselves to gain the approval of other women?

She decided to laugh it off. "I guess we all want something we don't have."

Devon chuckled, too. "How about Mandy and I pick you up about four for dinner?"

"Thank you, but I can drive. My right foot works, and I haven't had to take anything for pain today."

"We'll see you at four-thirty then. It'll be Mandy and me and a few people from around here. Very informal. I'm glad you're going to join us. 22235 Hibiscus Loop."

"Thanks again for inviting me. Scrumptious as it sounds, I wasn't looking forward to a Lean Cuisine turkey feast," Ceci said, envisioning a subdued holiday gathering with a group of lost souls who had no families and nowhere else to go.

CHAPTER SIX

"**G**ood Lord," Ceci whispered to herself as she exited her well-worn Hyundai Elantra at Devon's. "This is a two-million-dollar house."

Wearing a form-fitting coral cotton sheath accented by one multicolored sandal and one stylishly wrapped ankle, and her hair gathered at the nape of her neck in a loose braid, Ceci rested on her crutches and gazed open-mouthed at the goldfinch-yellow Key West-style home at the end of the shell-strewn drive. It was a dream house, with its wraparound veranda, second-floor balcony, and cypress double-door entrance. Inside the white fence stood a few artfully placed palms, and surrounding the house were well-tended beds of ferns, asters, cosmos, dianthus, and snapdragons. Shrub roses rioted along the porch. The whole place looked ready for a visit from *Architectural Digest*.

When Devon came to the door, Ceci caught a glimpse of the living space beyond. A wide-open expanse of bamboo floors topped with what appeared to be expensive and probably antique Oriental rugs, twelve-foot ceilings, and crown moldings. Off to the left was a beautifully appointed kitchen with a swarm of uniformed minions scurrying from refrigerator to island to oven as they served drinks and hors d'oeuvres. The Gulf glistened beyond the living room's wall of windows. Above, Ceci counted four bedroom suites. What the hell? she thought. She can't be more than a couple years older than I am and she works for the city, for Pete's sake. How is this house even possible? And catering on Thanksgiving?

"Devon," she said, swallowing her surprise, "your house is awesome."

"Thanks. It was my parents'. They built it three years ago, but then they went to Portugal, fell in love with it, and decided they wanted to live there. So they gave this house to me, lock, stock, and furniture," Devon said, gesturing like a game show hostess toward the center of the house.

"Well, frankly, I was wondering how you did it on a civil service salary."

Devon laughed out loud. "To tell you the truth, my parents are stinking rich, but only recently." Ceci tilted her head to listen as Devon went on—and on. "A year or so before I was born, my dad inherited some money from his grandmother, and he decided to invest it in a new stock. He bought a thousand shares. Every time it dipped, which happened fairly often, he bought more. My mother and all of her family thought he was nuts for holding on to a stock that tanked so regularly."

"I might have agreed with them," Ceci said, as the two moved through the foyer, Devon leading the way in wide-leg white pants and a vibrant green charmeuse sleeveless blouse that wrapped her waist. Ceci didn't think it was the most flattering look for a woman as short as her hostess, who was a bit thick in the middle and whose upper arms showed the first signs of the softening that would someday result in batwings if she didn't get going on the triceps exercises, but Ceci stifled the impression. I'm a guest here, she thought. Shut it down.

"They had some big fights about it, believe me," Devon bubbled on, "but he was intrigued with the company, and he kept the shares forever. It split three times, I think, and he ended up with something like twenty-thousand shares. It took off one day in 2012 and he sold it all, at close to the highest price in its history—at least at the time. If I tell you the company was named after a common fruit...?"

"Oh," Ceci said, once again surprised at Devon's willingness to discuss so many details of her life—and others'—with a relative stranger. She seemed to have no filter. "My parents were frugal people and they're enjoying their life now. But they believe in work. They said I could have the house, free and clear, but I'd have to pay the taxes on it and support myself and Mandy. The taxes are high, but not as astronomical as you might think, and the city's rich, so salaries are good, and without a mortgage payment, everything's great. I've borrowed a little against it, but it's manageable."

"I have to admit when I drove up, I thought you must be some kind

27

of heiress or something," Ceci said.

"Someday I will be, I suppose, but I hope that time is a long, long way off. My folks have always been my rock. Mandy adores them and vice versa. Can you make it downstairs okay? We're having drinks on the patio."

After crabbing her way down, holding the banister while Devon carried the crutches, Ceci was amazed to discover "we" was a much more substantial gathering than she had imagined it would be. As they snaked their way through a gaggle of children, Devon introduced her to two realtors who probably were salivating at the commissions they'd earn if Devon ever wanted to sell the house; the city attorney and her husband, he a full head shorter than she; a blond, green-eyed pilot Ceci took particular note of; a pediatrician, whose claim to fame was hands so gentle and needle skills so refined his patients never cried; his wife a brunette with narrow-set eyes and a permanent scowl; a banker and his stockbroker wife, whose jewelry screamed the couple's success; a charter boat operator with a permanent mahogany tan; and a squeaky-voiced friend of Devon's from Ocala. All of whom greeted Ceci warmly and seemed to know about her part in Mandy's rescue.

Ceci rescinded her initial assessment of Devon's friend-making capacity. She seemed plugged into nearly every aspect of the community and well-liked by everyone in the room.

Ceci was caught off-guard that Peggy and Matt were there, but not surprised to see Brian chatting comfortably with several people in the group. This was obviously the "later" he had mentioned to Devon. He looked even better out of uniform in twill pants and a cobalt blue polo shirt accenting the color of his eyes. Brown leather Top-Siders. No socks. Oh, yes, Ceci thought. Yes, indeed.

Rather than make an obvious beeline for Brian, she took a detour toward Peggy. "I saw you checking out the boss," Peggy said with a knowing smirk and a gleam in her deep-brown eyes. "Best to put your tongue back in your mouth, if possible."

"I know, but seriously, Peggy, is he not something you could eat with a spoon?"

"Not me, because A, he's a coworker, and B, I'm married."

"Is your husband here? I'd like to meet him."

"No, he isn't, but my wife is. Her name's Veronica. Ronnie. She's upstairs chasing our son around on the deck. He's three. I'll need to relieve her in a few minutes."

"Oh," Ceci said, taken aback. "I'll look forward to meeting them. How long have you been married?"

"Almost two years, and Gabriel came to us from Colombia six months ago," Peggy replied, with a wide smile. "We were married in Santa Fe because New Mexico had marriage equality and we'd never seen the West. It was a wonderful trip," Peggy hesitated, "but I see your mind is wandering. Let's go find a place to sit and I'll give you the 4-1-1 about Brian Walker—or maybe in your case the 9-1-1, since you might get hurt."

•

"First," Peggy said, leaning in and lowering her voice as the two sat on either side of a corner table far from the rest of the guests, "he isn't married, which is what most women want to know. Second, he was. For about three years when he was in his mid-twenties."

"Starter marriage?"

"No. She died. Ovarian cancer. It happened fast because it wasn't detected until it was advanced—and then it was relentless. From diagnosis to the end was about eight months. She's been gone now about as long as they were married."

"Did you know her?"

"No. I only met him a couple of years ago, but we've become good friends, so I've heard about her. She seems to have been a wonderful young woman with a lot of talent and promise."

"And he and Devon are an item?" Ceci asked, taking a glass of iced tea from a tray being passed by one of the servers. It was too highly sweetened for her taste, and she put it aside after only a couple of sips.

"She's a close friend of his, but I think she'd like to be much more," Peggy said. "They see each other pretty often, but when Rachel died, it was like something broke in him." Real sadness crept through her conspiratorial tone. "I watch him struggle with it. He gets into relationships, but I think he's afraid of loving someone and having something bad happen again. He and Devon have gone on longer than he does with most women. "

"But you don't think Devon's going to rope him in? They look pretty cozy right now, what with his arm around her and her hand on his chest."

"I think she's very serious about him. If he were serious about her, though, he wouldn't have been grilling me about you. What's her name? Where does she live? I know he visited you in the ER and was pretty dazzled."

"Really?" Ceci said, her eyes wide.

"Yep, but if you're interested, too, don't get in too deep," Peggy warned, her expression solemn. "He's dated lots of women and they always fall in love with him. He's gorgeous, yes, but there's a lot more to him. He's a genuinely good guy, and that makes him a rarity, I guess."

"So far, you haven't said anything to scare me off."

"He's not out to hurt anyone," Peggy went on. "He's clear about the fact he doesn't want a lifetime commitment, but each of the women thinks she's different. She's the one who'll change his mind. And they never do, and their hearts get broken. Some of them put on their big-girl panties and deal with it, but a few of the others have gotten pretty ticked off."

In her mind's eye, Ceci pictured an endless line of women of various heights, weights, and hair colors, all sporting bridal veils and holding out their left hands, waiting for a proposal and a life that would never come.

"I'm not looking for marriage, Peggy, so I promise not to cry over him or troll him on Twitter," Ceci said. When she looked up, Brian was glancing at her from across the room. She clambered up on her crutches to walk toward him. "I am going to say hello, though," she said to Peggy, who sighed, shook her head, and gave Ceci a sympathetic smile.

"Another moth to the flame," Peggy said.

I'm only on the Key for a few weeks, Ceci thought. Maybe a short-term dead end with a good guy isn't such a bad idea. Maybe it will wash away the taste of the one who wasn't a good guy. She felt a smile begin as she took her first steps toward Brian.

She heard Peggy's whisper behind her. "You'd be better off with the flyboy over there. Sean Bennett. He's easy to look at, too. And single. Don't say I didn't warn you."

•

It turned out Ceci spoke only briefly to Brian. Sometimes when she wanted to impress somebody, Ceci did what she called "dialing it up," which was her term for mounting a massive charm offensive.

Just to check his reaction, she dialed it up all the way to the top with Brian, but immediately felt uncomfortable about it, in spite of the fact he seemed happy to see her. His smile, when he saw her coming toward him, made her heart turn over. But Peggy was wrong. Brian and Devon were clearly a couple, and Ceci, though still intrigued and wanting to explore some more aspects of Brian's non-frog-like personality, dialed it back and went in search of other people to talk to.

It was impossible for her to turn off her growing fascination with Brian, though, and putting on her reporter perspective, she observed him with Devon. As she chatted with others, she covertly watched the couple and began to have a different feeling about them. Devon constantly touched him. She refreshed his drink and clasped his hand when she gave it back to him. As she passed by him, she often drew her fingers lightly across his shoulders. At one point, when he was sitting on the couch talking with the pediatrician, Devon leaned down behind him and put her arms around his neck, resting her head on his shoulder, her lips just shy of his cheek.

While he didn't seem to be ill at ease with the situation and did nothing to discourage it, Brian didn't appear to reciprocate. He was attentive and kind, but acted ever-so-slightly removed. Ceci reconsidered her conversation with Peggy, and it looked as if she might be right. This was a man who would go so far and no further. She found herself worrying about Devon, who was obviously invested in Brian. If she was one of the ones holding out her hand for the wedding ring, Ceci feared she'd suffer the fate of the others.

•

Ceci lingered a while with Devon at the door. "Thank you so much. Everything was perfect. You were so kind to include me." She reached out to give Devon a good-bye hug.

"Oh, I was glad to do it. Do you have enough of the leftovers? I don't want you to have to stump around your kitchen too much tomorrow. Just rest and recover. Did you meet everyone?"

"I did, and it was nice. I feel as if I have some friends now. I'm not here often, so knowing a few people is a big plus."

"I especially wanted you to meet Sean. Did you have a chance to talk with him?"

Ceci grinned. The plot was coming clear. Devon had picked out

Sean for Ceci. She really hadn't had much of a chance to get to know him, sandwiched as she was at a small table for six between the pediatrician and one of the realtors, who'd been having a spirited discussion about the relative merits of the stock market versus real estate as a retirement savings option, talking over her as if she weren't there the entire time. She did notice, however, that he, like Brian, was quite stunning, with nicely sculpted features.

At one point, she'd looked across the table at him and rolled her eyes at the conversation she was enduring. He caught it and laughed, but after dinner, he'd been scooped up by Devon's friend from Ocala, and the chance for further communication disappeared. As he walked away, she heard him say something about a concert at the Austen Theatre in two days, and she decided to go. Ceci loved music, and maybe they'd see each other there. Why not? He was alone at the dinner, didn't seem to be attached to anyone, and there was certainly nothing doing with Brian. She wasn't in search of a man for the long term because she might leave the Key at any minute for a new job, but she liked male company. So once again she asked herself, why not?

•

As Brian stood at the door with Devon and watched Ceci drive away, he was both excited and baffled. He'd felt her eyes on him throughout the party, but except for a brief moment when she'd come over to speak with him and Devon, she'd shown no interest at all. Most women did. He was used to female attention and the subterfuges women used to get him to notice them, but Ceci was off-hand and casual with him. She clearly had no interest in him, but she was on his mind quite a bit. It was driving him nuts. He'd never felt so confused by a woman in his life.

CHAPTER **SEVEN**

The following Saturday morning, which was foggy, with a sky as white as a sail, Ceci tried her first unencumbered steps, walking gingerly along the beach, letting the water spill over her feet and ankles. A flowered sarong skirt was tied low around her hips, the red bikini bottom peeking through as she ambled, with a barely visible hitch in her step, along the shore. She stopped in her tracks when she noticed Brian jogging toward her in shorts and no shirt. Seeing Ceci at the same moment, he slowed down and approached her.

"Well, look at you," he said, his smile nearly liquefying her bones. "No crutches. How does it feel?"

"Good. Ouchy, but not too sore. You were right about being able to walk on my own. The water helps. All's well. Aren't you working today?" She glanced down, then up under her lashes in a shamelessly flirtatious move that usually captivated men. Brian didn't seem to notice, though.

"I'm two days on and three off. This is the last of the off days."

"That's as crazy as a reporter's schedule," Ceci said.

Almost without noticing, Ceci found herself turning and falling into step with Brian as they meandered down the beach in the direction of her condo. Although she felt a current running between them that made her body tingle, she struggled to keep her excitement at seeing him under control.

"I was so amazed to watch you bring Mandy around the other day," she said. "I've always thought being a paramedic had to be one of the most rewarding jobs in the world. In the newsroom, I could hear all the scanners on the assignment desk. I'd listen to a call after cardiac arrest, and lots of times by the time the squad reached the hospital, the person had a pulse and sometimes was even awake and talking. It seems like magic to me. It must be exciting to pull someone back from death."

"It is," Brian responded, "but it's not magic. It's procedures. Following steps and watching results. Trying something else if we need to. Of course, we have a better chance of saving people today than we might have twenty years ago. Medicine's made advances, and we can administer more drugs than we could before."

"What about you, though?" he asked as they strolled along the water's edge. "You said you'd already worked in four cities. Where?" Brian picked up a sand dollar and handed it to Ceci.

Her face lit up. "How did you know?" she said. "Sand dollars are my favorite, and this one doesn't have any discoloration or even a chip. I'm always looking for one like this. Thanks.

"I started in news in Dayton," she went on, "which was fun because I'm from Cincinnati. But they had a purge and a whole lot of us were let go at once."

"Does that happen often?" Brian asked, surprise in his tone.

"More than you might think. New owners. New management. They want to bring in their own people. It's not personal, but I had to find another job. So I took a step back in market size and went to Huntsville—Alabama, not Texas. Best news director I ever had. She taught me so much and brought me along," Ceci smiled, remembering her mentor.

"I hated to leave, but she told me to look for a bigger opportunity because I was going to be locked in place in Huntsville. The anchors were hugely popular. So when Indianapolis called, I hustled up there and anchored the early morning show. The one before God gets up. But I got stalked there, and I decided to move on."

"Stalked?"

"It happens to female anchors sometimes. He never approached me, as far as I know. He might have, at a station event or something, but I wouldn't have known him." She paled a little bit as she always did at the thought of her stalker. Even though she hadn't heard from him in more than a year, she was still working on recovering her sense of safety in the world.

"Aren't people usually aware of who's after them?" Brian asked.

"This guy was different. He stayed out of sight. He wrote to me instead. Everything was hand-written in all caps. He wore gloves.

There was never even a fingerprint, except for postal workers'. Sometimes he delivered the notes to my door. He used those self-sticking envelopes and didn't have to lick the stamps. No saliva."

Ceci realized, embarrassed, she was babbling way too much, but Brian's interest in her seemed genuine and she warmed to his attention. She opened up much more quickly than she did with most people. Now, though, she paused and seemed to be focused on something far away.

"Where have you gone, Ceci?" Brian said, tapping her gently on the shoulder. "Was there more?"

"Some," she responded, still a bit removed from the moment. "It all started out as sort of 'fan-ish,' but then moved on to threats and gross sexual stuff."

"They never caught him?"

"Nope, and I never heard from him again after I left." With a quick shake of her head, Ceci snapped back to the present. "Then Orlando, which was a larger market, but obviously a big mistake. I anchored at five and five-thirty—and I did some serious investigative stuff I loved. And now here, without a job, trying to figure it out again." She sighed and raked her left hand through her hair, still abashed at how much she'd been talking. She wondered if he was interested in her story or her. She knew what she hoped.

"My parents used to like this TV show, *WKRP in Cincinnati*," Brian said, turning the conversation ninety degrees. "Except for the stalker part, it sounds like your life."

Ceci's face lit up. "Venus Flytrap? Johnny Fever? Jennifer Marlowe? I know that show. It's legend in Cincinnati, and I love old TV. It went off the air the year I was born, but I've watched lots of it on YouTube. Remember the Thanksgiving episode when Herb and Mr. Carlson threw the turkeys out of the helicopter? I watch it every year around this time."

"Oh, the humanity!"

"As God is my witness, I thought turkeys could fly!"

The two continued down the beach, laughing and bumping together like buddies, when Brian reached over to take Ceci's hand, squeezing it an instant longer than was necessary. "Your boss was a fool. You are plenty likeable. Beautiful, too, by the way."

"Really?" Ceci said, surprised as always when someone mentioned her attractiveness. She'd been gawky as a kid, especially in sixth and seventh grade, when she'd grown eight inches during the year. By the time she finished high school, she was five feet ten, with enormous hair and a mouth too wide for her face.

She hadn't grown into her looks until the summer before her junior year in college, when her wide mouth turned into an irresistible smile and she cut six inches off her hair, which instantly settled it down and made it possible for her to style in any way she chose. It became the talk of Tri Delt house. She ended up as the Sweetheart of Sigma Chi and never lacked for male companionship after her transformation.

But even then she often thought of herself as ungainly and clumsy. Alex had been able to make her feel oafish, too, because she was as tall as he. He always asked her wear flat shoes, which she disliked. She did it because he had some crazy notion the man must always be taller, and it was easier to slip on flats than trample all over his feelings of inadequacy.

Now, though, Ceci forgot the past and smiled up at Brian, slowing her steps as she neared her condo. The sun broke through the haze and lit her face. "This is where I live," she said. "You know what? The new boxed set of *WKRP* came out a couple of weeks ago—the one with most of the *original* music—not like the mess they made of it a few years ago. I bought it. You want to come over and watch it? We could binge." Although she wanted to appear casual, Ceci seemed unable to turn off the flirt. It was all she could do not to bat her eyes—and she knew mentioning binge watching conveyed the fact she wanted to spend more than a few minutes with Brian.

"Great idea," he replied, his expression reflecting he'd caught the drift of her invitation. "I'll call you when I'm off. Wednesday? I have to run now, though. I mean literally run. Have to stay fit for the job." He brushed his lips across her cheek, which both startled and stirred her up. "See you soon."

•

As the sun chased off the last of the fog, he stepped further into the shadow of a patio wall, watching her walk by with Hunky Shirtless Guy. She was so wrapped up in this new man she didn't notice him. It made him angry for the moment. But soon it would be *sayonara* to anyone else. She'd be with him and happier than she'd been in her life.

CHAPTER **EIGHT**

Ceci's walk with Brian hadn't been too taxing, so she was surprised to feel her ankle throbbing. She got off her feet, passing the time lounging on the lanai reading a mindless paperback novel—in between entertaining thoughts about Brian and what she'd like to do with him if the occasion presented itself.

A shadow crossed the page, and she looked up to see Annah Allenby, a snowbird from Canada, recently arrived with her two schnauzers, Thelma and Louise. Annah, in her late sixties, was one of her mom's favorite Florida friends and a sort of grandmother figure to Ceci.

"Ceci?" Annah said tentatively. "How long has it been?"

"A long time," Ceci said, rising to give the older woman a hug. "I haven't been here for almost four years. Moving around and all. The little girls are all grown up, I see." She patted Thelma as Louise pawed at the chaise for attention.

"I barely recognized you, dear," Annah said, "but then you probably wouldn't have picked me out on the street either. Lots more gray hair and wrinkles."

"I love the gray. And the haircut. All feathery and cute. You look wonderful. Is Hector with you?"

"He'll be here in a week or so. I came down early to check out the condition of the apartment and get the studio set up. Just got in last night and the girls were frantic to run," she said, laughing as the dogs took off for the beach. "Are your folks here?"

"It's only me right now."

Annah kept an eye on the dogs, who continued to zoom around, dashing to the water's edge and then retreating from the waves. "Last I heard, you were in Orlando. Still in broadcasting?"

"Not at the moment," Ceci sighed. "I am, as they say, between engagements." She decided not to get into the fact her other engagement also had been broken off.

"I'm sure you'll find something soon."

"I hope so. I have to say, Annah, this kind of leisure is a new concept to me. I feel lazy and kind of worthless if I'm not accomplishing something."

"Nonsense," Annah said briskly. "Enforced idleness can be very instructive. It helps you think about what really matters in your life. And what doesn't. Once you figure that out, you can recalibrate if you need to." She jumped up from her chaise. "I must run. It's poop patrol time. You know how people get if they encounter droppings on the sand. And it *is* bad for the beach environment. So good to see you, dear. Come by whenever. We can take care of each other until all the others arrive."

CHAPTER **NINE**

The Austen Theater was almost full when Ceci, who had dallied too long dreaming about her upcoming evening with Brian, hurried in for the concert that opened the Christmas season on the Key. Limping only slightly as she searched for a seat, she saw a man waving at her and pointing to an empty one next to his. She squinted at him as she moved toward Row F, finally realizing it was Sean Bennett.

"Thanks, Sean," she said, slithering her way past the two people on the aisle and the two beyond them. "These must be the best seats in the house. I wondered if I'd have to scamper up to the nosebleed section."

"I thought you might be here," Sean said, his eyes crinkling at the corners as he beamed at her. "I heard you mention you liked classical music, so I saved this seat...in case."

I don't remember talking about classical music, Ceci thought. Strange.

"I can't believe you even saw me in this crowd," she said.

"I was watching for you."

"Really? You must have sharp eyesight."

"Twenty-twenty uncorrected," he said, "and lots of training in noticing things. Pilot stuff, you know. Situational awareness."

"I'm so glad they don't have this concert before Thanksgiving," Ceci said. "I know I'm old fashioned, but I like my holidays one at a time."

"Not a Hallowthanksmas girl?"

"Absolutely not," Ceci said with a grin.

She shot a surreptitious glance at Sean as the lights dimmed. Captivating profile, she thought. And the close-cropped blond hair and sea-green eyes are easy to take. I guess there could be worse things than spending an evening listening to Handel with a guy who looks like an Air Force recruiting poster.

•

"How well do you know Devon?" Ceci asked Sean, as they strolled through the park after the concert on the way to what Sean promised was the best sandwich shop ever.

"Pretty well," he answered, "and she knows everything about everyone on the Key. She keeps me in the loop. I met her and Brian when I was dating one of her friends. She asked me to come to Thanksgiving because my family's all in upstate New York getting ready for the freezin' season. I like it better here."

"Where was the girlfriend? I didn't meet her."

"Long gone," Sean said. "It wasn't destined to be."

It's hard to find the one who is, Ceci thought, as they entered the sandwich place and found a booth. The server raced over with menus and coffee, lingering a bit longer than necessary to take in Sean's attractive features.

"I know you're a pilot," she said. "What airline are you with?"

"None. I'm corporate. I fly a lot of pretty high-powered business folks," Sean said. "They're nice people unless they develop a case of get-home-itis when the weather's bad. That can be ugly, especially if they're liquored up. Most of the time they're pretty reasonable, though. If I don't think it's safe to fly, they'll usually back down without too much fuss."

"I've flown in helicopters," Ceci said, "but I never made it into the corporate jet."

"I've seen you fly in a helicopter," Sean said.

"What?"

"I'm in Orlando a lot. At Thanksgiving, I was sure I knew you from somewhere, and when I heard you talk, I remembered seeing you on TV there. It was the Ceci Myers that threw me. You're Claire Cooper, aren't you?"

Ceci's expression became guarded and her heart skipped a beat. "Professionally, yes. Sometimes."

The server arrived with the sandwiches, but Ceci's appetite had deserted her. She was surprised at how fearful she was at hearing her alias again, especially from a man she'd just met and knew almost nothing about.

"Don't reporters use their own names?" Sean said, returning to the previous conversation.

"Often we do, but a couple of jobs ago in Indianapolis, I had a situation with a guy who was…maybe the best word is creepy," she replied, not wanting to blather on and on about it the way she had with Brian. "He was frightening and sometimes these guys really do carry out their threats." She discovered to her chagrin she was twirling a lock of her hair, something she'd done ever since she was a child when she felt fretful and a habit that had driven her mother to distraction. "When I went to Orlando," she went on, "I thought it was best to use a different name to make myself harder to find. And I dropped off Indianapolis TV overnight. No on-air goodbyes or anything.

"He didn't follow me, and I decided I'd had a pretty exalted view of myself to imagine he'd travel halfway across the country to find me. I hope he's forgotten about me. While I'm here, I'm Ceci, but when I go back on the air, I may be Claire again. Depends on where I go, I guess."

"Well, in spite of the fact he's probably not around, I insist on following you home," Sean said, placing Ceci's gauzy lemon-yellow shawl around her bare shoulders.

"That's very gallant, Sean, but certainly not necessary," Ceci replied.

"I think it is," Sean said, his expression serious. "I'll feel better when I know you're safe inside."

Boxing up Ceci's almost untouched sandwich, they made their way across the park to their cars.

CHAPTER **TEN**

O n Wednesday, Brian arrived toting a bottle of Sauvignon Blanc, Ceci's favorite. "How did you know?" she asked. "So many people only think of Chardonnay and Chablis when it comes to whites."

"Shot in the dark," Brian said, putting the bottle in the kitchen and glancing around the condo. "I like it, too. This is a nice place. It's big, but it's homey, not like most of the rentals. You know, the ones with the wicker furniture and the chartreuse parrot slipcovers. Pretty views, too. The gardens look great."

"My parents like to come down here a couple of months each year and they want it to feel comfortable for them. So no green parrots or palm-tree-covered shower curtains. The snowbirds seem to like it." She smiled. "I'd give it a little more spice, but it's not mine and it's free living this month, so I'm keeping my mouth shut."

Her nerves stretched taut by the nearness of this impossibly good-looking guy, Ceci prattled on. Why can I not shut up when I'm around him? she thought. I'm an idiot. "I haven't been back here for more than a couple of days for years, and I'd forgotten how much I love November on the Key. The Gulf's still warm, but the summer heat's gone. The sky is so sparkling blue. And hurricane season's almost over." She uncorked the wine and poured a plentiful stream into two stemmed glasses narrowed slightly at the top.

"What's changed the most since you've been away?" Brian said, taking a glass from Ceci and inclining it toward her in a little toast. She responded in kind.

"The beach. It's moved north."

"Sure has. It's taken a couple of years and a few big storms."

"And the Brigand Cove has closed. I loved it there when I was a kid. Sublime ribs and crispy fries."

"The owner died and the kids didn't want the restaurant," Brian explained. "It was prime real estate, and there are six new houses on the property now."

"So I noticed. But the pelicans and egrets and herons are still here, and I can still find perfect shells. The Gulf still calms me down. I can sit out there all day and listen or meditate. Did you ever notice that on a dead calm day an exhaled breath sounds just like an incoming wave? I'd have to say it's paradise on earth, the way it always has been."

"I agree. I was born and raised in the area. Not on the Key. This is way too rich for my blood. I live inland, but I love this part of the state. I really don't want to go anywhere else, unlike you, Bailey Quarters," Brian said, referring to a *WKRP* character.

"She was always my favorite," Ceci smiled. "The grill's fired up, but we have about twenty minutes before the coals are ready. Let's take our wine outside. It's fabulous, by the way. It finishes so well. Peachy, with some green notes underneath." She wasn't much of a drinker, but Alex had taught her a lot about wine. She'd learned all the jargon. "We're pairing with poultry, so it's exceptional."

They hung out on the chaises for a few minutes, talking about mundane things, when Brian suddenly asked, "What kind of accent do you have? I can't place it."

"I'm from Ohio. I don't have an accent. At least I don't think so. I speak General American. That's what broadcasting prefers. Heartland stuff, you know?"

"Well, it's something. You don't sound like other people."

Ceci giggled. "I know what it is, Brian. I enunciate. Most people don't. They swallow their words and sound all mushy. I had two great teachers, speech and English. I love words and I like to speak them properly. Is that a deal-breaker?"

He smiled in response. "Are we moving toward a deal?"

At a loss for an answer, Ceci jumped up to check the grill. She was acutely aware of Brian's face next to hers and his right hand on her left shoulder as he leaned over to assess the readiness of the coals.

"Fifteen minutes," she said.

"Ten," Brian responded.

"So we'll drink faster," Ceci said, trying for a nonchalant grin. But her knees had gone weak from his touch, and nonchalance wasn't in her repertoire at that moment. Her smile came out looking like Charlie Brown's spiky grin.

"If you want me to, I can handle the grill," Brian said.

"Excellent. You cook. I bake. We're a fine team." Oh, *that* was subtle, she thought, mentally face-palming herself. Maybe I should go straight to ripping his clothes off to show him I'm interested.

Brian glossed over the awkwardness. "*Did* you bake?" he said.

"I did. Double chocolate fudge cake. One of my specialties."

"Could we skip dinner and go straight to dessert?" Brian said, teasing.

I'd like to, Ceci thought, but the guy seems to be talking about food.

"Why not?" She headed for the kitchen island and returned with two generous slabs of four-layer cake filled with chocolate buttercream and topped with a rich ganache. She handed Brian a fork. "Money where your mouth is. Tell me what you think."

"Oh, my Lord," Brian said, after the first bite. "If you'd given this to your boss, you'd still have a job." He licked a couple of crumbs from the corner of his mouth. "Where did you learn to bake like this?"

"Mmm. That *is* good," Ceci said, taking a tiny bite. "My grandmother was my culinary maven. My mom has lots of admirable qualities, but she's a hopeless cook. So Minnie and I cooked and baked together every Saturday morning for years. She taught me everything I know, and I cooked most of my family's dinners. Except for meatloaf. Mom's hell on meatloaf, and she can manage a baked potato, but not much more. I don't know how she could have Minnie for a mother and not be able to boil water."

Taking another bite, she mumbled, "Everything Minnie touched was glorious. Her best was lemon meringue pie. It was so light I always thought it might float off the plate. I can't make it down here very often because it's too humid. I've tried, but the meringue is either flabby or chewy. I do great cakes and cookies and other kinds of pies, though. I used to make all the birthday cakes at work."

"This is the best thing I've ever had," Brian said. "You know La Patisserie down at the end of the Key? My buddy's wife owns it, but they don't have anything this good. Have you ever thought leaving broadcasting to bake?" he said, finishing the last morsel on his plate and looking longingly at the remainder on the cake stand.

"Right now, I'm thinking of leaving broadcasting for *anything*, but I'm lost about what it would be. I was trained to be a journalist, and I don't have a clue about how to revamp reporting into another career, except in public relations or something. I know I'm being childish. People get fired in TV all the time. But getting chopped twice in four years stings. Chocolate helps," Ceci said, taking the plates to the sink.

"Besides, broadcast is all about 'if it bleeds, it leads,' and I know there's more to news. I probably should be in print journalism where at least they occasionally do long-form stories about things that matter to a community. I'm sick of covering death and gore, but in local TV it seems that's all there's time for. People think reporters do their stories and go home and none of it sticks to us. But it does."

"Same with us," Brian said. "You can shake off the nonfatal heart attacks and sports injuries, but there are certain things you can't. They stay with you. What's the worst for you?"

"No contest," Ceci said, her face clouding as she turned back from the sink. "It's the sound a mom makes when her child has been killed. It doesn't matter how, and it doesn't matter how old the child is. Whether it's gang-related or getting hit by a car or some random thing like a lightning strike, the sound is the same. I've heard it too often. And they always say, 'My baby.'"

Brian looked startled. "For me, too. I've tried to resuscitate babies I knew were gone from SIDS and kids who've been in accidents close to home, when the parents are right there looking over my shoulder. And when it's clear it's too late, then you hear the mom. That scream. And you're right. They do say 'my baby,' whether the victim is two or forty-two. It doesn't matter.

"Everybody's beat up by it, but the guys who have kids take it hardest. They identify with the parents. When I saw you working over a child on the beach and then realized it was Mandy...," his voice trailed off. "But you'd done such a great job, Dev didn't have to go through it, and I didn't have to hear it. It sucks, though, and I've seen lots of guys cry in the truck."

"We cry, too," Ceci said. "We try not to do it on the air, although it happens sometimes. I've cried plenty at home. We have to do our jobs, like you, but sometimes it hurts a lot more than people think."

Though Brian looked at her with understanding, Ceci was surprised when he pulled her toward him, catching her hair in his fingers. He took her face in his hands and tilted it up to his lips, kissing her tenderly. "I'm guessing here, but I think you've been hurt more than you let on."

In spite of her astonishment at how fast things were moving, Ceci looked into his eyes. "Yes, I have, but things are looking up," she said, seeking his mouth again.

As Brian's kisses became deeper and more insistent, Ceci felt the familiar sting of anxiety in her throat. In spite of being drawn in by the unexpected softness of his lips, the beachy aroma of his skin, and the fire that rose in her wherever he placed his hands, she found herself pulling away. Perplexity showed in Brian's eyes, and she knew it was mirrored in her own.

"What's wrong?" Brian asked. "Too fast?"

Ceci took his hand, noting his palm was roughened, and led him to the couch, where they sat close together. She leaned forward, rubbing her temples. "Kind of. I'm sorry, Brian. I'm scared." Pictures of Alex raced through her mind as if the photo gallery on her phone had come to life to show her every minute of her time with him.

"Why?"

"I was supposed to be married in a few months. He broke up with me the day before I got fired. It was a crappy time. This feels pretty quick to me."

"Ah," Brian said.

"When you kissed me, I thought I might be ready again, but I'm not. I'm sure you can tell I'd like to take you upstairs right this minute, but sex is never casual for me. I get involved. I don't want to do that right now. I don't even know how long I'm going to be here. If I find a job, I could end up in Kansas City or Spokane or somewhere else the day after tomorrow."

"I'm sorry if I pushed you," Brian said, "but I'm a man, and it's normal behavior for a man who's fallen in love...for the first time in forever."

"You're in love with me?" Ceci said. "How is that possible? You don't even know me. You don't know a thing about me."

Brian leaned back against the arm of the couch with a lazy smile that almost enticed her into his arms again. It was clear to anyone with eyes he was significantly aroused, and she was sorely tempted to take advantage of his state. She held back, though, and listened to what he said.

"I'm not sure I can explain it," he said. "I wish I could. In the beginning I have to admit it was the red bikini and the body in it that attracted me. But when we were at Dev's, I couldn't take my eyes off you. There was something intriguing about you. You seemed very self-assured at her house meeting a roomful of strangers, but at the same time a little lost and vulnerable. I wanted to know more about you. I wanted to know *all* about you."

Ceci smothered a smile because Brian was so clearly stating her own thoughts about him.

"Why do you think I was running on your beach a few days ago? I don't have to come to the Key to run, for Pete's sake. I can run just fine on my own street. I was hoping to meet up with you. I didn't really expect to."

He spread his fingers through his hair as if he were trying to arrange his thoughts. "I couldn't believe you were on the beach then and walking toward me. And when you turned around to walk *with* me, I was very happy. You were so open and trusting, I just fell right into those beautiful eyes. By the time we got here, I'd fallen the rest of the way. I know it doesn't make sense. But I *am* in love with you, and I haven't been in love with anyone for a long, long time."

Ceci decided against mentioning what she knew of Rachel. "I have to tell you something," she said in a whisper. "I can't explain it either, but it's happened to me, too."

"What?"

"Oh, yeah. When I made my first little play for you...you did notice I was making a play, didn't you?"

Brian laughed. "I did. That little maneuver where you blink and look up through your lashes is pretty cute." He sat up and ran his hands down the backs of her arms. She shivered with pleasure as Brian lowered the strap of her dress to kiss her exactly where her collarbone reached her neck. Her resolve nearly shattered, but in spite of how much she wanted him, "Too soon, too soon" bubbled up in her brain. She'd learned to trust her instincts, so she gently moved away.

"I thought you'd be a nice distraction. Something to take my mind off what Alex did to me. Somebody to spend a few days with and then say goodbye to. But when you came to my house, I saw how much more there was to you besides your face and body, which are quite fine, by the way."

"You knew that was a ploy, didn't you?"

"I know I hoped so, but I wasn't sure."

She paused for a moment, wanting to say more, but afraid of revealing herself to a man noted for short-term relationships. In the pause, she decided to go for broke anyway. "When we were walking on the beach Saturday, something weird happened. Time stopped. I couldn't feel the sand or the water. I could barely have told you where we were."

She smiled up at Brian. "I told you I love words, and there's a word for what was happening to me. Ensorcelled. It means being bewitched. I was, and I wanted you. All of you. All the time. For good." She traced his face with her index finger as she leaned toward him again.

Brian kissed her again, this time at the base of her throat. She gasped but regained herself. "It was just you and me and feeling completely alone and yet at home with someone. It wasn't exactly love at first sight. But it was...is...something. Something really wonderful. And I don't want to mess it up."

"You're right. It is. And frankly I'd like to follow you up those stairs, but if you're not ready, you're not ready. I understand no means no. I might not like it, but I understand it. I knew I was moving fast." He grinned. "Doesn't mean I won't be thinking about it, though."

"So will I," Ceci said. "And perhaps action will follow thought before too long. The prospect is very appealing."

He stood up and bent down to kiss her on the forehead. "If we're not going to bed, we should eat. I'll go stoke the grill again and char dinner for us."

"And then *WKRP* or a walk or whatever."

"And more cake."

"Absolutely more cake. But we'll try this again another time, won't we?"

"We will. For sure. You're probably right, though. Very level-headed. I don't want this to be casual either. Let's figure out what the hell it's all about because I have to admit it's kind of strange. In the meantime, keep in mind that sex or no sex, I really do love you, and I'm as knocked out by that fact as you are." He kissed her again. "But sex would be good."

•

As Ceci lay in bed—alone—she pondered what Peggy had told her—that Brian was always very clear about not wanting any kind of lasting commitment and Rachel had spoiled him for other relationships. So what was this evening all about? Did Brian tell every girl he went out with he'd fallen in love with her? Was he only trying to get into her knickers? Or was he telling the truth? Was this the real deal for him?

All she knew for certain was she didn't care. Brian had awakened something in her she'd never felt before, even when she was planning her wedding to Alex. She was besotted. She knew it was only a raging infatuation, but the touch of his hands and the warmth of his lips extinguished her usual practicality. Whether her immediate, irrational passion for him grew into something permanent or sputtered out for any number of reasons, she was certain she'd cherish the memory of this night for a long time.

CHAPTER **ELEVEN**

Ceci was surprised to find Devon standing on her porch late the next morning. Even in the delirium of the night before, Devon had wormed her way into Ceci's consciousness, and she'd beaten herself up about the woman she had come to like but now saw as a rival. I'm a total bitch, she thought. Peggy told me how Devon feels about Brian, and I've seen it with my own eyes. It's hardly a secret. And yet I can't keep myself away from him. I can still feel his hands on me. I know how he smells. How he tastes. Almost everything. And I can hardly wait for everything.

She had sat at the kitchen table that morning for a half-hour, her head in her hands, her mind spinning. Alex and I broke up because someone got between us. Am I going to be that person now? The person I hated so much when it happened to me? I don't want to be, but I want *him*. Right away and for a very long time.

And now Devon was in Ceci's living room, bright and chirpy and unaware. "I have a day off. Want to do some Christmas shopping? I have to pick up a couple of things for Mandy. The mall will be a mess, but Ramiro Square should be less crowded this time of day. We can shop a little and have a bite at Antonio's."

"Sure," Ceci said, feeling caught. The guilt that had nibbled around the recesses of her mind the night before now threatened to eat her whole brain. There was no graceful way out, though, so she picked up her purse to leave.

"And, by the way," Devon said, lifting a glass sphere sitting at the side of the porch under the overhang, "someone sent you flowers. And not just any old flowers, either. No birds of paradise or gaudy tropical stuff. Hydrangeas and roses and a few sprays of freesia. All white. Very elegant." She was visibly curious.

Ceci felt a flutter of uneasiness. She'd received anonymous flowers several times in Indianapolis. Usually they were dead.

"Is there a card?" she asked, hoping there was.

"Right here." Devon presented it with a flourish as Ceci relaxed.

"I can't imagine..." she said, opening the flap. "I still do. B.W.," the card said.

A tiny, secret smile played around Ceci's lips, but she brought her face into neutral quickly.

"I saw that," Devon said. "That's a boyfriend smile."

"Sorry to disappoint. They're from an old friend. Betsy Williams. She's been really supportive during the job search. She's telling me she still believes in me." Ceci was horrified at how easily the lie slipped out. At least there *is* a Betsy, she thought, even though I haven't seen her since fifth grade. She almost showed Devon the card, but thought better of it in case Brian had written it himself. She tucked it into the pocket of her shorts. "Come on, let's hit the square."

•

Waiting for the light to change on the way to the parking lot after shopping, Devon shoved her sunglasses up on her head, where they perched hidden among the waves and whorls of her Goldilocks hair. "I had lunch with Sean Bennett a couple days ago," she said. "He said he ran into you at the concert." She appeared to be digging for details.

It was a little more than that, Ceci thought, recalling Sean had been waiting for her and holding an orchestra seat. "Yes," she said noncommittally. "It was a nice concert."

"He told me you went out after," Devon said, with a sideways glance.

"I wouldn't say went out," Ceci replied. "We went to a little sandwich place across from the theater."

"I think he's interested in you. Want me to invite you two to dinner or something?" Her eyes shone and her tone was light and breezy.

"Probably not a good idea. I have a lot to do on the apartment, and then I hope to find another job in God knows where. I'll probably end up in East Overshoe, Nebraska, or something. Best not to get started with anyone." *Except your boyfriend*, she thought, fighting off a wave of self-reproach.

"I wasn't trying to start anything. You don't have to marry the guy. I thought you might enjoy some male attention, that's all." Devon looked miffed and her tone was cool.

"I appreciate the thought, and I do like hanging out with guys," Ceci said. "Newsrooms are full of them, and I've liked most of them. But I'm coming off a bad relationship right now, so I'm not very interested in meeting someone." *Because I already have, and I hate what we're about to do to you.*

They stowed their packages in the trunk of Devon's Audi and eased into the traffic on Heron Way toward the Key. "So you were involved with someone?" Devon asked.

"I was engaged. Ring and all. He found someone else less than three weeks after he put it on my finger."

"Still have the ring? It sounds like you earned it."

"I flushed it. I thought he was going to dive in after it. But I was damned if he was going to reset it and give it to her. He said she was his soul mate. Now there's a phrase I hate."

"Oh, no, not a soul mate," Devon said, almost snarling. She slowed the car as a couple ran across the road in a mad dash for the beach. "That's what my ex said, too. I suspected there was someone else because the marriage had been rocky for a while. It made me sick, though, when he gave me the soul mate story. I don't believe in soul mates. And what was really funny was after six months or so his soul must have shriveled up or something, because her soul moved on to someone else's."

Devon's eyes flashed and her face reddened. "Now he's playing the field, which really ticks me off. If I had to give up my husband and Mandy's father, I'd have preferred it to be to the next Mrs. Carter, not a string of bimbos."

"I can imagine. It's like getting to the semifinals and losing. You want the team that beat you to win the championship. You don't want to lose to the loser."

"Exactly. I've never thought of it that way, but it's the perfect comparison. I think I've found my new BFF." Devon smiled her twinkly smile.

Oh, God, Ceci thought. What do I do now?

CHAPTER **TWELVE**

"**L**ook," Brian said, sitting next to Ceci on her living room couch and grasping both of her hands in his. The setting sun cast long pink and purple shadows across the walls. "It's not like that with us. I've known Dev for a long time. She's a good friend, nothing else. We've never talked about marriage or even a committed relationship."

"Oh, for Pete's sake," Ceci said, yanking her hands back. "You have eyes, don't you? Even half-asleep in the hospital I could see the way she looked at you. She's insanely in love with you. She can't keep her hands off you. I watched her on Thanksgiving. Are you so blind you don't see it?" She stood up and walked toward the open door of the lanai, letting the Gulf breezes cool her off.

"I was here when she came back to town after Patton left her. We went out. Dinner. Movies. I was a shoulder to cry on. She's a demonstrative person. It's nothing."

"To you, maybe. Did you ever sleep with her?"

Brian gazed up at the ceiling as if he'd find the answer written there. "Couple of times. In the beginning. Not now and not for a long while."

"She's all in, then. Vulnerable, and her old pal Adonis hustles her off to bed. Men never get this. For women, sex usually isn't just about sex. It's about loving somebody. She loved you and still does. And now we get to break her heart. Precisely the kind of situation I enjoy. Exactly what Alex did to me."

"That's different. You were engaged, for God's sake. With Dev, it's casual. We're friends. We've been friends for more than ten years. She's not all in. No strings. She's not in love with me, and I'm certainly *not* in love with her. I haven't been in love with anyone for a long time."

"Since Rachel," Ceci said, turning back from the lanai.

Brian recoiled in shock. "How do you know about Rachel?"

"People talk, and I was interested in what they had to say."

"Was it Dev? She never knows when to put a muzzle on her mouth."

"No, it wasn't. I protect my sources, so I'm not going to give him or her up. But tell me about Rachel. I've really heard very little about her."

Grief passed his face, and it looked fresh. He pinched the bridge of his nose with his finger and thumb and squeezed his eyes shut for a few seconds, as if to stop tears, but his tone was steady. "Rachel was my wife for thirty-four months. She was beautiful, she was funny, and she was pregnant before she got sick. Most people don't know that. She lost the baby at six weeks. A few months later she died."

Brian's head and shoulders drooped. "I wished I had died with her. But I had to find a way to make something of the rest of my life, so after some time off, I got back to work and took care of myself by taking care of other people."

"I'm so sorry, Brian," Ceci said, kneeling in front of him and holding his face in her hands. She wished she had the words to help him lift the burden of what clearly remained a devastating loss. Not knowing what to say that might make a difference to Brian, she fell back on what her dad always called funeral home platitudes.

"You two were so young, with your lives ahead of you. It must have broken your heart."

"It did," he said, looking into Ceci's eyes and seeming not to be put off by her trite phrases. "But finally the fog lifted. Then a few days ago I met you, and now I know what I'm supposed to do. Make a fresh start with you. It feels like a freaking miracle. I didn't believe in love at first sight any more than you do, but I'm damned glad I asked Dev to invite you to Thanksgiving."

"That was *your* idea?" Ceci sat back, alarmed.

"Yes. I met you during a rescue. It wouldn't have been professional of me to start calling you. But once we'd met socially..."

"I can't believe this! You asked Dev, a woman who is mad for you, to put us together?" Ceci's voice was louder than she'd intended it to be—and it seemed to reverberate through the apartment.

"No. I asked her to invite you because you'd saved Mandy," Brian said, irritation peeking through, and his voice rising to meet hers.

"I didn't mention my interest. Dev's a natural connecter. She loves making matches, although I think she probably had you in mind for someone else, maybe the realtor guy."

"No, it was Sean Bennett, but whatever, I'm sure she'll be über-thrilled about being used." Ceci paced onto the lanai again, taking a deep breath before turning to face Brian again. "Here's how I want to play this. I want to be with you, even if it's only for a little while, since I'm probably going to have to find a job somewhere far from here. But I hate sneaking, and I know she'd find out. You *have* to tell her about us."

"I disagree, but if you think it's important, I'll go by after I leave here. You want to come with me?"

"Why would I want to do *that*?" Ceci said, her stance rigid and her tone strident. "It's going to be hard enough for her without the new girlfriend looking on. No, thank you. I'll skip the goodbye scene."

"You're wrong about her. I think she'll be happy for me."

"We'll see," she said, her back to Brian once again.

•

As he walked by her apartment, he heard them bickering. Trouble in paradise already? He smiled. A few more days, and she'd be ripe for plucking.

CHAPTER **THIRTEEN**

B rian bounded up the steps to Devon's house. She saw him and opened the door before he knocked. "Hi, sugar," she said, a brilliant smile creasing her face. She hugged him briefly but tightly. "What's up? I didn't expect to see you today."

"I wanted to see you. I have a little news, and Ceci thought we should talk about it."

A range of emotions was reflected in Devon's face almost immediately, mostly curiosity and confusion.

"Ceci? What does she want us to talk about?"

The pair of them walked into the living room where they often sat together on the couch watching movies or chatting. This time, though, Brian sat in the chair opposite Devon. He looked uneasy. Ceci's words had caused him to think more about his relationship with Devon. He knew he was right—that she thought of them as friends and would want the best for him, even if the best was another woman—but maybe there was something he wasn't seeing, something Ceci had picked up with her woman's intuition or whatever. He tried to relax and choose his words with care.

"Dev, I'm going to start seeing Ceci." He wanted to say he'd fallen head over heels, but if Ceci was right, that wasn't what Devon would want to hear.

"*Really?* When did that start?" The smile again passed over Devon's face. "I tried to fix her up with Sean. I didn't have any idea you were interested in her."

"Well, to tell you the truth, it's barely started, but we've found out we're really intrigued with each other." Brian felt himself calming down because Devon was taking the news exactly the way he'd known she would.

"Well, terrific, but let me ask you a couple of questions. Not to throw cold water on it or anything, but isn't Ceci going to leave the Key fairly soon? She mentioned she wasn't having any luck finding work in this area."

Brian sighed. "We've talked about it, of course, but we've decided to see where this goes anyway. We'll try to figure something out. Long-distance is hard, but this is the closest to a real relationship I've had with anyone since Rachel died, and I don't want to let her go."

"I'm happy for you, Brian. I really am," Devon said, her expression somber and her brow furrowed, "but I don't want you to get hurt. It took you a long time to get past Rachel, and I'd hate to see you have to go down that road again if Ceci leaves."

Taking his cue from Devon's evident concern for him and lack of any hint of jealousy, Brian went on. "I won't. I know there are some potholes to deal with, but I'm willing to give this a real try. She's worth it. Funny, smart, and, of course, gorgeous." It came to him he was describing Ceci in almost the same words he had used to talk about Rachel earlier in the evening. "And it doesn't hurt she happens to be a terrific baker."

"A baker?"

"Oh, yeah. She made a cake that would have made me fall in love with her if I already hadn't."

"So this isn't a passing thing. You're really in love with her? So fast?"

"Yeah, I am, and I can hardly believe it myself." He took Devon's hands in his. "You know how much you mean to me. It was important for me to tell you this. I wanted you to know. I hope you two can be really good friends."

"I already like her," Devon replied. "And she did save my daughter's life, so I have a big debt of gratitude there. I think we're already on our way to being friends. And since *our* friendship is going to change…"

"We won't lose each other. Things don't have to change," Brian said.

"Of course they do, Brian," Devon said, with an edge to her voice. "No woman wants her boyfriend or lover or husband or whatever to have the kind of relationship with another woman you and I have. We tell each other everything. Even someone as nice as Ceci won't tolerate it. Believe me. I know women." She squeezed Brian's hands.

"We had our little fling and we have this amazing friendship. Now that has to change because you're moving on. Eventually I will, too. Since I struck out so sensationally matching her with Sean, maybe I should give him a try myself." She laughed unconvincingly, Brian thought.

"I'm going to miss you terribly, though," Devon went on, removing her hands from his. Brian was surprised to see her mood shift so suddenly from laughter to a glaze of tears in her eyes.

"Oh, my God, don't cry, Dev," he said, alarmed.

"Oh, come on. This can't surprise you. It's natural. We're no longer going to be best friends and it will be hard on me. I'm picky about who I let into my life, and what we've had is never going to be the same. I've got to mourn a little bit, don't you think?"

"I guess I just don't see it that way. I see you finding some great guy and the four of us hanging together for a long, long time."

"I hope so," Devon said, recovering her more cheerful mood. "Now tell me everything. I want to know all about the woman who's stolen your heart."

They talked until midnight. When Brian left because he was called in, he felt relieved and couldn't wait to tell Ceci everything had gone so well. He knew she'd be asleep, though, so his call would have to wait.

•

After Brian took off, Devon sat alone in the dark until nearly dawn. She had thought she might sob the night away, but she didn't. Instead she turned her brain inside out trying to come to terms with the loss of the friendship that meant the world to her and was now going to be so different.

Everything that had made her life meaningful now caused pain. The long talks into the night. Sharing nearly every aspect of one another's lives. Early-morning phone calls as they each got ready for work. Reliving, together, the pain of Rachel's death and Devon's divorce and her worries about raising Mandy alone. Sometimes reading the same book and discussing it for hours. Walks along the beach. Gone. All gone. Brian would now be enmeshed in Ceci's life, and the loss of him wounded her. Her whole body ached.

Sex, though it had been part of the relationship in the beginning, hadn't been for a long time. She didn't know why it had disappeared, but it was clearly Brian's choice. Devon had tried seduction and outright asking, but Brian had turned her wiles and entreaties aside, without much by way of explanation. She thought it had something to do with guilt about Rachel, but they never discussed it. She hung on, though, because the friendship was worth it. She invested hours of her life in him, dating only occasionally and always talking it over with him afterward. Almost three years of no one else. The feeling of loss engulfed her.

He was enraptured for sure. When he talked about Ceci, it was about her beauty, her wit, her charm, her warmth, her passion. His words came rapidly, almost as if he were high on something. She'd never heard him sound like that, and now she felt as if she were mired in mud while Brian enumerated all the reasons he was so in love in such a short time.

Despite Brian's assurances Devon would always remain in his life, she knew nothing could be as it was and she'd be the one left behind, as she often had been. She tried so hard to be liked, but there seemed to be something about her that kept others at a distance, even people she spent a good amount of time with. Maybe she was too competent or too emotional or too...something. She knew a part of her was lacking but wasn't sure what it was. Even her parents had always seemed to be behind a scrim. She loved them but she'd felt unable to reach them, no matter how hard she tried. She had friends—for a while—but then they were off to other adventures, forgetting to include her. Patton had broken through, but after several years, he, too, took a powder. And now this. The one person who seemed to understand her and love her as a friend, for herself, was leaving her, too. She liked Ceci. She really did, and she was immeasurably grateful to her. But Ceci already had everything. Why did she have to have Brian, too?

As the sun rose and she stumbled up the stairs to get ready for work, she decided to call in sick. She'd squirreled away weeks of sick time because she loved her job, often going in when she was under the weather. She was good at what she did, always able to ferret out a solution to a problem, even among people who seemed to have diametrically opposing views. Knowing where all the bodies were buried, she often could hammer out an agreement simply by dropping a hint of gossip that would suddenly dissolve a stalemate.

She sometimes thought of herself as a sort of Lyndon Johnson in her small territory, only her tactic was not arm-twisting, but information. She seemed to know everything about everyone, both the laudatory and the shameful, and having all the data made her proud of herself. Today, though, she was too strung out even to think of work.

Crawling into bed and wanting to dissolve into weeping, she found herself still unable to cry. She lay quietly trying to recall a line of poetry she'd heard. Something about thoughts that lie too deep for tears. The poet really knew the truth. She felt paralyzed and the tears were definitely buried.

After an hour of trying to calm herself down, she realized sleep wasn't going to come. She got up, showered and dressed, and drove in to work. It looked like a light day and maybe it would help take her mind off things. She hoped so.

CHAPTER **FOURTEEN**

When her cell beeped early the next morning, Ceci thought it was Brian, and she braced herself for news about Devon. The area code was familiar, but not the number, and she was surprised to hear Sean's voice.

"Since you've never flown in a corporate jet, I thought I'd invite you along on a little trip. No execs. I have to run over to Orlando. Got an AD, an Airworthiness Directive, from the FAA, so I need to have a system checked out. I asked my boss. He said I could take someone along. The whole thing should take about six hours. We can be back around five if we leave right away. Then dinner maybe."

"How did you get my cell number?" Ceci asked, ignoring his invitation. "I don't remember giving it to you."

"You didn't. I have ways." He was audibly grinning.

"No, seriously. Not very many people have it."

"Brian gave it to me. I saw him at the all-night pharmacy down the Key. He was on his way in to work. He was supposed to be off last night and today, but there's some kind of flu hitting the department, and he had to fill in. He didn't look any too great himself. Said he had a headache that would drop a moose. Anyway, I told him I had this trip to make and you and I had talked about flying. He suggested maybe you'd like to come along. See some friends in Orlando or whatever."

Ceci's mind raced. Why would Brian think she'd ever want to go back to Orlando—for any reason? Once security has accompanied you and your little box of personal belongings to your employer's door, you want to shake the dust off your shoes and never go back there. But then she knew why. He was getting her out of town. Obviously, it hadn't gone well with Devon. A hellacious headache, and now he was scooting Ceci out of the way until things calmed down a little. If that's what he wanted, she'd play along. "Love to," she said.

"Great. I'll be there in ten."

•

"Nice ride," Ceci said, climbing aboard the small business jet after accompanying Sean on his preflight walk-around.

"It's a good little plane," Sean replied. "Not ostentatious. Pretty quick. The whole flight should take about a half-hour. We'll be descending almost as soon as we get to altitude. Come on up next to me while I do my checklist and then we'll go."

"Somehow I expected your pilot suit."

"I save the uniform for the paying customers," Sean said, putting a finger to his lips. "I need to concentrate now."

Twenty minutes later, buckled into her seat, Ceci was enjoying the view of a deep blue cloudless sky from the co-pilot's seat. "Want to fly it?" Sean said.

"Really?"

"Sure. Put your hands here," he said, wrapping her fingers around the right-side yoke. "See the display in front of you? The artificial horizon's in the middle. Are we straight and level?"

"Looks like it."

"Good. Keep it that way. Now, check the center display. See any weather anywhere?"

"Yeah, but it looks like it's south of us."

"True. How about traffic? Use your eyes. Do you see anybody?"

"Yes, coming toward us. *Right* toward us." Ceci stiffened with alarm.

"Correct. Right toward us and about a thousand feet above us."

"Oh." Her shoulders relaxed. "It seemed so much closer."

"We're at altitude now, so basically we're on the freeway and he's on an overpass. We won't be anywhere near each other."

"Okay by me. I'd rather not know there's another plane anywhere in the sky."

"Oh, so you're fun at take-offs and landings, then."

"Not really. I hate them. I know they're the most dangerous parts of a flight."

"You do too much research," Sean said. "I'm letting go now. She's all yours."

"Oh, holy crap," Ceci said, delighted. "I'm flying 275 miles an hour."

"Yes, you are," Sean laughed, "but not for long. We're at altitude already, and because this is such a short flight we'll begin our descent in only a couple of minutes. I'm going to have to take her back soon."

On the ground, Ceci was exhilarated. "Here we are, Claire," Sean said as they taxied. "Back at the scene of the crime."

When the engines were turned off, Ceci turned to him, gently placing her hands on his forearms. "Sean," she said, "could you call me Ceci? I lived with Claire here because I had to, but hearing it now reminds me of the reason I changed it in the first place—and it kind of freaks me out."

He looked chagrined, but his expression morphed smoothly toward compassion. "Of course. It's just that Claire is my favorite name. I've always thought if I ever had a daughter, it's the name I'd choose. And if I were you, it's the name I'd want to hear every day. But if you prefer Ceci, then Ceci it is."

•

"We may have a problem," Sean said as they approached the Key in their landing pattern on the way home. "I'm almost certain we don't, but I'm not getting the lights that tell me the gear is locked. I know it's down. I felt it, but we're going to fly around a little bit while I recycle it a couple of times."

As Sean nosed the plane up and then down, Ceci's serene expression masked her mounting fear. "No change," Sean said, "so I'm going to fly by the tower and have them tell me what they see."

Ceci froze. She wanted to ask questions, but Sean was speaking quietly to the tower. Something about three greens. He turned back to her. "It's good. All three wheels appear to be down and straight, but I'm still missing the lights. I'm sure it's a sensor thing and not a mechanical. Even if something folds up on us when we're on the runway, though, I know what to do. I don't think I'll have to. I think everything's going the way it should. Don't worry."

"Okay, I won't." Ceci worked to keep her nervousness under control, but her palms were slippery with sweat.

"I'm going to put her down now."

Ceci closed her eyes and waited for the plane to make contact with the ground. "We'll land soon, won't we?" she asked after a moment.

"We've been on the ground for about fifteen seconds, kiddo."

"I didn't feel anything!"

"I didn't want to break the eggs," Sean said with a laugh.

"You must be the best pilot ever." She exhaled as the fear exited her body.

"Let there be no doubt," he grinned.

"Why is there a fire truck over there in the grass?"

"I asked for the equipment just in case. I have some precious cargo here. Didn't want to take any chances."

CHAPTER **FIFTEEN**

"Feel like an early dinner?" Sean asked, as he and Ceci left the airport.

"Not really. I want to go home, if you don't mind. You did great and everything, but I'm kind of shot. Lots of excitement in the last week. This kind of put the cherry on the parfait for me."

"If you don't want to go out, how about pizza at your place? Romano's makes a great one and it's practically next door to your condo."

"Okay. I'm surprised at how hungry I am after those huge sandwiches in Orlando." She and Sean had spent the afternoon dawdling over lunch and talking about his job, her job, college days (his at Purdue and Embry-Riddle and hers at Ohio University), politics (on which they disagreed), and their shared fondness for Words with Friends. "I'll whip your…well, your lovely derriere," Sean had said.

"You'll have trouble. I'm very good at words," she retorted, as her mind flashed to her use of ensorcelled only a couple of days before, "and the only way you can beat me is if you use cheats. I never do, so if you do it's a Pyrrhic victory. That's p-y-r-r-h-i-c. Any questions?"

Their camaraderie was easy. "Siblings from another mother," Sean said. "I have three brothers. Always wanted a little sis. I think you're it."

As they waited for the pizza, Sean checked out the apartment. "Did you know you have a broken window here?" he said, calling to her from the second bedroom. "It looks like somebody tried to pry it open."

"Oh, geez," Ceci said, entering the bedroom. "Sometimes the renters don't think. I ran into some people from Breakers and

Banyans, and they said their renters used a hibachi in the middle of the living room! There was a huge ring of grease the carpet cleaners couldn't get out. They had to replace it all. I'll have someone fix the window."

"I'll take a look and see if I find anything else," Sean said, as Ceci answered the door for the pizza delivery.

"Your slider's off the track here, too," he said.

"In the front room?" Ceci said, her voice rising. "It was okay yesterday."

"Not now," Sean said. "I tried to manhandle it a little bit, but it didn't work. Have your guy look at that, too. You don't want anyone in here who doesn't belong."

CHAPTER **SIXTEEN**

"The trip was fine," Ceci said, in answer to Brian's question the next morning. "I was kind of surprised you gave my cell number to Sean, though. I keep it private. Almost nobody has it." She put the phone on speaker as she picked up her favorite mug and poured the day's first coffee.

"I didn't," Brian said. "I saw him in the drugstore last night. He said you told him you'd never been in a corporate jet and he was going to ask you to try it out. I had to go in to work all of a sudden and wasn't going to be able to see you, so I thought you might enjoy it. But I didn't give him your number."

"He said you did. How could he have gotten it?"

"Honey, I don't know, but it wasn't from me."

The "honey" softened Ceci's indignation as she picked up her phone and took the coffee upstairs to her bedroom. In bed, she leaned back against a phalanx of pillows and set the coffee mug on the side table to cool. "I thought you were getting me out of town because it had been a big mess with Devon. Why else would you send me to Orlando, of all places?"

"*Orlando?* He said he was going to Gainesville."

"It was Orlando, believe me."

"Hmm. Two lies. One to you and one to me. I don't like it."

"Me either, but I really want to know is how it went with Devon. Is she okay?"

"It went the way I thought it would. We spent a couple of hours talking about it. Our being together has been a transitional thing for her and a high school halfback – cheerleader thing for me. So it wasn't some weepy goodbye or anything. She's sad we won't be seeing each other as much, but she seemed to be pretty chipper when I left."

"That's surprising. Whenever I've seen the two of you together, she's always had that 'he's mine' kind of look about her. When Sean said you had such a terrible headache, I figured it had been all emotional and horrible."

"Nah. I had a monster sinus thing going on. Took some decongestant and everything's fine now. But I have to stay on duty for another day. This flu is really ugly. Everybody's sick. Do you want to paint tomorrow?"

"I was hoping I could put it off forever, but I got a text from my parents last night. They're driving down in ten days or so, even though my mom's still in the immobilizer for her knee. Since I'm here and it's already icky in Ohio, they've decided to do Christmas on the Key."

"You pick up the paint, and I'll see you tomorrow. We'll paint, we'll fool around, and we'll see where it goes from there."

"Painting, like flattery, will get you everywhere," Ceci said. "I hate painting."

Carrying her empty mug back to the kitchen, Ceci noticed the envelope under the door. Probably a notice from the condo board, she thought, but she sucked in air as she saw the handwriting on the front. All in caps.

GOOD MORNING, CLAIRE.

She opened it.

GET RID OF HIM.

CHAPTER **SEVENTEEN**

That night, in the murky state between waking and sleeping, Ceci heard the glass door slide open. Unnerved, she reached for her phone. It slipped from her fingers and fell to the floor beyond her grasp. Seeing her move, he yanked her from the couch by her hair and dragged her across the lanai toward the beach. The tide was high as he hauled her into the water. She couldn't find her voice to scream. No matter how she thrashed and kicked, his strength was overpowering. He pushed her head into the waves; she gulped water and felt it burn her throat. Panic consumed her. She heard Brian's voice from too far away. She was alone. And dying.

She woke fully. "Oh, God, not again," she said to herself. "Not this."

She went to the kitchen, grabbed a bottle of water from the fridge and guzzled it. Sinking down on the couch, still unnerved, she tried to calm herself without success.

She felt the familiar prickling above her knees on the backs of her thighs. "No," she said. "No." As she fought against it, the trembling began, first in her legs and slowly moving up to envelop her entire body. The tremors gave way to uncontrollable chills. Cold crept over her; sweat poured down her forehead. Her entire face ached as she tried to stop the quivering by clenching her jaw, even though she knew it wouldn't work. Her bones felt frozen. Grabbing a throw from the back of the couch, she tossed it into the dryer for a couple of minutes and wrapped herself in the warmth. It was comforting, but the shaking continued.

She paced, frantic, and stared at her face in the bathroom mirror. It was bright red, and her pulse raced so fast she couldn't count it.

You know what this is, she said to herself, her thoughts careening almost out of control. It's a panic attack, and it won't kill you. You've been through it before. You know your blood pressure is way up, but it will come down on its own. You don't need to go to the emergency room again. TV won't work. Reading won't work. Only distraction works. Write this out. She grabbed her journal and scribbled whatever came to mind.

As she wrote, her hand twitching to the point her words were almost illegible, she became aware of how terrified she was of the stalker himself and by the thought of dying young. All she had to do was think of Rachel to realize no one was immune from untimely death, and the threats she had received concerned both torture and killing. The thought of having to deal—again—with someone unknown who wished her real harm felt like more than she could bear.

She realized she was struggling not only with what, but also with why. *I'm a good person*, she wrote. *I don't hurt people, at least never deliberately. What have I done to him? To anybody?*

The act of putting her thoughts down on paper brought her a degree of calm; the shaking slowed. Reading more of what she'd written, she realized something else that was troubling her: a pervasive sense of failure. *I've always been good enough*, she wrote. *Always. It was expected. One day I came home with a report card that was all A's except a B+ in history. I remember my dad looking at it and saying, "Why did you get a B?" There was no condemnation in his tone, no anger. Only surprise. I think that was the day I began to believe anything less than perfection was unacceptable, even though he never said anything to make me think so. That's all on me. And now I've failed at my job and at a relationship I thought would make me happy for the rest of my life. Maybe I'm not good enough*, she'd written, underlining *not*.

And last, Brian himself. *Can this possibly be real? How can I have swung from loving one man to loving another so much in only a few weeks? Is it really love or is it some sick dependency? Am I a weakling who has to have a man in her life? Can't I stand on my own? Am I my mother's daughter, after all?*

This is ridiculous, she thought, as she read her scribbling. The guy who's after me is nuts, not someone I hurt. It's not my fault. The break-up with Alex wasn't my fault, either. He's a deceitful, lying bastard. I loved him, I thought, and I was good to him—faithful, kind, loyal—a real Girl Scout.

I got fired because Jake and I weren't good together and he had seniority. It doesn't mean I'm lousy at what I do. The first firing had nothing to do with me at all, so why am I letting it bother me now? And Brian? Brian is a gift from God and I'm lucky I found him and fell in love with him.

Her body finally calmed itself. Breathe in and out now, the way you learned in yoga, she thought. Slowly she felt the last vestiges of overwhelming anxiety lift like a vapor.

Sighing, she checked the doors and went upstairs to bed, where exhaustion from the rush of terror overcame her.

CHAPTER **EIGHTEEN**

Every building on the Key was an ideal representation of Florida Modern, except for the police station, which looked like a Wild West lock-up. Ceci expected to see wanted posters for Butch and Sundance or Billy the Kid. The worn wooden floors were permanently pockmarked from the sand tracked in by generations of residents and occasional miscreants. Ceiling fans moved the air only slightly.

A young woman who had to be the department's newest recruit led Ceci and Brian to an interrogation room. It was a study in decrepitude, except for the walls, which had been painted a bright, nauseating pink.

"Oh, my God," Ceci said. "Nobody's used Drunk-Tank Pink since the Seventies. Do they still have the rubber hose and bare bulb, too?" If she hadn't been as upset as she was, she would have laughed, but now she wondered if the Key police were up to the task of dealing with any crime more serious than joyriding or disorderly conduct.

She and Brian sat side by side at the table in the center of the room—a table so dilapidated its fourth leg was held up by two beaten-down, cobbled-together soft drink cans. The wooden chairs were hard on the hips. If I had to sit in these for more than a couple of hours, I'd confess to anything, Ceci thought. Don't they have any budget at all? Her skepticism must have shown in her face. Brian patted her hand. "It'll be okay," he said.

She felt better when the department's lone detective, Zach Smallwood, took a place at the wobbly table. Ceci thought Zach looked precisely like what he was. A tall African American with close-cropped graying hair, skin drawn so tightly over his high cheekbones it looked burnished, Ray-Ban aviators folded up and the temple piece jammed between the first and second button of his white dress shirt. Amber eyes. Cop shoes. He didn't seem as world-worn as a lot of the urban police Ceci knew, probably because he didn't see much violent crime on the Key. She wondered how he kept his investigative chops when he had so little practice, but at the same time admitted the possibility that maybe he was the greatest detective since Sherlock Holmes and chose to work on the Key because he liked the weather. Brian had called him when he heard about the note, and now the three of them had gathered for a debrief.

"Let's start at the beginning, Ms. Myers," he said, his faint drawl pure Kentucky, the prettiest of Southern accents, which Ceci recognized from spending nearly her entire life in Cincinnati. He pulled a long, slim notebook and a pen from the inside breast pocket of his blue blazer. "Who's Claire?"

"I am," Ceci said, noticing even from upside down Zach's handwriting was as exquisite as a monk's calligraphy. She wanted to ask him how he learned to write like that, but she kept her eye on the ball and her mind on the question. "My name is Claire Cooper Myers. C. C. I've been called Ceci since I was a baby and all the way through school and college. Almost nobody knows my real name."

"I certainly didn't until a few minutes before we came in. I assumed it was Cecelia," Brian said to Zach.

Ceci was shaken. *How could I have fallen so far in love with a man who doesn't even know my name?* But then it occurred to her she'd never told him. Swept up in a passion she'd never felt before, she was dismayed to realize this was a man she didn't know. What was she doing?

She dragged herself back to Zach's interview. "When I worked in Indianapolis, I had a stalker," Ceci said, turning to the detective. "He knew me as Ceci. I used my real first and middle names when I went to Orlando to throw him off the trail if he was of a mind to follow me. I knew it might not work. Anybody with access to anything about changes in television could find me in a few minutes just by comparing pictures and stuff, but not everybody knows about those pages. I was kind of hiding in plain sight when I got to Orlando."

She drew a breath as she spit out the rest of her story, her throat tight and her breathing shallow. "Once I arrived there, it stopped. Not a peep. I thought I was free of him until today. I'm sure it's the same guy because he acts the same way he did up north."

"Which is?" Zach asked, peering intently at Ceci.

"No personal contact. No pictures of his privates to my email—and nothing ever to my social media sites. It was a very personal, intimate situation, which made it even more frightening. All I ever got were notes making it clear he was close by every minute and waiting for an opportunity to hurt me or someone who mattered to me. He's meticulous. If you try to find anything on this envelope or piece of paper, the only things you'll see are my fingerprints."

Her voice became even more strained, as if her vocal cords were tightening as she spoke. "My station in Indianapolis knew all about it. I never went to or from the parking lot alone. Everything was reported to the police, but they never found him. And there wasn't too much they could do about it anyway. They said I should file a restraining order, but I didn't know who he was, so I couldn't. I can put you in touch with the detective there. Her name's Charlotte Baird. Charlie. She has a file and copies of all the notes. I have the case number here, too." Zach nodded.

"Zach, I was scared to death all the time. He threatened rape or torture. He said he would kill me. Constantly. And not just me. He threatened anyone he thought might get between us." Her hands trembled. "He was like the air. No one ever saw him come or go. After a few weeks, I couldn't sleep. I didn't eat. I lost weight and always looked like hell on camera. Going out was hard. Staying in was harder."

She took a deep breath and went ahead. "I don't know how you feel about civilians and guns, but I finally got a concealed carry permit. I had a gun close by most of the time in my apartment, even though my roommate wasn't crazy about it. I took training at a target range. I kept the gun in the car, too.

"The guy hated it if he saw me with another man, even if it was someone from work," Ceci talked on, the color draining slowly from her face. "I pretty much stopped dating. I didn't want to be responsible for some poor guy getting beat up or taking a bullet because we went out for a burger."

Zach sat quietly for a moment, watching Ceci and Brian. "Ms. Myers," he said finally, "you were Claire Cooper in Orlando. Is there anyone on the Key who would be aware of that name?"

"Only one I know of. Sean Bennett. "

"How would *he* know?" Brian said, his voice hard as flint.

Ceci could feel her relationship with Brian blowing up in her face. "He flies to Orlando a lot. When I sat with him at the concert, he said he'd been trying to remember where he'd seen me before. He called me Claire."

"He sure as hell didn't mention any of that to me," Brian said. "He told me you'd been together at the concert. Period. Kind of a big omission."

"I don't know why he didn't tell you. Maybe he thought you already knew. Or he shouldn't talk about it. I don't know. I'd give him the benefit of the doubt."

Zach continued to observe the byplay between the two of them and then tapped his pen on his notepad, with a tinge of no-nonsense impatience. "If we could get back to my questions. Did you explain to this guy—Bennett—why you changed your name?"

"Yeah."

"Did you give him any details about the way you were stalked?"

"Not really. I don't share that with just anyone."

"Zach," Brian interrupted, "Ceci was with him yesterday, and there was some weird stuff happening. He told me he was going to Gainesville to have something checked on the company plane. He invited Ceci to go with him, but they didn't go to Gainesville. He took her to Orlando instead. And he told her I'd given him her cell number, which I didn't. I'm not about to give her private number to some other guy." He covered Ceci's hand with his own. The storm seemed to have blown over.

"And you know what?" Ceci said. "There was one other thing. When I went to the Christmas concert, he said he'd heard me say I liked classical music. It bugged me at the time because I know I never, ever said that to him. The only place he could have heard it was at Thanksgiving dinner at Dev Carter's, and I'm sure I didn't talk about music there."

"Has Bennett ever been to your apartment?"

"Yesterday. We had pizza after the trip." Brian slowly withdrew his hand from hers. "I didn't want to go out and we were both hungry, so we sent out for Romano's."

"Were you with him the whole time?"

"Mostly. I told him he could look around the apartment while I was setting the table. He found some things that needed to be repaired."

"Like?"

"A window and…" Ceci paused, "he said the sliding glass door was off the track and he'd tried to fix it. But when I'd looked at the door the morning we left, it wasn't broken. I'd swear to it because I locked it. Do you think someone tried to get in while we were gone?"

"I think we'd better talk to Mr. Bennett," Zach said, replacing his notebook and pen. "Your stalker disappears for a year, you tell Bennett about it, and within twenty-four hours the guy's back. Could be a coincidence, but Bennett knows where you live and your real name, so I'd say he's of interest. We'll chat and see if we can clear a few things up."

"Wait," Ceci said, pointing at Zach. "Maybe you don't have to. He *can't* be the one. I came downstairs today about eight-thirty to get the paper. The note wasn't there then. I went back up to the bedroom and after I talked to you," she looked at Brian, "I read the paper and dozed off for a while. I didn't come back down until about nine-thirty and that's when I found the envelope. So it showed up in the hour between 8:30 and 9:30."

"Go on," the detective said.

"Sean was flying this morning at seven-thirty. He had to be at the airport by seven o'clock. The company president and the attorney were going to North Carolina. Sean couldn't have done it. He wasn't here."

"Easy enough to check," Zach said. "We'll find out if the flight was delayed and if so, why. Whoever is doing this meets the Florida definition of aggravated stalking and a credible threat. But since we don't know who it is, we don't have anyone to arrest. We really don't have anything to go on, but I'll give this as much attention as I can, informally for the moment. Brian saved my dad when he had a heart attack. It's the least I can do, even if it's kind of unofficial right now."

CHAPTER **NINETEEN**

After Zach left, Brian wheeled on Ceci in the Pepto-colored room. "Anything else you need to tell me?" he said, his eyes narrowed.

"I think you know it all now. I've already been interrogated once today, and look, it's not even noon," she said, irritated. "I'm in no mood."

"Sorry, but pizza and apparently cozy conversation with the pilot? I didn't know I was in a competition."

She tried a smile. "I'm surprised at this, Brian. You and Sean are friends, aren't you? I got that impression from him."

"We're acquaintances. Dev and I had dinner with him and his girlfriend a time or two. I sure wouldn't call us intimate friends."

"Whatever. You suggested the trip and sent me off with him. I had no idea why. I thought it was because Devon was upset and going to confront me or something, but I didn't know for sure. Maybe you were throwing me at him for another reason. Maybe she'd gotten you into bed for a last-call, one-for-the-road pity-screw and you'd changed your mind. I didn't hear anything from you."

"I *didn't* suggest it to him," Brian said, his annoyance matching Ceci's. "He suggested it to me, and then he lied about how he got your number. I had to go in to work fast and the night was nonstop. There wasn't any time. Between the non-breathers and the bleeders and the diabetic coma and the barfing kids with nervous moms…oh, crap, those are all bad excuses. I should have taken a minute to call you." His tone moderated, the air leaving the balloon of his indignation. "It didn't occur to me you'd be worried. I told you everything would be okay, and it was."

"I have to admit I was kind of petrified about what might be going on with the two of you. And now I'm worried about what happened this morning. I don't even know who this nut case is warning me to stay away from—you or Sean—since I know Sean isn't our guy."

Brian looked down at Ceci, his eyes shining. The expression on his face warmed her. "Good morning," he said, extending his hand to her. "My name is Brian Walker. Would you like to start over?"

The thrill of his touch zinged all the way up her arm. "I would," she said. "I really would."

•

Starting over began at the beach. It was overcast, but the sun was making its way through the clouds. The repetitive sound of the waves was comforting as Brian and Ceci walked aimlessly, stopping once to sit on the sand and play with Thelma and Louise. Freed from confinement in their apartment, the dogs ran in circles, yipping and chasing each other.

Ceci felt more at ease than she had all day. The panic attack of the night before was behind her. She'd decided not to tell Brian about it because she was sure it was a one-off, something that had zapped her because of a bad dream. Brian was at her side, the tension of the morning with Zach had dissipated, and everything felt right again.

The two of them chatted briefly with Annah, but once she had called the little terriers inside, Ceci and Brian continued to walk hand in hand. "I'm almost afraid to hold your hand in public," Ceci said. "I don't know where Mr. Nutso is. Is he watching? Has he walked by us right on this beach? Does he live around here? Are you in danger? Is Sean?"

"Look," Brian said, "this guy might not be dangerous at all. He gets off by scaring you to death. He's never made a real move on you or hurt anyone close to you, and it doesn't seem like things are getting any worse. He's a sick twist for sure, but if you can, try to stop worrying about him."

"I'd like to. Coming back from Orlando yesterday was enough worry for me for a while."

Brian stopped suddenly. "Did Sean do something to you? In the plane?"

"No. He did something for me. He did some great piloting."

Brian wrapped his arm around Ceci's shoulders as they walked along. "You better tell me about it. I don't want any more surprises where this guy is concerned."

Ceci explained the events of the flight, her fear, and Sean's coolness under pressure.

Brian pulled Ceci closer. "Everything was down and locked," Ceci explained, "but I was petrified about landing. I saw a belly landing once in Dayton. It wasn't pretty. People usually walk away, but that time three people got hurt. It was my rookie story, and it stuck with me. Sean got us down fine and we taxied straight to the shop for an inspection. Since he left early this morning, I'm sure he was right about the sensor. He must have had it fixed."

Brian fell into a deep silence for a couple of minutes. Finally he said, "I hate to bring this up, but is there a possibility there was nothing wrong and he was trying to frighten and impress you all at the same time?"

"Wow! What a leap." Ceci peered up at him, disbelief in her eyes. "He tried to recycle the gear twice and he talked to the tower. It seemed like a real problem to me. I didn't hear him do it, but he asked for fire equipment."

"Think about it, though," Brian said, stopping again. "He says there might be a problem with the landing gear and then does all these things to make you believe him. Did you know where to look for the sensor lights? They might have been on the whole time. The tower had no way of knowing whether they were on or not. He's lied to you, he's lied to me. Maybe he cooked up a simple, unprovable crisis. And when he gets you safely on land and it turns out to be nothing, he's a hero. He gets closer to you."

"Now who's paranoid? I know you don't like whatever relationship you think Sean and I have, but he can't be the guy who stalked me. It started two years ago, and he's never lived in Indianapolis."

"He wouldn't have to live there. He could have been in and out, the way he is in Orlando. It would be interesting to see flight logs over the last few years."

"But if he knew I was in Orlando, which he did, why didn't anything happen there? My face was on the air for a year. Nobody bothered me. You know how I was wrong about Devon?" Ceci continued quietly. "I think it's your turn."

"Let's not talk about this anymore," Brian said, as they washed the sand off their feet and entered Ceci's condo. "Let's do something normal. If you'll go pick up something to eat, I'll stay here and get the paint and brushes ready to tackle your renovation project."

●

As they scrubbed, masked, and painted walls and cabinets throughout the afternoon and into the evening, Brian and Ceci caught up on what they'd missed.

"Parents," Brian said.

"Richard and Kimberly, never Kim," Ceci answered. "Private banker and homemaker, in that order. Yours?"

"My dad was Mark. Killed by a drunk driver when I was ten," Ceci's face showed her surprise and sympathy. "He was a high school science teacher and a great guy. Mom's Sally. She's the office manager of a huge medical practice in Tampa. Siblings?"

"One younger sister. Her name is Gigi, honest to God."

Brian threw back his head and laughed. "Seriously? C.C. and G.G.?"

"Yep. Gloria Grayson. I think my folks went temporarily insane. She's in PR in Michigan. Ann Arbor. Your turn."

"Younger sister Ashley. She's a teacher like our dad. Married to Jack Brannon. She lives on the mainland not too far from me. Younger brother Jeffrey in Atlanta. He's a web designer. His middle name is Joseph and, yes, we do call him J.J."

"No, you don't," Ceci laughed. "Change of subject. Blake Shelton or Luke What's-his-name?"

"Johnny Cash. Leaves the new boys in the dust."

Ceci dipped her small roller into the paint tray. "Ketchup. In the refrigerator or the cabinet?"

"Are you kidding me? Fridge. Potato salad. Eggs or no eggs?"

"I'm from Cincinnati, Brian. *German* potato salad. No eggs and no mayo. Vinegar, sugar, and bacon, though. Mercedes or BMW?"

Brian turned from rinsing his brush. "Jaguar. How are we doing?"

"I'd say we're great. Agreement on almost every important matter. French toast or pancakes?"

"Pancakes."

"That's only because you haven't had my strawberry-stuffed brioche French toast."

"Can we have it for breakfast?" Brian said, laying the brush on the newspaper beside the sink and wrapping his arms around Ceci from the back, nuzzling her neck.

"I have strawberries and oranges. I have brioche. Cream cheese, milk, eggs, and vanilla. Come back tomorrow at nine."

"I'd rather stay."

"I'd rather have you stay. I'm not some quivering virgin trying to make you crazy by dangling 'maybe' in front of you. This is not my first rodeo. To be honest, though, I haven't had a lot of partners. The college boyfriend, one drunken New Year's Eve with a co-worker in Dayton, which I will regret for the rest of my life, and the idiot fiancé are the sum of my sexual experience."

Ceci turned to face Brian, her arms around his waist and her head against his shoulder. After a moment of feeling secure in his arms, she looked up. "I've thought about it a lot, and what I've come down to is if we have sex now, it will feel like revenge for me, like I got back at Alex—fast—for how he treated me. I don't like the feeling and it's really unfair to you. You're not someone I want to *use*. I'd rather come to you with a full heart and no lingering anger toward anyone else. I want you in every way possible more than anything, but I also want it to be right. Does that make any sense?"

"Even though it's obvious I'm thinking with something other than my brain, I guess it does. I have to say, however, we've got a real Henry the Eighth – Anne Boleyn thing going here."

"Oh, please," Ceci laughed, "she kept that poor guy on the string for seven years before she opened her legs. We've known each other, what, ten days? And then he cut off her head."

"Yeah, but each day without having you is like a year, so I've been waiting longer than Henry. And please don't even mention the word head. Will you still fix the French toast?"

"I will, and I guarantee you're going to want me even more once you taste it."

"I'd rather taste you."

"That's allowed," Ceci said, pulling him to her and parting his lips with her tongue.

CHAPTER **TWENTY**

"I talked to Zach this morning," Brian said the next day, as Ceci laid the platter of French toast and sausage on the breakfast bar, which was still littered with paint cans and brushes.

"On Sunday? Did he find out anything?"

"Lots of contradictory stuff," Brian said, drowning the toast in maple syrup. "Sean *is* gone, apparently where he said he was going. He's due back late today. But, and this is interesting, he never asked anybody in the shop to check the sensors. I thought you were with him when he was supposed to have done that."

"No. He tossed me his keys and asked me to pick him up at the front of the drive-through joint at the airport. The Autopilot. Then he went into the shop." She speared a couple of sausage links as she moved her chair close to Brian's.

"I think he sat around shooting the shit with the mechanics for a while and told you another lie."

"But why? What does he gain?"

"Like I said before, hero status."

"That's crazy. He said he had three brothers and I felt like a sister to him."

"You didn't fall for his crap, did you?"

"Brian, I'm not stupid. He wasn't putting me on. He's become a friend. Nothing else."

"Maybe. But I'd like you to move into my house for the next two days. I'm off and I'll stay here to see if anyone shows up or to take anything that might get delivered. I'll feel a lot better knowing you're out of harm's way. No one will know where you are. If anyone asks, you're interviewing for a new job."

Ceci was immediately on her guard. "You want to put me on the mainland and leave me there alone when this guy seems to know where I am all the time? I don't want to do that. At least here I have lots of people around. This isn't a big complex, but everyone's coming and going all day. And even so, the nitwit got through to me. I don't think I'd feel safe on the mainland where I don't know anyone."

"Don't worry. At my place, the people really look out for one another. There's a neighborhood watch and we all take it seriously. It's safe."

"Frankly, the idea creeps me out." She gathered up the dishes and headed for the other side of the island. She poured some Dawn into the sink and busied herself with creating suds. She needed to think. Brian was a smart guy who wouldn't endanger her. At least she didn't think he would, but the idea of being alone in a strange place frightened her. Although she'd slept well the night before, the dream and the panic attack from a couple of days before were still with her. In only a few minutes, though, she decided to stop being a scared little mouse and take her life back. She put her reservations to sleep and capitulated to Brian's suggestion.

"Don't take much," he said. "Just a toothbrush and a couple pairs of shorts and shirts. If somebody's watching, we don't want him to see you with a suitcase. Shove all the stuff into a grocery bag."

"But, Brian, if I'm interviewing and staying overnight someplace out of town, wouldn't I have a suitcase? You're being overly analytical."

She started for the stairs. "May I take my underwear and make-up—and maybe some shoes?" Ceci asked. "I assume you have a hair dryer." She grinned at him as she went to round up two days' worth of necessities.

•

It began to drizzle as they left the condo. Just before they stepped into Brian's vintage Honda, Ceci stopped still. "Smell that," she said.

"Smell what?"

"The scent of the rain. It hasn't rained here for quite a while, and the earth is releasing some compounds that make up the sweet smell. There's a word for it: petrichor."

"I have a feeling I'm going to be in for an English education. Where did you ever pick up that word?"

"My roommate in Indianapolis. She's a meteorologist. Knows all kinds of arcane weather words."

"I'll try to file it, but I'll probably forget it. I doubt if comes up much in conversation."

"Not too much," Ceci said, sliding into the car.

•

"I love your house," Ceci said. "Somehow I pictured you in a leather-upholstered man cave with a 5,000-inch TV."

Brian grimaced. "I'm not a frat boy. I'm thirty-two years old, and I have at least some taste—and Rachel had a lot more. We were lucky to get this house. It was a foreclosure and we snapped it up really fast. We expected to get into a bidding war, but it didn't happen. I've always felt a little guilty about it. The original owners were another young couple and they had to give up their dream when the recession hit. I wonder about them sometimes.

"It's not a very big house. About fourteen hundred square feet," Brian went on, as he led her down the hall outside the kitchen toward the bedrooms, "but I like living here. It's a community. People buy in this area and they stay. The folks on either side have been here since before Rachel and I moved in."

Looking around Brian's home, Ceci remembered her mom talking about the karma of a house. "Take the house we had on Fairfield," she had said. "It was our first one and the house we brought you and Gigi home to, which makes it my happiest house, but at the same time, it was the saddest because it's where we lived when I had those awful postpartum depressions. I thought about suicide constantly because I knew I couldn't make it through another day. I think a house breathes in all those things from everyone who ever lived there. It's why some houses feel comfortable to some people and others wouldn't live there on a bet. It's more than colors and kitchens and where the bathrooms are. It's in the walls. Some people think you can feng shui it all out, but I'm not so sure."

Ceci felt at home at Brian's, almost as if Rachel had left a personal benediction behind for her. Everything in the house looked like something she would have chosen herself. "The art is spectacular," Ceci said, entering the small bedroom Brian used as an office. She leaned in to look more closely at a painting—a professional-quality water color of the house—that hung over the couch. "Rachel did this?" she said, noticing the artist's signature.

Brian nodded. "She was a graphic designer, but her real love was painting. She did most of what's hanging on the walls." Ceci looked more closely at a stunning still life of flowers and fruit and a whimsical portrait of a dog that looked as if it could come to life at any moment. What a talent, she thought, wondering again about exactly what kind of woman Rachel would have become. She had died almost a girl, with so much promise. Ceci was sure she would have liked her.

She glanced at a silver-framed color photo on the desk: Brian and a woman as arresting as he, with black hair and dazzling deep brown eyes flecked with gold. Her seemingly pore-free oval face glowed with natural color. "Rachel?" she said, nodding at the photo.

"Yes. Our wedding picture."

"You both look so happy. She's ravishing, and I don't think I've ever used that word to describe a woman before."

"It's a good one. She was."

"I noticed a menorah in the china cabinet," Ceci said. "Are you Jewish?"

"No, my family's kind of eclectic," Brian chuckled. "We were all baptized Catholic at Hell's Angels by the Ocean, which is what J.J. and I called Holy Angels at the Shore. I'm more skeptical than I once was. I like this pope, though. My brother's a Presbyterian, and my sister is a Druid." A look of surprise crossed Ceci's face.

"Not really. It's just she's more in tune with nature and 'the unity of all creation,' as she likes to put it. Pretty poetic for a science teacher. Rachel was Jewish. Her birth name was Feldstein. Her parents weren't overjoyed with her choice."

"That sounds like my brother-in-law's family. They're Catholic, too, and we're Episcopalians. It's not much of a jump, but I think his folks wanted to bring back the Inquisition."

"All that stuff is crap," Brian said, showing Ceci out the patio door. "My mom was fine with whatever we wanted, but we couldn't invite her to the wedding and not have Rachel's family, so we were married at the Muni by the mayor. Worked for us. He took the picture."

As she stepped onto the brick patio, Ceci was entranced by its beauty. "It's gorgeous, Brian," she said, taking in the complex patterns and whorls, almost like a labyrinth. "The masonry is off the hook."

"Thanks," he said, putting his arm around her shoulders. "I laid every damn brick myself. It took weeks, but I think the result was worth it. I started last fall and did the plantings in the spring."

Ceci sighed with relief. Not only did she feel at home at Brian's, but it was clear he wasn't being driven only by painful memories. He mentioned his wife easily and her presence was everywhere, but the small, beautiful patio was something he had done for himself. He was continuing to move on and build a life beyond what he had shared with Rachel. It was clear he would always cherish her, but he had come to the place where he knew all the wanting in the world couldn't bring her back. Ceci sensed what a hard lesson that had been for him.

"It's beautiful," she said. "I've never seen a garden with this much blue and purple, and the white makes it feel restful and calm. So many colors here seem too bright. Kind of garish, you know?"

Brian looked at her with appreciation and placed a soft kiss on her temple. "That's why I did it this way. I wanted something peaceful to come home to. I sit out here a lot and decompress, especially if the day's been really stressful. "

As they finished the tour of the house, Brian said, "You can sleep wherever you want. The guest room is probably the nicest one, but if you want to sleep in mine…"

"And imagine you there next to me?" Ceci said. "I like that thought. I think I'll feel safer there."

"I have t-shirts in the bureau. Sleep in one of those. I'll be thinking of you in it."

CHAPTER **TWENTY-ONE**

With no reason to get up early the next morning, Ceci slept in, checked her phone to see if there were any responses to the résumés she'd sent out, and padded out of the bedroom, wearing only Brian's t-shirt and her bikini underwear. Although she'd tried to keep it at bay, worry licked at her. Her father had taught his girls to squirrel away six months of salary in case of emergency, but she'd had a lot of fun in Orlando and the savings had dwindled to about three months' worth. Although she didn't have rent to pay for a couple more weeks, she'd have to leave the Key soon. She needed a job. I'm *not* moving back home, she thought. Several of her friends were boomerang babies, living in their parents' basements and sucking funds Mom and Dad had put away for retirement. Ceci couldn't imagine it.

To take her mind off her predicament, she fumbled through the kitchen cabinets to find the ingredients for an apple tart she was experimenting with. "This man is not an organized cook," she muttered, sighing and shaking her head in exasperation. She finally located the cinnamon and was measuring dry ingredients when she looked up, startled to see a woman standing on the porch. She was holding a vacuum cleaner.

I didn't know they sold vacuum cleaners door to door anymore, Ceci thought. The woman rapped on the window and then, to Ceci's amazement, unlocked the door and barged in. Dressed in yoga pants and a cotton man-tailored shirt covering what looked to be an eight-month pregnancy, she stared at Ceci in surprise.

Vacuum Woman spoke first. "I'm Ashley Brannon," she said, her face flushing from her neck to the hairline. "Brian's sister. He let me borrow his sweeper. Mine broke and I'm having people for dinner and I needed to clean and I thought I'd bring it back while I was out running errands." The words gushed out in one long sentence without punctuation. "I'm sorry. I don't usually ramble on like this. I didn't see Brian's car, so I didn't expect anyone to be here."

Ceci stepped forward, trying to maintain a matter-of-fact attitude to cover her own astonishment. "I'm Ceci Myers," she said, extending her hand. "A friend of Brian's." Ashley's eyebrows rose almost imperceptibly as she took Ceci's hand. "He's letting me stay for a few days. He's not here right now," she continued, becoming aware her breasts were visible under the light fabric of the t-shirt. She was thankful that at least her lady bits and buttocks were covered. "Let me put on a robe or something and we'll talk."

"Again, I'm sorry I startled you," Ashley said.

"Don't worry about it. I'm sure it was surprising finding me here."

She scurried into the bedroom, mortified and embarrassed, emerging a few minutes later, fully dressed, from Brian's bedroom, a detail Ceci was sure Ashley hadn't missed. She quickly brewed some tea and sat down with Brian's sister in the living room. "Brian is at my place on the Key for the next couple of days," she said, as she began the explanation of the reasons for her residence at Brian's house.

"Wow, how awful," Ashley said, adding cream and sugar to her tea. "And you have no idea who it is?"

"Not really. It might even be two people. One who stalked me in Indianapolis and gave up when I moved, and a copycat here. Brian has a suspicion about who it might be. I think he's wrong, but I agreed to come here to get away from the Key for a few days."

"You're comfortable being here alone?" Ashley asked. "I don't think I'd be."

"I wasn't at first," Ceci said, warming to Ashley, "but Brian told me he'd let the police know I was here and why, and they'd keep an eye on things."

"I'm sure they will," Ashley said with a little chuckle. "They've known Brian since high school. The fire and police departments here are in one building, and he's wanted to be a firefighter since he was sixteen, after 9/11. He was always hanging around the fire house. When he was old enough and had the training, he did ride-alongs. That made him even more determined. "

"I know he's a paramedic, but I didn't know he was a firefighter, too. He never told me."

"He isn't yet, but it's his dream," Ashley said, stirring another half-teaspoon of sugar into her cup and settling into the sofa as comfortably as she could. "When he graduated from high school, he went to a community college to go through their firefighting academy and took EMT training at the same time. The Key fire department is small and every firefighter has to be a paramedic even to be considered. He loved that part of it and pretty much sailed through the three levels of training."

"So what's left to do?" Ceci asked.

"The chief's interview." Ashley suddenly winced, stretched her left leg and pushed the heel forward. "Leg cramps. It's the worst part of pregnancy as far as I'm concerned. I eat tons of bananas, which I hate, and I still get cramps." Continuing to wiggle her lower leg, she went on. "Anyway, when the Key announced they had one position open, they got two hundred applications, and he's made it into the top three."

Standing up, Ashley braced herself on the arm of the couch and stretched her left hamstring. "He has a real chance now," she went on. "He's passed the psychological and physical tests and it's down to the wire. It all depends on the interview now. He's preparing every minute, and I think he has an advantage because he's been with the department for a long time. But if someone comes along and knocks the interview out of the park...well, I don't want to think about it. He wants to be chief someday, and if he doesn't get in now it may be years before they test again. Nobody ever leaves the department."

Ceci felt uneasy as Ashley spoke. When was Brian preparing? She didn't see it. Instead of concentrating on the thing that mattered most to him, he was spending his time trying to protect her from a man who was ratcheting up his intimidation again. And why, when they'd become so close so quickly, hadn't he even mentioned this important part of his plans?

The back door opened and Brian appeared in the living room a moment later. "Hey, Ash," he said, dropping a kiss on his sister's strawberry-blonde hair. Her blue eyes, almost the same shade as her brother's, lit up as she grinned at him. "I see you two have met. How's little Brian?" he said, patting Ashley's belly.

"Is Brian the baby's name?" Ceci asked.

"My brother would like to think so, but he isn't entertaining the possibility of a girl."

"You don't know the sex? My sister couldn't wait to get her ultrasound. Gigi's not much for suspense. When Jane was born they were all ready."

"Oh, what a great name! I'm so tired of all the trendy names," Ashley said. "My name was kind of trendy once, and I hated it. There were four Ashleys in my class. We never knew who the teacher was talking to. Our doctor knows the sex, of course, but Jack and I decided we'd rather be surprised, and she's kept the secret very well. We'll find out in January, and I hate to tell you, brother dear, but Brian is not in the running. It will be either Elaine or Mark."

"Oh, well," Brian said. "Dad would like that. And there's always the next one." He turned to Ceci. "I have news," he said. "But first, I have something more important to do." He crossed the room, caught Ceci up in his arms, and kissed her full on the mouth.

"Well, lookie there," Ashley said, with the teasing tone siblings reserve for one another. "From what Ceci said, I thought you were helping out a pal. I didn't realize you two were so...close."

"We'll tell you about it later, sis, but I have some information for Ceci right now."

"Have you found the person who's been bothering her?" Ashley interrupted before Ceci had a chance to speak.

"Not really," he said, glancing at Ceci, "but we might be getting closer to ruling someone out."

"Sean?" Ceci asked.

"I was at your place when he showed up," Brian said. "He wanted to know where you were, so I used our cover story and told him your stalker was back in business."

"How did he take it?"

"Fine. He said he wasn't sure I'd known about it, and that's why he hadn't mentioned it to me."

"I believe that's what I told you," Ceci said with a self-satisfied half-smile. "He was being cautious. I know I'm right about this guy."

Brian wandered out to the kitchen to get coffee. As he clattered around, he shouted toward the living room. "Then you'll be real happy about this part. I asked him why he flew you to Orlando instead of Gainesville like he told me. Turns out the place he usually takes the plane for service is in Gainesville. He called them in the morning, and they couldn't take the job because a repair they were doing got more complicated. They didn't have enough time to do the system check, but they called around and Orlando did."

"Two down," Ceci said, studying her manicure.

"Don't get too cocky," Brian said, emerging from the kitchen. "When I asked him why he told you he got your cell number from me, he went up like a rocket. Said he was through with the cross-examination, and he was out of there like a shot. And I hadn't even gotten to the question about why he jimmied your patio door."

"I don't think he did. I don't know how it happened, but I think he was trying to help."

"Maybe, but he sure as hell didn't have an answer for me about the phone. He got caught and he couldn't cover it."

Ashley leaned forward as far as she could. "So you think this Sean might be the one who sent the message?"

"I do," Brian said, "but Ceci's not sure. She likes him."

"That's right, and so far he has good explanations about the things that were bothering you, Brian," Ceci said. "To me, the most important thing isn't whether he lied. People lie all the time for a whole bunch of half-assed reasons. What matters to me is whether he was in town when the note was delivered. If he wasn't, I'd say he's off the hook. Has Zach found out anything?"

"Not yet, but he's poking around."

"Well, when we have the answer to that, we'll know. Until then, I'm withholding judgment about him."

"Brian usually has pretty good instincts, Ceci," Ashley said, a wary look crossing her face. "Please be careful around this guy."

"I will, but I think everyone's barking up the wrong tree."

CHAPTER **TWENTY-TWO**

Slightly after midnight, Ceci sat up in Brian's bed as an unexpected violent storm lit the sky and shook the house. The power failed, and in the dark she searched for candles or flashlights, using the beam from her cell phone. "Come on, Mr. Medic, prepared for anything," she muttered to herself. She giggled when she found the stash of condoms in the bedside table. "Well, I guess you're prepared for *some* things."

Wandering into Brian's office, she said, "I've got less than one bar on this phone and no way to charge it. Where do you keep your flashlights?" Reaching into the back of his desk drawer, she found one and turned the base. "Aha!" she said, as twenty-eight tiny LED bulbs brightened every corner of the room. The light on the phone faded as the battery gave up the ghost.

Oh, crap, she thought. No TV, no phone, no charger, and a whole night to go. She padded out to the living room couch, the best place to watch the pyrotechnics produced by the storm. As she glanced out, a forked bolt of lightning illuminated the entire street and someone running to the north, where the cross street led straight to the highway.

It's someone who got caught in the rain, she thought. Nothing more. Don't let the crazy take over. But her heart sped up, her skin prickled in fear, and she felt nauseated and fragile. Taking a butcher knife from the block in the kitchen and locking the door to Brian's room, she crawled back into his bed, hyper-alert. Even as the storm passed, she was keyed up, not falling asleep for hours, the knife finally dropping from her hand.

The clarity of the late morning erased any lingering qualms, and Ceci set about cleaning up palm fronds and debris the storm had dumped on the patio. The next-door neighbor, busy with the same chore, looked up as Ceci dumped the leavings into the yard waste bin. "Hi," he said. "I'm Stan Porter. And you are?" Ceci caught the suspicion in his tone.

"I'm Ceci Myers. Brian let me use the house for a couple of days while my apartment's being painted." She wondered why she was explaining herself with a lie, but conceded Brian had been right about the neighbors. They did look out for each other.

"Were you expecting someone last night?" Stan said. "I noticed somebody at the door, but when you didn't answer he took off. Fast, too. Probably didn't want to get any wetter than he already was."

"Did you get to see what he looked like?"

"Nope. It was raining so hard, all I could see was a shape. Kind of medium height in a slicker with the hood pulled up."

"Thanks," Ceci said. "I'll check it out."

She knew what she'd find on the porch. The soggy note was tucked into the screen door. The ink was running, but the words were legible.

DID YOU THINK I COULDN'T FIND YOU? IF
YOU CARE ABOUT HIM YOU KNOW WHAT
TO DO. IF YOU CARE ABOUT YOURSELF
YOU'LL DO IT NOW. I'D HATE TO OFF HIM
ALTHOUGH I'D ENJOY DOING YOU AFTER.

CHAPTER **TWENTY-THREE**

B rian drove as fast as he could through the early-morning tie-up on the bridge connecting the Key to the mainland. Ceci had sounded nearly hysterical on the phone. He called her back as he drove. She seemed more collected, but still frightened. This was the dumbest thing I've ever done, he thought. How could I have left her alone in a strange place, even if I thought it was safe? She didn't want to do it in the first place. She felt protected at the condo and I sent her packing to my place, just because I thought it was a better idea. Damn! Why do I always think I know what's best?

•

"I'm so sorry, Ceci," Brian said, as she sobbed in his arms. "I love you, we're in this together, and I left you alone." His voice caught. "It never occurred to me there'd be some reason you couldn't call me or the police if you had a problem."

"Made me kind of wish I had my gun back," she said, wiping her eyes as her tears subsided. "The only place Stan was wrong was he thought the person knocked and I didn't answer the door. Nobody knocked. We both saw whoever it was, but neither of us got any kind of a good look. It's so frustrating. And it was my fault there was no phone. It was in my purse and I forgot to charge it. If I had, I could have used it when the storm came."

"I don't know how anyone could have known you were here. We didn't tell anyone but Ashley, and she knew it was important not to say anything."

"And this time, it wasn't only a threat against me," she said, her head still resting on his shoulder. "It was against you, too. If something happened to you because of me..." She began to weep again. She looked up, surprised to see that Brian's eyes were wet, too.

"And vice versa," he said. "Let's go back to the Key. I think you were right. You are safer there, and we need to talk to Zach."

•

"This is definitely an escalation," Zach said. "And I don't think it's the same person who stalked you before. It could be a more dangerous situation."

"Really?" Ceci said, looking agonized and twisting the lock of hair nearest her face. "Why do you think it's someone else?"

"I called Indianapolis to get copies of the notes from there," he said, indicating a thick file with her name on it. "The detective you told me about, Charlie, had retired, and the new guy wasn't up to speed at all. I gave him the case number and he reviewed it while we were on the phone. It seems your successor at the station had filed a couple of complaints about someone harassing her. Notes and dead flowers. Just like you talked about."

Ceci gaped at Zach, amazed. "And he didn't put two and two together?"

"As I say, he was brand-new and he was following her case instead of yours. She hadn't mentioned it to anyone at the station yet, so *they* didn't put two and two together either. Equal-opportunity screw-up. Anyway, they caught him."

"What? And nobody told Ceci?" Brian said, irritated.

"*I'm* telling her," Zach answered. "Criminals aren't always the brightest bulbs on the porch. This dipshit had gotten away with it for so long he got careless and apparently didn't remember to wear his gloves when he sealed the last note. He hand-delivered it and left four beautiful prints, uncontaminated by anything from the post office. They were like the wedding album of fingerprints." Zach's high, light laughter seemed out of character coming from someone so tall.

"Matching them took about thirty seconds. He also stalked his ex-girlfriend, and when he violated the restraining order she had on him, they took his prints. Unfortunately, he left zero evidence in your case. He looks good for it, but there's nothing they can take to court."

"So that part of the mystery is solved," Ceci said, "and it's the best news ever, and I'm very grateful. But now what do we do? Today's note was as threatening as anything I got in Indiana."

"Yep, and I'm sorry to say, Brian, it looks like your hunch about

Bennett was wrong. The flight to North Carolina *was* delayed. That made me suspicious, but I have about a million witnesses putting him at the airport from six until nine in the morning. He flew four take-offs and landings. Told the guys in the shop that the sensor worked twice and failed twice, but the gear was down and locked every time. He and his passengers left about nine after he scheduled the repair in Charlotte. They stayed an extra day to make sure of the fix."

"It's somebody else," Ceci whispered, as she covered her face with trembling hands.

"Probably," Zach said. "Brian, I have a couple of questions for you. Ceci told Bennett about the stalker, but no details. You're the only one who knows the details."

"Are you looking at *me* for this?" Brian said, his low-pitched tone boiling like lava.

Zach reached across the table and slapped Brian on the side of the head the way a big brother would do. "Of course not. What I want to know is if you told anyone about it."

"We told Brian's sister, but only yesterday, after I'd already received the first note. Can you think of anyone else?" Ceci said, turning to Brian.

"Yeah," he said slowly. "I can. I told Matt. And Dev."

"Oh, holy crap. You told the Voice of the Key? I'm surprised it isn't all through the Muni by now," Zach said, frowning.

Ceci's strained voice overlapped with Zach's. "When did you tell her? And why?"

"The night I went to see her about us. She said you'd had a good time together and she wanted to know more about you."

"And *that's* what you told her?" Ceci tried to think of the word describing how she was feeling and came up with violated. She had shared intimate details of her life and he had taken them to Devon with no regard for her feelings.

"You told Sean. What's the difference?"

"Well, there is one," Ceci said, her face reddening. "I chose to do that and I was very careful about what I said, but you made the choice to tell someone else without checking with me about whether I wanted it shared. That information was between you and me, not between you, me, and Devon. I would have told her about it myself if I'd wanted it to go further."

"And you don't think Sean might have told her?"

"Not the details. He didn't have those…by design."

Brian gave up. "I'm sorry," he said. "You're right. I didn't see it then, but I do now."

"You're right, too," Ceci responded, downcast. "If I didn't want anyone else to know, I shouldn't have told anyone."

"I know she talks a lot," Brian said. "But she's a good friend, and I think she's been discreet."

"That'll be the day," Zach interjected. "So at this point, we don't know how many people have heard about it. Maybe Matt's wife, maybe their friends, and whoever Devon might have shared it with. Depending on how far it's gone, a ton of people could know by now. Not a lot of crime in this area, so a stalker is kind of juicy. And if there's somebody with a screw loose and he's heard the details, whether from Devon or someone else, he could be our guy."

"Isn't that more of a problem, then?" Ceci asked, naked fear in her eyes. "We could be dealing with anything from a teenager who thinks this is funny to an honest-to-God psychopath."

"Right," Zach answered. "There's a slew of possibilities."

"Damn," Brian said, shame contorting his features. "Honey, I don't know what to say. You know I wouldn't…"

"I know you wouldn't," Ceci said, wrapping her hands around his.

"Here's what I don't want," Zach said. "I don't want you two trying to outsmart him with a dumbass thing like that bait and switch operation you pulled. We both know how to save lives, Brian, but we do it in different ways. You stop playing junior cop and let me do my job."

CHAPTER **TWENTY-FOUR**

The next morning, still enervated and shaky from the events of the day before, Ceci leaned against her car pumping gas at the Key's only service station. Her eyes closed, she didn't notice Sean pulling up into the next bay. Putting his pump on autofill, he stormed toward her. "I try to be nice to you," he said, his tone yanking her out of her lethargy, "and the next thing I know I've got a detective and two cops swarming around where I work like a bunch of goddamn hornets. Didn't look good to my boss, I'll tell you. And the suggestion there was nothing wrong with the plane? What planet do you live on, anyway, lady? I'm a professional. I don't pull crap like that. You're not worth the effort."

"I'm so sorry, Sean," Ceci stammered, lowering her voice as she realized others who were gassing up had heard him and now were straining their ears to catch her end of the conversation. "It's just that right after I talked to you about my stalker and how I hadn't heard from him in months, he showed up again, and the only other person who knew about him was Brian."

"And it couldn't be the golden boy, could it?"

"No, it couldn't be," Ceci said becoming defensive. "Because I was on the phone with Brian when the stalker dropped off a note at my door."

"Have you ever heard of a cell phone? He could have been anywhere. But maybe it came from someone else you've treated like shit along the way. Check your roster." He spun on his heel.

Her eyes fiery, Ceci followed him to his truck, now beyond caring who heard what. "I'm not known for treating people like shit, Sean," she said, "and it would be nice if you answered two questions for me. You're not the only one affected by this, you know. I'm the one getting threatened with rape and worse."

She detected a softening of his features. "All right. What?" His tone remained hostile.

"Question one. How did you get my cell number and why did you lie to me about it? And two, why did you say I mentioned liking classical music when I never said that?"

Mortification crept across Sean's face. "I guess you do need an explanation. I liked you. I wanted to see you again. When you went to the ladies' room at the sandwich shop, you left your phone on the table. I used it to call my phone, which gave me your number. I was ashamed of doing it, and I gave myself the worst cover story possible. Of course you'd check it with Brian. And the music? One night when I saw you on the news in Orlando, you'd just hosted some teen chamber music event and you talked about how well they played such difficult music and how much you liked it."

Ceci tamped down a smile. "You could have asked me for my number. Simple. Clean. Easy. And why all the deception about the music?"

"It wasn't complete deception," Sean said, answering her with a half-grin. "I did hear you say it, just not here. And as for the phone number, I wanted the right one. Look, I may be a pilot and all, but pilot doesn't always equal suave. I'm actually kind of a nerd. I was afraid you might give me some bogus number, like the time and weather, and then I'd feel like a fool."

"Really?" Ceci said, her voice rising an octave. "Really? I might do something like that in a bar if you were being a jerk, but I was having a good time with you. I'd have given you my number."

"I'd seen you on the beach with Brian, so I figured he had the drop on me."

"Well...he does," Ceci said haltingly, trying for diplomacy, "but that shouldn't prevent us from being friends, should it?"

"No. I guess not." Sean's fixed smile widened, but his eyes didn't take part in the transformation.

"Good," Ceci said, as she gave him a peck on the cheek. "I need all the friends I can get."

As she walked back to her car, Sean's words echoed. "Ever hear of a cell phone?" But it couldn't be Brian. It couldn't. Why would he have taken me straight to the police? Why would he have come back to his house and left a note when I might have seen him? Why did I see tears in his eyes? But Brian intimated Sean had frightened her so he could be the hero. What if Brian wanted to be her hero? He was, after all, in the hero business.

Her mind whirled. But then it settled on Zach. Zach knew Brian, and his behavior showed he didn't have Brian on his list of suspects.

"I'm nuts," she said as she started her car. "I'm seeing this guy around every corner, just like I did in Indianapolis. I need to calm down. There's not a snowball's chance this is Brian."

•

Who the hell is *that?* he thought, as he watched Sean and Ceci from across the street. Another one? Too damn many men when the one she needs is standing right here.

CHAPTER **TWENTY-FIVE**

Whonenen Ceci checked her caller queue, she found a message from a station in Augusta, Maine, where she'd sent her résumé. The assistant news director wanted to interview her by phone the next day. Thank God Brian's on duty today and tomorrow, she thought. This might be a dud and there's no sense in getting us both agitated about breaking up before we've even gotten started.

Still, it was time to think rationally about the possibility she and Brian weren't going to walk hand in hand into the sunset, no matter how much they wanted it. She replayed Ashley's comment that Brian's dream job was to be on the Key. If she got the job in Maine, she would have to leave the only place he wanted to live. "It's a Catch-22," she said to herself. "I need to talk to Lee."

•

At seven in the evening, when her best friend and one-time Indianapolis roommate Lee Sanchez was off the air, Ceci made the call. "How's life in the world of Miami weather?" she asked.

"Oh, you know, highs and lows," Lee said.

"That's lame. Get some new material," she laughed.

Ceci knew Lee was destined for big-city broadcasting. With a bachelor's degree from the University of Oklahoma and a master's from Cornell—both top atmospheric science programs—she also had a minor in communications. The network kept calling her to New York to fill in on the morning show, so Ceci knew it was only a matter of time until Lee moved on from Miami.

"She has the triple minority thing going, too," Ceci had told Brian, "but she doesn't lean on it. She's just plain good."

"What triple minority?" Brian asked. "I get Hispanic and female, but what else? Is she in a wheel chair or something?"

"She's Asian," Ceci said, with a chuckle, "which always surprises people. Her birth name was Li-Mei Han. The Sanchez comes from her stepfather, who adopted her when she was a baby. Apparently, Mr. Han decamped as soon as he made her legitimate."

"Sounds like an interesting gal," Brian said.

"She is," Ceci answered. "She's stunning and fluent in Spanish, English, and Mandarin. She also has a mouth like a trucker and can blister you in all three languages, so look out. You'll love her."

•

"Let me get this straight, Myers," Lee said. Ceci could visualize her friend with her feet on the desk and her long, straight black hair streaming over the back of the chair as she teetered precariously on its two rear legs. She was no doubt a vision in three-inch heels and some jewel-toned, flattering dress that never strobed or bled on the air. "You've found the man of your dreams and the two of you declared yourselves by the end of your first real date. He's fabulous, wonderful, the handsomest man on earth, and it's not the sex haze talking because you haven't had sex. Which, by the way, makes no sense to me."

"I knew it wouldn't," Ceci said with a sigh. "You're more adventurous in that arena."

"What's the matter with you, girl? You love him, he loves you, but you're holding back. And don't give me all the bull about revenge sex. That might work for him, but I know you. What's really wrong? Alex the Asshat doesn't still have a hold on you, does he? He's a sociopath."

Ceci was silent for a moment. "Nice alliteration, Lee, but I wouldn't go so far as to call him a sociopath."

"I would," Lee responded abruptly. "Let's tick off a few points. Charming? Check. And great at reading cues so he knows just *how* to charm different people? Check. Super smart? Check. Risk-taker? Oh, yeah, with other people's money."

Ceci leaned into the conversation. "But, Lee, lots of successful people are smart and charming and risk-takers. You can't be as successful as he is without taking risks."

"Oh, stop making excuses for him. He's not just a sharp, aggressive businessman. He doesn't have a heart. He doesn't have a conscience. Let's go back to our list. Does he have any sense of guilt, remorse, shame, or empathy? Nope, at least not when it comes to you. Did he ever apologize to you for what he did? Did he show even one scintilla of compassion when he told you to vacate his place?"

"Can't say he did," Ceci admitted.

"I rest my case. If you won't go for sociopath, how about at least self-serving narcissist? An asshat."

Ceci laughed without humor, pulling her knees up under her big nightshirt as she sat on the floor of the condo. "Whatever we call him, I don't think it's Alex himself. I think it's what he did to me. I'm scared, Lee. I'm totally in love with Brian. I mean like never before with anyone."

"So what scares you? The dead wife? Afraid you can't measure up to the first love?"

"Not really, even though she was enchanting and talented, and he still speaks of 'us'."

"May I remind you that you are enchanting and talented and now speak of 'us'?"

"What I'm worried about, I guess, is what his partner told me in the beginning. After a while he cools off. I don't want to jump any further than I have and get tossed aside again. I really don't think I could stand it. Alex was bad. This would be so far beyond bad I can't even think about it. It's one thing to *have* to break it off, which we might have to do because of work. It's another thing to be dumped." Ceci tugged at the lock of hair she'd been twirling at warp speed.

"You know, the two of you sound kind of alike. This partner says Brian was afraid of getting hurt, and now you're afraid of getting hurt. This is not the Ceci I know. So the son-of-a-bitch Alex broke your engagement. Happens to hundreds of couples every year. Big deal. He was screwing somebody else and he did you a terrific favor. If he hadn't cut you loose, you'd have married an unfaithful pig and you wouldn't have met Brian. Can I get an amen, sister?"

"Amen," Ceci said, dropping the tendril of hair.

"Look, I don't mean to diminish what happened. Remember I was the one who listened to you cry for four hours when you found him doing the Girl with the Plastic Ta-Tas, but I can't *believe* you're questioning yourself like this. That he made you doubt yourself so much. Maybe Brian broke up with the other women because he figured out they weren't right for him. He says you are. He says you're the one he wants. Do you trust him?"

"With my life."

"Well, then, what's your problem? Do you know how many women would change places with you?"

"I do. But I'm not hanging back only because I got my feelings hurt. I have work I love, Lee, not just some job. Sometimes I wish I were my mother. She's been a housewife all her life and for some reason that fulfills her. She doesn't understand why Gigi keeps working now that she has a husband and child. She knows I have to support myself, but if I were to get married, she'd expect me to quit my job and live the way she has."

Walking into the kitchen with her cell, Ceci turned on the oven light to check the newest version of the apple tart. "I chose something totally involving, though. It's a lot of who I am. I've looked around here. There's nothing, and I mean nothing, for me in this market. I have a phone interview tomorrow with a station in Maine, and you know I give great phone."

She could hear Lee giggling. "But if Brian is chosen after his interview, this is where he wants to be for the rest of his life. His sister told me he wants to be chief."

"I don't understand. It's just geography. If you two are so much in love and you found a job somewhere else, couldn't he be a firefighter anywhere?"

"That's what I thought, too, but it's not so simple. There's really no such thing as a transfer. Say there's a job in Augusta. There would probably be a couple hundred applicants. He'd have to jump through all kinds of hoops, work his way to the top of the candidate pool and then maybe lose out to someone else. He has a much better chance here because he's a known quantity. Somewhere else would be much harder."

"So no trailing spouse."

"Not unless there's an opening, and there usually isn't. I'm not going to say anything to Bri until I know if they're going to ask me to visit the station, but I have to go through the process. If it pans out, Maine is way too far away to make a long-distance relationship work, and I'm really not sure I can deal with that. Someone like Brian will happen once in my life. But if I choose him, the person he loves now might not be the person he gets because I won't have my work anymore."

"Go ahead and do the interview," Lee said. "It's almost the holidays. They aren't going to bring you in for a sit-down until after the beginning of next year. They probably have other interviews to do and tapes to look at. If he gets the job and you get yours, you guys have decisions to make. But right now you're working from if-come-maybe. I know you're a planner, but you've got to live in the moment. Don't miss today because of what might happen tomorrow."

"How very New Age of you," Ceci volleyed back, with a smile.

"I mean it, Ceci. You don't know what might come your way. Don't believe the way things are now are the way they'll always be. Life changes every day."

"You're right, of course. My only practical problem is the condo's rented right after the holidays. I won't have anywhere to stay while things are working out...or not."

"You always miss the obvious. Move in with him."

"He hasn't asked me to."

"Give him a nudge," Lee said. "Carpe diem."

"And that's why I love you. Best advice ever." Ceci hung up, shaking her head, still laughing.

CHAPTER **TWENTY-SIX**

L ee was right. Life changes every day, but Ceci hadn't expected Alex to show up the next afternoon, soon after she'd finished her interview and a quick trip to the grocery. But there he stood in her courtyard, peering around trying to locate her condo. Alex, with his open face, his approachable manner, his *friendliness*. All the traits that drew people to him and made him a trusted high-net-worth financial adviser. The trousers breaking just so over his instep, and his blue blazer tossed over his shoulder, suspended from his right index finger. The crisp, spotless shirt monogrammed on the cuff, certainly different from Brian's blues with "Walker" embroidered over the breast pocket.

Her arms full of grocery bags, Ceci stared wordlessly at Alex, as he, seeming to sense her presence, turned around. He held out his arms to her, as if the two of them were stars in some cheesy romantic movie where they would run to one another in slow motion across a golden, dappled field. Her ears buzzed and she stood still, holding the grocery bags in front of her like a shield.

"What are you doing here?" Ceci said, without a trace of welcome in her tone.

"I came to see you," Alex said, lowering his arms and looking hangdog at the attitude she was giving him. "When you left, I wasn't sure where you'd gone, but I remembered you sometimes mentioned the Key, so I took a chance. All I could remember was Los Olas, so I dropped by the Municipal Hall, and somebody in the office knew the rest of the name."

"It's 'Las,' and what difference did it make where I was? You told me to get out and I got out. There's no reason for you to be here."

"Let me take the groceries and we'll go inside. I really need to talk with you."

Ceci clutched the bags tighter as her mind flashed to the conversation she'd had with Lee right after Alex bolted. "What are you going to tell him when he comes crawling back? Because he will. Once he realizes she's not the fucking goddess he thinks he deserves, he'll drop her like a bag of flaming feces because she's disappointed him. He'll want you then. My crystal ball tells me it will take about three months. He knows, or thinks he knows, you'll take him back if he acts contrite enough. Are you going to do that, idiot?"

It had barely been six weeks, but if this impromptu visit was about a reconciliation, Ceci had her answer ready.

•

"Okay," Ceci said, sitting as far away from Alex as possible on the lanai, "what do you want?"

He sighed. "This is hard," he said. "I took some time off to spend here. I've been on the Key for several days trying to get up the nerve to talk to you. I've been sort of lurking around, seeing you here and there, but I didn't know how you'd react if I suddenly popped up on the street."

"Now you know. I'm not glad to see you. And I repeat, what do you want?"

"I made a mistake, a big one. You were right for me. Nicolette wasn't."

"Too bad."

"I want you to come home."

"People in hell want ice water."

"I shouldn't have done what I did to you."

Ceci snorted. "You mean the lying, the cheating, the sneaking around with someone I thought was my friend, all the while asking me to marry you? Putting my suitcases in the hall outside our condo?" As Alex talked, memories of the fun she'd had with Nicolette flashed through her mind.

Nicolette was a five-foot-tall tornado. Her teeth were too big, her gums too prominent, and her hair was mouse brown, but she had confidence to burn and undeniable magnetism. She'd started her thriving online accessories business with a $500 loan from her mother and had built it by cajoling virtually every investor, male and female, in the Orlando area. She'd already banked her first million, and her five-year plan was more than ambitious. No one doubted she'd hit the target, though.

Ceci had interviewed Nicolette during a women's business segment and been impressed with her drive and determination. Nicolette called to thank Ceci for the interview, a nicety most people forgot, and their initial conversations developed into a friendship. They lunched and shopped together on weekends. They went to movies and bars, and sometimes bagged groceries at a food pantry.

After Ceci and Alex got together, the two of them often dined with Nicolette and her latest Mr. Right Now. As she had struggled with Alex's betrayal, Ceci had to admit he and Nicolette often spent more time talking with one another than they did with their respective dates. At the end of her engagement, Ceci chastised herself for not seeing what was right in front of her. Her fiancé and her friend hadn't gotten where they were by being self-effacing and empathetic. Once Ceci's eyes were opened, she realized they were as ruthless—and lethal—as Bonnie and Clyde.

Ceci had often thought how different Alex was from her dad, even though both of them were in finance. Richard spent his days helping people save for their kids' educations or retirement. He was a solid, conservative Cincinnati adviser at a solid, conservative Cincinnati bank, not like Alex, who helped the preposterously rich become obscenely rich with what Ceci considered risky concentrated positions in leading-edge stocks. She had to admit his clients had considerable tolerance for risk and liked to fly high. If they lost, they shrugged their shoulders, but Alex succeeded far more often than he failed, and his clients frequently thanked him for making their third vacation house—the beachfront condo in Maui, the palatial ski-in, ski-out home in Aspen, or the *pied à terre* in Paris—a possibility. During her months with Alex, she often thought of those multi-million-dollar "extra" homes and wondered how far the money spent there would go toward housing homeless veterans.

She tuned back into Alex's words. "Once you took off, she and I spent more time together. That's when I realized I missed your sizzle. She's very one-dimensional. She has no sense of humor, and let's face it, she doesn't have your body, in spite of the recent surgery." His smile held the faintest trace of a leer.

"Don't you *dare* sit there and run her down. Is that what you did with her? Did you two lie around in bed and tick off a list of *my* faults? At least have the decency to keep your mouth shut about the women you screw. Sorry she's a little more…pillowy…than you'd like. Looks like she fed you well, though. Do I detect the outline of a soon-to-be expanding paunch?"

"I know you're mad, Claire, but I think we're good together and I got sidetracked and forgot that. And that's why I'm willing to sit here and take whatever you have to dish out. Get it out of your system and then we can move on."

"I'm speechless," Ceci said.

"And yet you're talking," Alex shot back, trying another smile, this one without the leer.

"You arrogant prick! A minute ago you said I was right for you. Did it ever occur to you you're not right for me? No, of course not, because I should be honored just to be in your presence, right? Well, fuckface, I'm not, and I'd like you to get the hell out of my house. Right now." Ceci tried to watch her language, but when her reptilian brain overran the prefrontal cortex, she often channeled her grandfather, a man with an astonishing command of expletives, which he rarely, if ever, deleted.

"You forget I know you," Alex said, leaning back on the chaise, his hands behind his head, the picture of ease and confidence. "When I met you, you were a scared little girl, running from Indianapolis because some guy was threatening you. Six months later you still had the shakes so bad I had to take you to the hospital. Twice. Most guys wouldn't stick around. I did. I made you feel safe again. I put you on an even keel, and we were happy."

Ceci had to admit that part was true, at least for a while. "We were happy until you double-crossed me. Until I saw you for what you really are."

"I know. It was terrible mistake."

"Oh, wait … a … minute," Ceci said as realization dawned. She stood up and bent over him, a broad grin on her face. "The picture is coming into focus. She dumped *you*, didn't she? And now you don't have a hot girlfriend anymore. You know what I think, Alex? I think you always have your eye on the main chance. She was better than I was. I was only a sub-anchor, not the real thing. Not six and eleven. Not the face of the station."

She laughed. "And Nicolette, the Entrepreneur of the Year, with all her success and being featured in every newspaper and style magazine in the city, was better arm candy, even though those teeth make her look awfully horsey. You're still calling me Claire, like you always did even when we were at home. I think you preferred Claire, the TV personality, to plain old Ceci, which is who I am. You like to be seen with women who are known and recognized. You're an attention whore and you don't know how to get it for yourself."

"But you have *no* cachet now and here I am, asking you to come home," Alex said, sitting up. "When this anger blows over, you'll see things more clearly. You'll realize I'm good for you."

"You're good for me like Ebola was good for Africa. I've moved on, Alex. I'm in love with someone else. I don't love you. I don't even like you. It's time for you to leave now. I mean it. Go back to Orlando and find some other rich-bitch society queen. I'm never coming back."

Alex rose, crowding Ceci's personal space. "I know you've moved on. I told you I've been here a few days. I've seen you on the beach with a guy several times. I assume he's the new love because you've been climbing him like a scratching post." He gave her a sly, sidelong look.

"So now you want what you can't have? You'll *take* second best because you can't stand *being* second best? If you've seen me with someone else, take the hint. Get out." Alex didn't move, the supercilious smirk still on his face, unlike the affable expression he showed the public.

"Yes, but I know you already have someone else on the string, too," he said.

"What are you talking about?"

"I happened to be across the street from the gas station yesterday and there you were, fighting and making up with Guy Number Two. Looks like Guy Number One should be careful. He'll be slipping on a wet deck one of these days."

"One of your more repulsive sailing metaphors," Ceci spat out, "and from you it's even more nauseating since you were mooring in two harbors at the same time. And if you don't leave right now, I *will* call the police. They know me. They'll show up in a hurry. Get your ass out of my house."

"I don't think so. I'll be here a few more days, ready to pick up the pieces and take you back with me when the whole mess falls apart. It will, and then you'll be looking for me."

"You're delusional."

Alex reached for her, pinned her arms behind her back, and kissed her with both anger and passion, biting her lip. Her own blood flowed into her mouth.

She stepped away, wiping away his kiss with the back of her hand. "Leave now and don't ever come near me again."

"When you get rid of him, I'll be here. And you'll be glad. You'll come running."

•

Ceci rushed to the bathroom, retching violently. Anxiety threatened her, but she beat it back by sheer force of will. Stumbling to the kitchen, she made an icy compress for her lip, praying she could stop the puffiness before Brian showed up at midnight. A bite on the lip from an old lover wasn't something she wanted to explain to him.

Surveying her reflection in the mirror after a half-hour ice treatment, she saw that the swelling had gone down, and a careful lipstick application could cover the discoloration. She pressed her fingers against her mouth. It smarted, but she'd live with it. She wasn't going to back away from Brian's kisses, even if they stung. She would be composed and serene.

CHAPTER **TWENTY-SEVEN**

Her resolve didn't last. When Brian arrived just after midnight, Ceci was still agitated, stomping around the kitchen, burning a loaf of cranberry orange bread, and swearing like a sailor. "Oh, fuck it all to hell," she cried, as she stuffed the loaf, pan and all, into the trash. "I turned the oven to 450 instead of 350. No wonder the thing looks like a shit briquette."

"Honey, what is it?" Brian asked. "You're all crazy pants."

"Alex showed up today."

"What did *he* want, for God's sake?"

"Well, if you think I'm crazy, he's certifiable. Nicolette told him to take a hike and he says he wants me back."

"Too late. He can't have you." Brian paused, his expression a mixture of alarm and bewilderment. "Or can he? I've never seen you this upset. Are you thinking about going back to him?"

"Is *everybody* nuts?" she said, picking up the oven mitt she'd thrown on the floor and tossing it onto the counter. "Of *course* I'm not thinking about it. I don't know how I could have gotten mixed up with him in the first place."

Brian let out the breath he'd been holding. "Thank God," he said. "But he must have had something going for him if you were going to marry him." He gave Ceci about a quarter of a smile. "Let's get you away from hot water and sharp implements for a while." Guiding her to the dining table, he took a seat across from her.

Ceci sighed. "I didn't want to talk about this, but I guess we have to. In the beginning, he was a nice guy. He's very personable. Successful. Excellent education. Cleans up well. Good on paper. We enjoyed each other's company."

She wrestled with how much Brian might want to hear, but he

wasn't backing away, so she went gingerly. "He has a sailboat. I've only sailed a little, so it was fun to learn. We kind of fell into the romance part." She willed herself not to think about the long days on the water, some of it involving champagne and various states of undress. She smiled at Brian. "It wasn't like us. No thunderbolts.

"He helped me get through the aftermath of the stalking," she continued. "I was pretty beat up after a year of looking over my shoulder and being afraid every second. He knew all the details..." She stopped speaking and her body went rigid.

"What just happened? What are you thinking?"

"He knew *how* I was stalked. The letters. What they said. Everything. He never called me anything but Claire. And he told me he'd been on the Key for several days. Yesterday was the twelfth. I got the first note a week ago."

Ceci jumped up and stood behind a dining chair, her hands grasping the top until her knuckles blanched. "He said he'd seen us together, and what he said about me was so crude and dirty. He's never showed that side of himself. At least to me. He was always a gentleman, but not today. He was like a different person, and he didn't make any sense. He honestly believed I'd go back to him. He said I'd need him when I got rid...." She stopped again, her hand to her mouth.

"Go on."

"When I got rid of you. Just what the first note said. It's nobody here on the Key, Bri. *It's him.* He was so nasty this afternoon, and his eyes looked sort of crazed. He hurt me, too."

"Hurt you? How?" Now Brian was standing, too, facing Ceci from across the table.

"He jerked my arms behind my back and kissed me. It wasn't a pleasant, come-back-to-me kind of kiss. I thought my arms would come out of the sockets. He bit my lip."

Brian leaned over the table, his color high, peering into Ceci's face. "I see that now, and I'd like to kill him with my bare hands. I think you have it right. The timeline fits, and he gave himself away. We'll call Zach in the morning, and I'm staying with you tonight. No discussion."

"No discussion, but I'm too upset for..."

"I'm just staying, Ceci. This isn't the time for anything else."

CHAPTER **TWENTY-EIGHT**

"I'm sorry, Bri," Ceci said, when the shakes hit her an hour after midnight. "This is anxiety, but something else too. I'm so angry at Alex. This is the way I was in Orlando. So scared I could barely breathe. I got over it, slowly, and Alex helped with that. He really did. And now he's the one doing it to me. Why would he think scaring the hell out of me would make me come back? The look on his face this afternoon was pure evil. How could I not have seen that side of him?" She slid into Brian's arms and felt comforted, even as the tremors continued.

"He knows how all this affects me and he doesn't care. When I have one of these attacks, I feel like I'm going to die. He's seen it. He knows I'm shaking myself nearly to death and hyperventilating because my pulse races and I can't breathe. I can't function. No matter how he feels, why would he want to put me through this again? I'm not the one who left. He did. I can't imagine why he'd hate me so much he'd want to cause me this kind of pain."

Brian drew her down next to him in her father's oversized recliner, taking her pulse. "You're plenty scared," he said. "It's one-thirty."

"I know. I know exactly when it hits that number and goes beyond it. I can feel it. I hate this so much. My body aches all over when I shake this hard."

"What helps you the most when it happens?"

"Mostly I write. If I can get myself completely out of the situation mentally, then the physical stuff starts to go away, too. But I don't want to do that now. Could you just talk to me? Sometimes talking helps a lot."

"Sure," he said. "Do you want to hear about my funniest case ever?" Ceci nodded as Brian pulled her onto his lap and held her more tightly. "It didn't happen here. It was over on the mainland. There was this middle-aged couple, and the woman's sister came for a visit. They all spent a lot of time outside working in the garden, but one day it was really hot and the sister went inside to take a shower. The wife was in the kitchen making a sandwich, but her husband didn't know that and thought *she* was the one in the shower."

Brian's smile grew wide. "So he goes into the bathroom to surprise her. Strips off his clothes to jump into the shower with her. Pulls back the shower curtain and kaboom! It's not his wife. The gal screams, jumps up, falls down, and hits her head on the spigot. Puts a gash in her forehead. The man is nuts because he's naked in front of his sister-in-law. He trips over the bath mat trying to get away. Falls ass over tea kettle and breaks his arm."

As her shaking subsided, Ceci said, "This can't be true."

Brian raised his right hand. "Swear to God. The wife comes in and finds her naked sister bleeding with the shower still beating on her and her naked husband with a busted arm. She's confused, but she pulls herself together enough to call us. You should have seen *that* report."

Ceci laughed and cuddled up even closer to Brian, her quivering now reduced to an occasional spasm in her arms and shoulders. "I got a million of them, honey, all for your listening pleasure," Brian said, "and I'm also your own private paramedic. You're safe."

"I feel safe with you, but I want you to be safe, too."

"We'll both be safe. We're going to get this guy sooner rather than later," Brian said. "Come on. We're going to sleep."

They lay locked in each other's arms on the couch until dawn. And in the morning, the note was on Brian's car.

> FINALLY GOT IN HER PANTS I SEE. HOPE IT
> WAS WORTH THE WAIT BECAUSE IT'S THE
> LAST TIME.

CHAPTER **TWENTY-NINE**

Ceci met Zach at the front door of the condo. It was his day off, but nonetheless he appeared in knife-pressed khaki shorts and a carefully laundered button-down short-sleeved plaid shirt. Zach was a big guy and Ceci was surprised at his long, slender legs. I know women who'd kill for those legs, she thought. She handed him the latest note, sealed in a plastic bag.

"Ceci," Zach said, somewhat gruffly, she thought, as he sat down at the kitchen counter, "why don't you have a security system in here?"

"We never needed one," she said, offering him a piece of the finally perfected apple tart—the dish she hadn't thrown away in fury the night before. "But I'll talk to my folks and have one installed as quickly as I can. Today, if possible. I'll tell them there's been a series of break-ins around here. I don't want to worry them."

"Find out who your parents want to use and I'll have the company expedite it. It sounds like you're having a rough time, and I'd feel better if you had some relief. Now tell me about this Alex guy."

"God, I'm tired of talking about him," Ceci sighed. "His name is Alex Buchanan. He was my fiancé. He broke up with me for someone else. They split, and he decided he wanted me back. I told him to go pound sand down a rat hole. That's an old Midwestern expression. It seems to fit this situation."

"We have a few of those expressions down here, too. You think this is the guy, though."

"I do. He knows everything about the previous episodes, so he can mimic it exactly," she said, refilling Zach's plate, satisfied the tart was a winner since he had gobbled the first slice in about a minute.

"He's been on the Key for enough time to have sent all the notes?"

Zach asked.

"Yes. And he's been spying on me for sure," Ceci added. "He admitted as much. He's seen me with both Brian and Sean, and he tried to make something filthy out of that. He was a one-hundred-eighty degree different person from the guy I was engaged to."

"They don't call jealousy a monster for nothing," Zach said. "And he sounds like a bit of a squirrel. Do you have any pictures of him?"

"I burned most of them, but I think I still have one or two." Ceci went up to her bedroom, pulled a shoebox of pictures from under the bed and retrieved one of her and Alex on the boat.

"It's blurry," she told Zach, "and he's kind of a medium guy. Medium height, medium weight, brown hair, brown eyes, medium Florida tan. No distinguishing marks, unless you count a really ugly attitude."

•

"We're watching him when we can, and so far he's been very quiet," Zach told Ceci a couple of days later. Looking around the condo, he said, "Your security system is top of the line, from what I can tell."

"It is, but the beat goes on. I just picked up the mail and there was another note. This one came from the post office. It says, 'Did you think a security system was really going to help? I can get either one of you anywhere and anytime. I know where you are. I know where you go. You'll never be safe.' I bagged it for you."

"I'll take it with me. How are you feeling?"

"Zach, it's strange. I feel calm. Or maybe just numb. I'm not sure. I'm glad the system's in, even if he doesn't think it will stop him."

"We're a small force and we can't keep an eye on this guy twenty-four-seven, especially when we're not sure he's up to anything at all, but I don't think he's been out of his apartment in the last day. He's been hanging around the pool deck reading and on his phone a lot. He's not far away, though. Just down the road at the Cowrie Shoals."

"Zach, that's almost next door to the post office. He could be at those outdoor collection boxes in thirty seconds. And here in two minutes. Obviously, the letter was mailed yesterday, so it doesn't matter much if he's home today."

"I know. Watch yourself, and we'll watch you, too."

CHAPTER **THIRTY**

"**W**ant to forget all this crap and go to a Christmas party?" Brian said, calling from the firehouse.

"I'd really like to," Ceci said. "I just heard from my mom, and Daddy has a bad case of bronchitis. His doctor says no travel for a while. He's had some heart issues, and he's pretty sick, so they're staying close to home."

"Do you need to go to Ohio? Maybe your mom would like you there."

"I don't think so, Bri. If things get worse, yes, for sure. Mom told me it was nasty, but not dangerous. He just needs to rest rather than get on a plane right now. Gigi's going to go down to Cincinnati to get the lay of the land, and if she thinks I should fly up there, I will. So when's this party, and where?"

"Day after tomorrow. The town plaza. I'm on that night, so I might be in and out, but it's time for you to meet the brothers and a couple of sisters, too. They've heard a lot about you. Oh, I signed us up for bringing dessert."

"Us, you say? And your contribution will be what? Chips Ahoy?"

Brian laughed. "I was wondering if you'd bake the cake that made me fall in love with you in the first place."

"It *was* the cake? And here I thought it was my sparkling wit and shapely bod."

"I have to admit I'm intrigued by those perky breasts and gorgeous backside."

"Not from the firehouse, you perv," Ceci snickered. "There are parts of your anatomy I'd like to explore too, but in person, not over a public phone."

"I'm on my cell, which you'd know if you ever looked at the caller

ID before you answer."

"Okay, then, and yes, I'll make the cake. Anything else?"

"How about the dark chocolate pie with the phyllo dough."

"Sure. And if we're going with death by chocolate, how about a yule log?"

"And those huge cookies with the sesame seeds?"

"Okay, but that has to be it. Any more and I'll need a sous chef."

"Is everything okay there?"

"Yep. I'll do a grocery run to stock up for marathon baking—and I'll see you Thursday. These three days on are killer."

"I know. I can't wait to lay my hands on you, and my mouth," he paused, "around that cake."

"I'm hanging up now," Ceci said, grinning. "Go save lives." She picked up her bag, happy once again she hadn't yet heard from Maine.

•

Checking the grocery list on her phone, Ceci wasn't paying attention when she slammed into another cart. The woman pushing it looked up, annoyed. "I'm so sorry," Ceci said, seeing Devon and wishing she could run in the other direction.

"It's okay, Ceci." She peeked into Ceci's cart. "Wow," she said, "what in the world are you cooking? It's all chocolate and sugar. How do you stay so skinny?"

Devon's tone was friendly, and Ceci answered her smile. Maybe Brian had told the whole truth and Devon didn't harbor any ill will toward her after all. "I'm not eating it by myself. I was invited to a party and apparently I'm in charge of a few desserts. I decided to do a variety, but most of them seemed to come out chocolate."

"The firefighters' party?"

"Yes." Ceci decided to plunge ahead and offer up the name of her date. "Brian asked for a special chocolate cake, and everything sort of mushroomed from there."

"It's a great party," Devon said. "Live music, dancing, lots of food. I'm going, too." Ceci's heart flipped in her chest. So the Ghost of Christmas Past will be there, she thought. Yippee.

"All the city services, except the police, are on the plaza, so that's where they set it all up. Everyone from every office ends up at the party for at least part of the night. It's a bash, but it's kind of tame because lots of people are on duty and the others want to make sure they don't do something stupid. I'm taking a couple of salads, so maybe that will balance out some of your calorie fest."

Devon's comment felt like a dig, but Ceci couldn't put her finger on why. Maybe I'm just being overly sensitive, she thought.

"I'm sure it will all be yummy, though," Devon went on. "Brian mentioned the cake the night he came over to talk to me about the two of you. I'll have to try it, unless the recipe's a secret or something."

"I guess he's been telling me the truth, then. He said the cake is what reeled him in," Ceci said, trying to lighten the mood and quell her mounting discomfort. "The recipe is pretty easy. I can give it to you—and I promise not to leave out a critical ingredient."

The two women checked out at nearly the same time. "Let's go sit at the tables outside for a minute," Devon said. "We'll get some coffee or something."

The last thing Ceci wanted to do was have some kind of heart-to-heart with Devon, but she didn't see a way out that wouldn't be transparent, so she acquiesced. The first moment passed in uneasy silence because Ceci couldn't find a way to broach any subject but Brian. Somehow the weather or the firefighters' party didn't seem to work.

Devon dived into the quiet, placing her hand on Ceci's arm. "Look," she said, "I can tell you have some worries about Brian and me. You didn't break us up. There was nothing to break up. We've been good friends, and yes, once or twice we had a roll in the hay, but it didn't mean anything to either one of us. People took us for a couple, but we weren't." She leaned in closer. "I was mourning my marriage, and I think he'll mourn Rachel forever."

Devon averted her eyes and spoke softly. "We were both lonely and hurt, and we ended up together. And now it's over and he's moved on. We always knew one of us would. I'll be honest. I always hoped it would be me first, but that's not the way it worked out, and I'll miss the closeness he and I have had for the past few years. You should know I told him it would be hard to give him up. I love Brian. Always have. Since high school. But I've never been *in love* with him. I hope we can all be friends, however this all plays out."

What an odd phrase, Ceci thought. Her gut told her it hadn't all played out for Devon. Not by a long shot. Well, then, game on, sister, she thought. Game on.

CHAPTER **THIRTY-ONE**

The night of the party, Ceci dressed with special care in a tissue wool white mini that showed off her long, shapely legs, which her high school boyfriend always said went all the way to the ground. She chose a cream silk tank, and because it felt chilly for an outdoor party, added a navy textured-knit moto jacket shot through with gold threads. She'd broken out the flat iron and her hair fell straight to her shoulders. Checking her reflection, she nodded in approval at the smoky eye she'd created and the softer palette on her lips. "Good," she said to herself.

Brian's expression when she entered the party told her all she needed to know. "There's a word for what you're doing right now," she said.

"Oh, no doubt," he said, rolling his eyes. "And I'm sure you know what it is."

"I do. It's called apodyopsis. It means to mentally undress someone."

Brian was nonplused and then burst into laughter. "Well, when you're right, you're right. But I learned a word, too. I went to some list of weird words on the internet, and I found this one. He reached into his shirt pocket, pulled out a folded Post-It®, and read it to her. "Basorexia."

"And it means?" Ceci asked.

"An overwhelming desire to kiss someone."

"Correct. And guilty as charged. We'll get to that later." She set her array of desserts on the long table in the center of the plaza, which was lit with white lights that were also wrapped around the surrounding trees.

"Now I'm going to introduce you to about a million people whose names you won't remember tomorrow," Brian said. "I guarantee they'll remember you, though. You look sensational, and with your hair down you look really young. Like sixteen. Everyone here is going to think I really am a perv, as you put it so nicely on the phone." He squeezed her hand. "Let's go."

They moved around the plaza, meeting and greeting, Brian never releasing her left hand. Out of the corner of her eye, Ceci noticed Devon chatting up the police chief and the chair of the zoning commission. She, too, had tried the flat iron, with mixed results. Recalcitrant curls coiled up here and there like minuscule mattress springs, fighting with the smoothness Devon had tried to impose on her hair.

Though Devon appeared animated, Ceci saw her customary dazzle was attenuated, her vivacity absent. Her eyes were empty, and whenever they locked on Brian, she looked agonized, although she managed to keep the smile plastered on her face as she conversed with the city officials.

So much for "it didn't mean anything to either of us," Ceci thought. She hurts a lot, and I can barely stand myself that I brought that about. But as she and Brian remained connected hand to hand, she couldn't feel sad at the outcome for the two of them.

After a couple of hours, while Brian was on a squad run, Ceci checked the dessert table to see how hers were faring. The cake stands and cookie plates she'd brought were empty. Excellent, she thought, noting many of the other goodies were untouched. I must have made the right selections for this crowd.

She watched as an attractive, somewhat plump fortyish woman whose brunette hair was artfully highlighted picked at the last piece of the chocolate pie, tilting her head as if trying to identify the ingredients. "This is a dynamite pie," she said to Ceci. She brandished another fork. "Want some?"

"No, thanks," Ceci said. "I made it, so I know how it tastes. I'm glad you like it."

"You made this? It's so creamy. I love the orange flavor. I'm betting it wasn't part of the original recipe."

"How did you know?" Ceci asked. "It was vanilla. I tried it with almond, and it tasted a little like a Hershey bar. Pretty good actually, but then I substituted a chocolate orange bar for the unsweetened, cut back the sugar, and this version is my favorite. It's pretty intense."

"Raspberry might be good, too. Did you make anything else?"

"I made the yule log, the sesame cookies, and…"

"Let me guess. The four-layer cake."

Ceci beamed. "You're right. How did you know?"

"It was a cut above. Like this pie. Very professional. I'm Christine Robinson, by the way. Chris. I own La Patisserie, and I know another baker when I meet one."

"I'm Ceci Myers."

"Brian's Ceci? He said you were a dazzler. He was right."

Turning away the compliment, Ceci said, "I've heard about your bakery, but I haven't been in yet. It's fairly new, isn't it?"

"We've been in operation about ten months."

"Opening your own place is such a gutsy move," Ceci said, feeling drawn to this friendly, unpretentious woman who'd made her bakery a Key destination in a less than a year. "My dad is a banker, and I've heard him talk about all the perils of going out on your own."

"It's a risk, no question about it, but I have a good business plan and a couple of solid investors. I'm satisfied we're going to make it."

The two women moved toward a couple of empty chairs on the perimeter of the plaza and sat down knee to knee, Chris taking small bites of pie. "I'm always looking for talent," she said. "We need to put on another baker. Are you interested?"

Ceci's eyes widened in astonishment. "I'm afraid not. I'm a reporter, but I'm flattered. I love baking, and I've taken lots of classes as I've moved around. You really think I could make a go of it?"

"Absolutely," Chris smiled. "If full-time doesn't work for you, we have a cooperative kitchen on the Key where you could work occasionally and supply the bakery. You'd have to get a food handler's license, but I'm sure you could do that easily. You're very good. Those sesame cookies were just the right savory bite in the midst of all the cakes and cookies and pies."

"I'm so excited you like what I did, but I may not be here much longer. I'm looking for a broadcasting job, and pickings are mighty slim around this part of the country. Thanks for the offer, though."

Brian appeared at Ceci's side. "It's 12:01," he said, "and I'm officially off duty." He greeted Chris with a hug. "Jim should be back soon. A food-on-the-stove run. Lots of greasy smoke on the walls, but no damage and all contained."

"So you two are on your way?" Chris said. "Have a good rest of the evening."

"We will," Brian said, as he moved Ceci toward the plaza gate.

"Steady, cowboy, I need at least one dance," Ceci said. "I like to dance and I'm good at it."

"Well," Brian said, bowing to her, "I love a challenge. You happen to be in the company of one of the best dancers around."

The excellent combo that had been playing up-tempo numbers all evening was replaced by a DJ who apparently was in a more mellow mood, leading off with the Etta James classic "At Last."

Brian drew Ceci into his arms and held her close, their faces only a kiss away from one another, their eyes locked. Abandoning the standard dance position, he placed his fingers around her palm and both of their hands on his chest. With her fingers extended, she could feel his pulse alternating with her own. He took the first step, his gaze never leaving hers. When he changed the position of his left hand, now entwining his fingers with hers, she felt as if he had entered her body. With not a scrap of light between them, she became aware of his desire, and her passion matched his. The music lifted her and they moved as one.

The music stopped and Chris crossed the dance floor to whisper something in Brian's ear. He smiled at her.

"What did she say?" Ceci asked as they walked to the edge of the plaza, his arm still around her waist.

"She said we should get a room."

"I agree."

"If you do, we need to get the hell out of here right now."

"I'll go get my car."

"Is it locked?"

"Yes."

"Then leave it—and everything else. We can pick it up tomorrow. Come with me. Now."

As they hurried from the party, once again hand in hand, Ceci caught of glimpse of Devon driving away. Reflected by the glint of the sparkling Christmas lights, her face was shiny with tears.

•

Standing in the bedroom of the condo, Brian held Ceci close, his cheek resting on her hair. "Are you still sure?" he said.

"I am," Ceci replied as she slipped out of her dress. "You're a little smoky, though. Shall we take a shower first? Lots of room in there for both of us."

•

The water cascaded down her back as Brian anointed her with body wash and gently massaged it into her skin, working his way from her feet to her shoulders, slowly, in small circles, until she quivered and asked him to stop. "Let's prolong it, shall we? I'm so close to the edge now that all you have to do is touch me one more time and it will be all over for me. I'd rather be in this together."

Brian smiled. "I like the way you think."

She bent and licked the droplets from his chest and started to move down. "You taste quite delectable."

He groaned. "*You* have to stop now. You're not the only one who wants to make it last. Come on. I'll dry you off."

The first time was awkward, as they discovered they seemed to be better at dancing than lovemaking. "Oww," Ceci said, "your elbow's on my hair."

"Sorry," Brian responded, embarrassed. Rolling her on top of him a bit too enthusiastically, he took a knee to a groin. "Oh, baby," he laughed through the pain, "if you want me to use those parts, you have to treat them more gently."

"Sorry," she said. He kissed her and handed her a condom. "Why don't you put that on for me?" he said, with an enticing, seductive look on his face. As Ceci rolled it down, she stopped suddenly in the midst of her passion, snickering. "Bri, you could drive a truck through the hole in this thing."

Brian put the second condom on without assistance, but even though Ceci was determined to make the encounter perfect, the two had trouble adjusting to each other's rhythms and languages—and what they experienced was less than ideal. "Sorry" seemed to be the word of the night.

Later, Ceci lay back on her pillow, while Brian wrapped his arms around her from the side. "Stop giggling," he said, although there was a grin on his face, too. "I'm usually pretty good at this. It's humiliating."

"The end was excellent," Ceci smirked. "Exceptional, actually. I have high hopes for us."

"I'm grateful for your optimism," he said, as he once again pulled her on top of him. She relaxed, and this time their closeness was what Ceci had always dreamed sex could be and never had been before.

"Turn on the light," Brian said. "I want to see all of you." She straddled him, rolling her hips in time with his thrusts as he rose and fell beneath her. He looked into her face, watching, then pulling away and holding back, forcing her to slow down before he led her on. She moaned and bit her lip as she approached a climax again and again while he teased her by withdrawing.

"Please, Bri," she begged. "Please. Now."

He pushed further into her and her pleasure forced a scream from her throat. She felt him grow inside her and shudder with release as she collapsed against his chest.

They were wordless for several moments, catching their breath, their perspiration mingling. She finally moved away and onto her back. "That was better, wouldn't you say? I don't know where I was. I think I left my body."

"You were right here with me, sweetheart," Brian said. "Right where I want you all the time."

CHAPTER **THIRTY-TWO**

The next morning, as Brian slept, Ceci couldn't. The Nanday parakeets—nine of them—were shrieking on the wires outside the condo and she waved at them as she crept out of bed. She stole down the stairs noiselessly, although she felt like pirouetting on each step. She was loose and free, a sensation she had experienced only rarely. Her father used to say Ceci was "tight as a tick," but now her cells felt detached from one another. She was sensation without substance.

It's not the sex, she thought, smiling, although it had made her nearly delirious. Obviously, she'd had sex before. With Blink, her college boyfriend, so called because of the tiniest droop of his left eyelid, it had been mostly bump and run. He was young, virile, and not able to contain himself for more than the briefest time, so for Ceci it had rarely been satisfying. Since most of their encounters took place in the Sigma Chi house, she also had struggled with the fear of being walked in on by Trip, Spinner, Gus-Gus, or another brother—or even more unnerving, the house administrator.

With Alex, it had been better, but still somewhat like a business transaction. Put a hand here, put a hand there, signed, sealed, done. She had never experienced what she'd felt with Brian. As a bridesmaid at four weddings, she'd heard the words but never quite understood the concept of "the two shall become one flesh." That morning she did.

Ceci slipped out to the lanai and watched the Gulf as the sun rising behind her painted the crest of each wave with fire. As the water fell over into its trough, the gold transmuted to frothy silver. She was transfixed by the colors, the movement, and the raw power of the waves. For several minutes, she stood awestruck, caught up in the beauty unfolding in front of her. Her heart overflowed with feelings of thanksgiving for that moment and for the gift of her new relationship with Brian.

As she turned back from the lanai, however, she became uneasy about the communication she was sure to come from whoever was watching them. It sickened her that the ecstasy she had experienced would be reduced to an obscene, threatening comment sure to come from Alex.

As the day wore on, though, there was nothing. Although her mood lightened, the silence was unnerving.

CHAPTER **THIRTY-THREE**

When the next day passed without any more interruptions, Ceci felt she could take a breath. For the next couple of days before Brian's hours on duty, they reveled in time together. Ceci rose early and made gooey breakfast pastries. They carried them in paper sacks into the waist-deep tide and out to the sandbar, where they sat and gorged themselves on butter and sugar, rinsing their fingers in tiny swells thick with the smell of brine. They watched the water change its colors and smiled as an unexpected pod of dolphins breached and twirled in the sunlight like so many synchronized divers.

Later, they walked the beach gathering coquina shells. "They're so beautiful," Ceci said. "I've always wanted to make clothes in these colors and designs. The pinks and blues and browns are so subtle. I'd make dresses and shirts and pants, and I'd call my store Coquina Creations."

"I don't think that's going to happen," Brian said with a playful smile. "I've never seen anyone draw blood sewing on a button. You should tell your friend Annah about it. She could probably whip up a quilt and since it was your idea, maybe she'd give it to you."

"That's certainly the only way I could afford one of her pieces," Ceci replied.

The next day, they did nothing more strenuous than scarf down what they agreed were the best hamburgers they'd ever had. They walked them off along the bike path that circled the Key.

"Listen," Ceci said as they ambled along. "How many different kinds of birds do you hear? What else do you hear? The ocean? Cars? The school bus squeaking as the driver opens the door?"

"To tell you the truth, I've never thought about it much."

"I do," Ceci continued. "My mom used to take Gigi and me on what she called attention walks. They were so much fun. Each day, we'd concentrate on only once sense at a time. Sometimes it was seeing. And when you do that, you see things you've barely noticed before. Red geraniums in a blue pot on a white porch in the summer and a red cardinal against a snowy tree branch in the winter. Other times, we paid attention only to what we could hear. The most fun days were when we concentrated on smelling or touching. It helped us learn to notice things. I still love those walks."

"Well, let's see what we see today." Brian slipped his arm around her waist and she reciprocated. They walked along in the silence of people who know they don't have to fill the air with chatter to be close.

But then Ceci had a question. "Do you remember the first night you came to the condo?" Ceci asked as they continued to stroll along.

"It would be hard to forget it," Brian said.

"I agree, but in the midst of all the sexual tension we had a conversation about how we dealt with tragedy in our jobs. I was thinking about that today when I saw a quote on the Web. It said something like 'Only three kinds of people run toward danger: firefighters, police, and journalists.' I know you're not on the service yet, but have you ever been in danger on a rescue?"

"Got shot at once," Brian said laconically.

"Really? Here? On the Key?"

"It was way inland. It was a drive-by shooting and I was patching up the guy who got shot. He was lucky. It was a through-and-through shoulder wound. He needed to be transported, though. When I bent over to strap him onto the cot, I heard a bullet go by my head. Apparently, the shooter realized he'd mucked up the job and came back to finish it. I don't want to come that close again. You?"

"Nothing quite so dramatic. I was working an odometer story. This sketchy dealership in Huntsville was rolling back the mileage on every car. We nailed the guy, and when I did my 'gotcha' piece, he shoved the camera into my photog's face. Broke his nose, and then he literally chased me off his property. Poor Ask was bleeding all over his face and shirt and the lens."

"Ask? What kind of name is Ask?"

Ceci laughed. "His name's Asclepius Christopoulos."

Brian looked dumbstruck. "Asclepius? Like the Greek god of

medicine? Do all of your friends have colorful names?"

"His parents wanted him to be a doctor. How he ended up in a newsroom I'll never know. Great shooter and funny as all hell. Handsome, too. He *is* kind of a Greek god, even with the broken nose, which was never was quite right again."

"So then what happened to you and the Greek?"

Ceci was still laughing. "I was trying to run away in three-inch heels, so of course I fell and sprained both wrists. Ask and I had to hold each other up when we got back to the station. He was bloody and I was barefoot and both my arms were scratched and swollen. We were giggling like fools, though, the way you do when something is just ridiculous. The video was clear enough to support an assault charge, which put the bad guy out of business. Very satisfying. You and I each have our ways of doing good, I guess."

The next day, Ceci showed Brian one of her favorite places to enjoy the Gulf: a small sand cove cut into a higher beach. "I read here all the time," she told him. "The cove is a shelter if the breeze gets chilly. I snuggle back in there and never get cold." Brian jumped into the depression and pulled her down with him. They spent the next hour in each other's arms. Since sex was out of the question on a public beach at two in the afternoon, they restricted themselves to kisses—every kind of kiss, as if they'd just discovered this pleasurable pastime.

"This basorexia stuff is pretty damn good," Brian sighed.

"Oh, yeah. Quite a fine idea."

But late in this second day of their mini-idyll, while Brian was on a grocery run, the call from Augusta came. The news director wanted to see her on January fifth. Ceci agreed to go and then paced the floor, agonizing over whether to tell Brian or not. Everything he wanted, except her, hinged on his chief's interview, which would take place on the second day of the new year. If she told him about the possibility of a job at the other end of the country, would he take his eye off the ball, worrying about what would happen to them? If she didn't get the job, she would have upset him for nothing. If he wasn't selected for the open position, it would be her fault because she'd distracted him—or so she thought.

On the other hand, if she didn't tell him and got the job, would he feel sandbagged when she told him she had to leave the Key? And if he didn't get the job, he'd be miserable and she'd be gone.

She could easily go to Maine for the interview by faking a brief trip to Ohio to see her folks. Then if the job didn't work out, he'd never know, so no harm, no foul. It might work. But if he got the job...her thoughts caromed like pool balls inside her brain.

"I wish Minnie were still alive," she whispered to herself. "She'd tell me what to do."

Ceci had always depended on Minnie for advice, which was consistently hard-headed and practical. Minnie had surmounted hardships brought on by her father's death at Pork Chop Hill just weeks before the armistice in Korea. It had unhinged her mother and forced Minnie to become head of her family at the age of sixteen. Her marriage a few years later softened some of the rough edges but never penetrated the bedrock of her inner toughness. She took life as it came and made the best of whatever it handed her.

It didn't occur to Ceci to call her mother. Everyone said Kimberly was a lovely woman, and it was true, but Ceci felt her mom couldn't advise her now. In Ceci's opinion, Kimberly had settled for a diminished life, a channel as narrow as the grooves on the vintage vinyl records Ceci and Minnie listened to when they cooked together.

While her girls grew up, Kimberly ran volunteer boards, raised money, chaired events, and even pushed legislation. Ceci had always believed her mom would have made a formidable executive, but the role didn't interest her. She was happy at home—and Ceci didn't understand how her current life could satisfy a woman as able as her mother.

On a recent visit home she'd tried to question Kimberly about it, and her mother had smiled her tranquil smile as she answered. "I thought feminism was about choice, Ceci. You and your sister have made your choices, but that doesn't mean mine isn't right for me. You think of my life as confining. I think of it as deep. You've already lived in four cities. I've lived in one place my whole life. One place where I know everyone from the mayor to the people who come to the food pantry and where I can make a difference because I have a big network. I can make things happen, maybe not as dramatically as you can. The things I do take longer to accomplish, but the results are worth the time. You say you want more—and that's fine. This is *my* more, and I'm happy with it."

•

After Brian left for work the next morning, Ceci knocked on Annah's door and was greeted by a welcoming smile from the older woman.

"Could I talk with you, Annah? Are you working?"

"Not at the moment, and even if I were, fiber art is often forgiving of time. Come in. You look perturbed. I was just about to take the girls down to the beach. Want to come with me?"

"Sure."

As Annah disappeared to gather up Thelma and Louise and their leashes and treats, Ceci walked around the living room, mesmerized as always by the quilts hanging on the walls, works of art that filled the space with color and texture. Each one suggested some aspect of life on the Key: the waves, the sand, the flowers, and in one more-representational piece, people walking on the beach watching the dolphins play. As the quilts sold, Annah replaced them with new ones, so the apartment never looked the same from year to year.

Entering the older woman's studio, Ceci stopped still, riveted by a work in progress. "Annah," she said, raising her voice to accommodate Annah's slight hearing loss, "this quilt is *beyond*. It looks like an Impressionist painting. And the colors! I've never seen anything so beautiful. How did you *do* that?" She stared at what appeared to be thousands of tiny pieces of material worked into a garden design as subtle, incandescent, and ethereal as a Monet. It was a stunning departure from projects she'd seen in the apartment, at the local gallery, and on Annah's website.

Joining her, Annah placed Louise's leash in Ceci's hand. "Thank you for the compliment, dear. Hector and I were in France recently and we went to the Musée Marmottan. It had a huge collection of Monet's work, and somehow it was calling my name. I started as a painter, you know, but I couldn't make the brush do what I wanted it to. I can manipulate fabric, though."

That's a bit of an understatement, Ceci thought, coming from one of Canada's best-known art quilters.

•

Stepping onto the beach, Annah skipped any preamble. "What's on your mind?" she said. "Something is. You seem quite troubled."

"I've always thought of you as a wise person, Annah, so I'm wondering if you could give me some advice." As they walked, she sketched out her job/love/relocation dilemma in quick sentences.

"I'm not sure I'm comfortable stepping into this," Annah said, running her fingers through her cropped silver hair. "Why aren't you asking your mother? I'm really not some tribal elder with all the answers."

"Mom would have *one* answer. If I love Brian, and I do, I'd chuck the job and stay with him, no matter what happens."

"I think you underestimate your mother, but let me think about this." They followed the dogs in silence for so long Ceci wondered if Annah had forgotten the question.

"Ceci," Annah said finally, turning to her, "I've always believed honesty works best. It can be uncomfortable sometimes, but it's so much easier than lying or even shading the truth. Maybe you try the excuse of going home to your folks. Then you get snowed in in Maine when the weather in Ohio is unseasonably spring-like. How do you explain it? You tell another lie. One lie begets another and another as you cover up the original one. Nothing kills a relationship faster."

•

After Annah had gone back to her apartment, Ceci sat on the beach, turning their conversation over in her mind. She had explained to Annah that she and Brian had discussed her need to find a job that probably would be far from the Key and from him.

"You may have talked about it in general terms," Annah had answered, "but that's far different from reality. I know how hard it is to think about walking away from someone you love to do work you want to do."

"You do?"

"I do." Annah had stopped and turned toward the Gulf, a smile playing about her lips as she looked back on earlier times. "Hector and I had just been introduced, and we were lost in each other from Day One."

"Really?"

"Oh, yes. It's why I understand what's happened to you. I know it's rare, but it's priceless when you find the person who fills your mind and heart almost from the moment you meet one another."

Ceci felt more at ease as she had listened to Annah's words. She hadn't wanted to admit even to herself that things with Brian might be moving too fast and maybe what she felt was nothing more than overwhelming physical attraction. She was so happy, so content, and comfortable with Brian, she knew it had to be right, but she'd be lying to herself if she didn't admit the whole situation had unsettled her.

As Annah had explained it, about six months into her relationship with Hector, he received a faculty appointment in British Columbia and she was offered a coveted fellowship that would support her work for a year—in New York. "I was at the beginning of my career and dying to take it," she said. "I knew it would open so many doors for me, and I was hungry to build my reputation. Like you."

"What did you do? Obviously, one of you made a choice. You've been together a long time."

Annah had walked on, keeping a watch on Thelma, the more energetic of the two dogs. "I suffered...and then I married Hector and moved to British Columbia. I couldn't lose him to my ambition. I also thought that if I was destined for the success I wanted, God, or fate, if you prefer, would make it possible."

"Didn't you feel you gave up a lot?"

"In the beginning, yes. God didn't get it in gear fast enough for me. But after a couple of years, we moved to Toronto and over the next decade or so I found my voice as an artist and a whole community of other artists like me. Hector and I stayed together, and it gets better for us every year, even though we're not young anymore. I guess you could say I got everything I wanted by trusting in something greater than myself and following my heart. I don't know if it's what you should do. That's for you to decide."

Ceci made her decision that afternoon. She would tell Brian right after Christmas.

CHAPTER **THIRTY-FOUR**

eci stood in front of the display case at the La Patisserie talking with the saleswoman when Chris emerged from the back of the chic, French-inspired bakery. Although Ceci never had been to Paris, she thought the shop probably looked like one she'd find there.

Dressed in a sky-blue t-shirt, black sport shorts, and Nikes that had seen better days, Ceci was out of breath from her jog down the bike path to the bakery, but managed to gasp hello to Chris. "After we met the other night, I thought I'd better check this place out," she said. "Everything looks delicious."

"It is, if I say so myself," Chris laughed. "You like croissants?"

"Love them."

"Wait here, then. I just pulled some out."

Delivering the croissant with a small ramekin of raspberry butter, Chris waved away Ceci's attempt at payment and joined her at a small round table by the front window of the bakery. "How long have you and Brian been together?" she asked.

"We met a couple of days before Thanksgiving, so it's been a whirlwind. I could never have planned anything like it."

"Jim and I have known him for a long time. He's a super guy and a wonderful friend, but we've always found him to be sort of…veiled. He was there but not there, if you know what I mean. I haven't seen him this happy and unguarded for years. He recovered from Rachel's death the way people do from any loss, but it was like there was a hole in his heart. It seems to be filling in now."

Chris's words, no doubt meant to be complimentary, raised considerable angst for Ceci. Once she'd made the decision to delay telling Brian about her plans, she spent her days fretting. She, too, felt there but not there. What would be the best way and time to let him know what was happening with her professionally? When he was going on duty so he'd have things to distract him from the news or during an off-duty day so they'd have lots of time to discuss it? The choices chased each other around, and Brian had commented about the fact she seemed distracted and hard to reach.

After Chris left to attend to another patron, Ceci leaned over the table, enjoying the croissant and reading the *Key Daily*. Although she found some coverage of national news, the *Daily* mostly concerned itself with events that directly affected the twenty-eight square miles comprising the Key. She perused stories about builders' plans to develop the south end and residents' plans to prevent the development, a lawsuit filed by tenants against their condo management company, adult education classes, robberies and car accidents, social news, and a feature about city employees. Staring up at her from the paper was Devon's face.

"Devon Carter," the profile said, "earned a master's degree in public administration from the University of South Carolina. She is known for her responsiveness to residents and her attention to detail. If you want to know anything about the Key and the people who live here, just ask Devon. The daughter of Mary and Finn Reynolds, who now reside in Portugal, Devon was formerly married to Patton Carter of Greenville, South Carolina, and has a daughter, Mandy, who attends St. Agatha School in Naples."

Ceci was surprised at the master's degree. Devon seemed like more of a lightweight than that. She reminds me of some of the on-air traffic reporters I've known, she thought. Shiny hair and straight teeth. Pretty and pleasant, but not too much upstairs. I guess I was wrong. She does seem to be effective at what she does. The city runs smoothly and at least some of that has to be her doing. I probably misjudged her because we're in love with the same man, and I trust her about as far as I could throw a baby grand.

And St. Agatha's? Ceci didn't realize Mandy didn't live full-time with Devon. She seemed very young to be in boarding school a hundred miles away, she thought. Her dad disappears from her life and then her mom packs her off? Who does such a thing?

Still mulling it over and taking her last bite of the airy, buttery croissant, Ceci froze when she heard Chris say, "Hey, Mr. Buchanan. You must have been away for a couple of days. *Pain au chocolat*? I don't sell as many of those when you're not around."

"It's Alex," he said, as Ceci's stomach turned over and she tried to make herself invisible in the corner. "You know my habits already, Chris," he said in the sincere, cordial voice that had both attracted and comforted Ceci for several months and she'd only recently come to despise. "I was in Orlando for business, and I certainly missed these. They're exactly the right way to start the day. Café au lait, too, please." He made a show of inhaling the aroma of the almond pastry puffed around a slim cone of bittersweet chocolate, a flirtatious look in his eye.

Alex would put the make on a parsnip, Ceci thought. Pretty soon he'll be telling her about the bakeries he used to frequent in France when he went to school there. Phoniest man on the planet. I wish I'd known it before I got involved with him. He won't get anywhere with Chris, though. Brian says she and Jim are joined at the hip.

"How's the croissant, Ceci?" Chris said, forcing Ceci to look up from the newspaper she'd been hiding behind since she'd heard Alex come in.

Alex spun around, trapping her. His eyes glowed with malice. "Yeah, *Ceci*, what do you think of it?" All the previous warmth had disappeared from his tone.

"You two know each other?" Chris asked, clearly uneasy at Alex's spin from his practiced congeniality.

"Only slightly," Ceci said.

"Well, a bit more than slightly, Chris," Alex said. "We were engaged."

Chris retreated, seeming to know she'd wandered into the muck. "I'll leave you two to catch up, then, while I check on some things in the back."

Alex took three steps, landing in front of Ceci's table.

"Don't speak to me," Ceci said, as quietly as possible, barely moving her lips, as she shrank from him. "Get out of my sight."

"Darn," he smirked, "just when I was going to sit down and shoot the breeze with you about your boyfriend Brian. A paramedic and budding firefighter from a community college? That's what you're shooting for now? What's the attraction? Can he lick his eyebrows or something?"

"You're revolting. Get away from me." She edged by him, slamming the screen door as she escaped from the bakery. She ran, rather than jogged, back to the condo, her mind racing as fast as her feet. Alex had been away when the notes stopped coming, which made her more certain he was the one who was terrorizing her. As she ran, she wondered how he had found out so much about Brian—and then she knew. Convincing Brian of it would require considerable finesse.

•

Ceci stopped at the condo office on her way to her apartment. There was something in her mailbox.

> I HOPE YOU HAVE A MERRY CHRISTMAS.
> DON'T DO ANYTHING TO MAKE ME ANGRY
> OR IT WILL BE YOUR LAST. AND HIS TOO.

Her hand trembled and tears rose in her eyes.

CHAPTER **THIRTY-FIVE**

"Honey, I'm sorry," Brian said, when Ceci raced to grab her cell phone. "I wish I hadn't had to come in to work. Are you feeling any better?" The night before hadn't been a good one as Ceci fought through the anxiety again. The attack had lasted longer than usual, and she was worn out. She was glad to hear Brian's voice, but wondered whether he'd really forgiven her for some of the awful things she'd said when she was in the grip of the terror. He'd certainly responded in kind, but she had to admit she'd thrown the first grenade.

During the turmoil of the night, Brian suggested she start on some anti-anxiety medications and offered to make an appointment with his doctor. Ceci rejected the idea out of hand and everything went downhill from there.

"I'm not starting on some mood-altering drug that will make me an addict. I'm not interested in being on the nod all day," she said. "As soon as I'm not being threatened with murder every day, I'll calm down. This is a legitimate response to real danger."

"Of course it is. I'm not suggesting you drug yourself into oblivion, and I'm not saying you take it for the rest of your life. But it might give you some relief from the physical symptoms. There's no reason to suffer any more than you have to. It hurts to watch you."

"Sorry if it makes you uncomfortable. It hurts to *be* me, too." She tried to stop the full-body shaking by squeezing her hands as tightly as she could. It didn't work. And like ugly toads, words she had never expected to say leapt from her mouth. "You know, even Alex didn't ever suggest I needed chemicals. He thought eventually the attacks would stop—and they did—when the notes didn't come any more. He didn't think I was crazy."

"*I'm* not uncomfortable," Brian said. "I've seen worse than this. I'm worried about you, and there are some meds that could help your muscles relax so you don't have so much pain. I don't think you're crazy, for God's sake. You don't have to be crazy to benefit from medication now and then." He loosened the embrace in which he'd been holding her. "And by the way, I don't appreciate being lumped in with the guy who came in and roughed you up a few days ago. But if you want, I can call him," he said, testy and irascible. "Maybe when he's not writing letters, he could be more helpful than I am."

The fight escalated and Ceci's anxiety mounted until she vomited a couple of times. At that, Brian backed off to reduce her increasing agitation, but the air was still heavy with anger and misunderstanding. When the attack eventually slowed and ended, the two went to bed without speaking, and the next morning Brian left for work while Ceci slept.

Now, though, things seemed to have blown over to some degree. "I have some good news," he said. "J.J.'s going to be able to come down from Atlanta for Christmas at Mom's. Ashley and Jack were already planning to be there, so why don't you and I go, too? I have Christmas Eve and Christmas off, and the next day, too. Let's go to Tampa and have a nice family Christmas since your folks aren't coming down. We'll come back on the twenty-sixth."

"It sounds wonderful, Bri, but it scares me a little."

"Why? It's just my family. They aren't too scary," he said, with a laugh.

"It's not that. I'd love to go. But maybe it's one of the things that would make Alex 'angry.' He's threatening both of us, so part of his problem is we're together."

"We'll get away from him for a couple of days. He won't know where we are. We can even take separate cars if you want, but I think that's overkill. We can do another cover story though. I'm taking you to the airport in Tampa so you can catch a flight to Cincinnati, and I'll be picking you up when you come back from Ohio."

Ceci's shoulders relaxed. The story sounded plausible, and escaping the incessant drumbeat of fear was attractive. "You're convincing me. I really liked Ashley, and I'd love to meet the rest of your family. Another reason not to start on meds. I'd like your family not to think I'm some stoner, and I know they'll make me slow and sleepy."

"Okay. I get it. I'm not going to suggest them again, even though

I think they'd help. Let's leave Christmas Eve morning about eleven. Does that work for you?"

"Anything works for me if I can be with you." She hung up the phone with relief. She'd worried her first big disagreement with Brian about something as intimate as her inability to control her own body might have put him off. "Come on. He's not a jerk," she said to herself, as she gathered up her keys. She felt better in a crowd, so she headed to the mainland mall to pick out Christmas presents for Brian's family.

CHAPTER **THIRTY-SIX**

Brian called Ceci several times when he was on duty, and she reported no more untoward events. "Maybe Alex has decided to give me a Christmas reprieve, or maybe he's gone back to Orlando for the holiday," she said. "I wish Zach had been able to find something, but he can't watch the post office or put uniforms on Alex's apartment all day without any real cause. He does scare the hell out of me, though. It's like he's turned into Mr. Hyde."

Brian came off duty at midnight, slept a little, and now, Christmas Eve morning, he and Ceci were packing up his car for the drive to Tampa. "It's not much of a trip," he said. "Three hours, tops, depending on the traffic."

As Brian put the last gifts and his suitcase into the trunk, Devon pulled up next to them in the parking lot. "I was on my way back to the Muni and noticed your car. You two packing up for a Christmas getaway?" she said, looking as if the corners of her mouth were being manipulated like a marionette's. The attempt at a smile didn't work.

Brian gave her a quick around-the-shoulder hug. "Nothing too exciting," he said. "I'm going to my mom's for a few days, and Ceci's on her way to Cincinnati. I'm giving her a lift to the airport." He lied well, Ceci thought, his voice smooth as silk, giving nothing away. "What are your plans?"

"Very quiet," Devon said, with more than a tinge of sadness in her voice. "It's my merry little Christmas alone this year. Patton has Mandy. He picked her up last night for the trip to South Carolina. They're in Charleston with Andrea and Beau until the new year, which means they'll fill her head with poison about her awful mother and she'll go back to school thinking I'm the wicked witch…again."

"That sounds awful," Ceci said, stepping up between Devon and

Brian, and taking Devon's hand.

"Not much fun," Brian said, "even for Mandy."

"Who's going to be at your house?" Devon asked, turning toward Brian and removing her hand from Ceci's. "Is Aunt Judy coming? I've always thought it was nice she and your mother remained such close friends."

"I imagine she'll show up at one time or another, but I don't know when exactly."

"How about Aunt Nancy and Uncle Chaz?"

"Nah. The rich branch of the family will be in San Francisco this year, visiting Karl and Lauren. They just had their first baby, so the new grandparents can't wait to get there."

"Really? Boy or girl?"

"A girl. Riley."

"Oh, that goes nicely with Evans," Devon said, her eyes twinkling.

Ceci felt sure the sparkle in Devon's eyes wasn't reflective of any joy about the new baby, but instead carried a flash of malevolence. This conversational display was designed to show Ceci just how much Devon knew about Brian. How familiar she was with his relatives and friends. And how she hadn't given up on him in spite of what she'd told Ceci.

Time to bring down the curtain on this performance, Ceci thought. "Honey," she said to Brian, all sweetness and smiles, "we probably ought to get started if I'm going to make my plane." She deposited her carry-on bag next to Brian's and closed the trunk.

"Right," Brian said, settling into the driver's seat and putting down the top of the convertible. "See you, Dev. Merry Christmas. At least as merry as it can be."

•

As Brian and Ceci headed north to Tampa, Ceci tried out the theory she'd developed on her run from La Patisserie a few days before. She'd wanted to tell him sooner, but she felt the discussion needed to be in person and at the right time. Given their recent arguments, the time hadn't arrived until now. Tread carefully, she thought. You could be way off base.

"Bri, I've been thinking about something," she said tentatively, although she didn't feel in the least tentative about what she was going to say. "When Alex came to the condo the first day, he said he hadn't been sure of the name of the complex."

"Yeah." Brian kept his eyes on the road.

"He told me that a few days before he'd stopped by the Muni to see if anyone there could help him. He said someone did, and I'm thinking maybe it was Devon and she filled him in on us. When I saw him at the bakery and he was so hateful, he knew your name, he talked about your going to a community college, he knew you were a paramedic, and even that you were in the running to be a firefighter. For sure he's been sneaking around and seen us together, but I certainly didn't give away any details about you. How would he know your name or anything else if someone hadn't told him?"

Brian turned to stare at Ceci. "And you think that someone was Dev?"

"I'm sure it was innocent. The first day, he probably said he was looking for me and couldn't remember the name of the place I lived. I'll lay down big bucks he told her my name and she gave him my address. She knew I wasn't with my fiancé anymore and it was an ugly break-up, but I never told her his name. I'm sure she wouldn't have given me up if she'd known who he was." Ceci wasn't sure of Devon's innocence at all, but she didn't want to share her doubts with Brian.

"I know him," Ceci went on, choosing her words with care, "and I can almost guarantee how this all went down. He saw us together. He wanted more information. He knew Dev and I were acquainted. So a day or so later, back he goes to the Muni. He asks her out for coffee to thank her for her help. He's an attractive guy, so she went. And then he pumped her for every detail. He's good at getting people to open up, and she's an easy mark. Everybody says she never knows when to stop talking. Even you admit that. I'm sure she told him everything she knew and he used it to his advantage."

"We're a suspicious twosome, aren't we?" Brian said. "First I think it's Sean because I'm jealous, and now you think it's Dev because you are."

"I'm *not* jealous of Devon!" Splotches of color rose in Ceci's cheeks.

"Could've fooled me. You put on quite a show back there." Brian lifted his voice an octave and batted his eyes. "'Honey, we should leave now.' I call you honey, but you've never called me that. Not once. Did you think I didn't notice what you were doing?" He was grinning as he patted her knee. "I loved it. Very flattering."

They drove a couple more miles in silence. Then Brian spoke up, his expression and voice troubled. "I have to admit what you're saying might be plausible. They could have struck up some kind of friendship. Maybe she thought she could bring you two back together or something. Rachel always said Dev was a yenta, constantly yammering away, gossiping and matchmaking."

If she was trying to bring Alex and me back together, it had nothing to do with assuring my happiness. It was to get me the hell out of the way. "Those two certainly would be an unholy alliance," she said. "There's actually a word for it."

"Oh, God, and you're going to tell me what it is, aren't you?"

"Not if you're going to behave like that," Ceci said with a snicker.

"Oh, go ahead. All this vocabulary-building is good for me, even if I never use one of your words again—ever."

"It's concilliabule. It means to have secret meetings to hatch a plan."

"You really think that's what they're doing?" Brian sounded disbelieving, and Ceci decided to back off.

"I don't know, Brian. He wants me back and she wants me out of the picture. It would make sense. In spite of what I did to save Mandy, she really doesn't like me at all. She may have felt some momentary gratitude, but it evaporated the moment she heard about the two of us. She's still in love with you, no matter what you think."

"And you have figured this out how?" Brian said with a slight smile.

"All I have to do is look at her face when you're somewhere in the vicinity. As my grandmother used to say, it's as clear as mud in a washtub."

Brian's face clouded again. "Do you really believe she fell into an arrangement with Alex out of spite and jealousy? I've known her a long time, and I know she can be petty, but this is way beyond anything she's capable of."

"I think this is far more than petty, but I'm willing to believe it was unintentional, at least in the beginning. But if they're in cahoots now, I'm not so sure. The motive might be love, not jealousy. But whatever it is, she could be egging him on."

Ceci decided to let it drop and fell into a deep stillness, her thoughts turning on the events that had occurred since the day she met Brian. Emerging from her meditative silence a few minutes later, she looked as if a revelation had come to her. "Now that I think about everything, Bri, there's one thing I know. No matter what Alex has been up to, he doesn't have murder in him. He's definitely an asshat, but he's not a killer—or a rapist.

"As you said in the beginning, he gets off on power. I don't know why he's chosen to do this to me, but he won't step over the edge. He likes his lifestyle way too much to risk sharing a toilet with a guy named Stinky in a six-by-six cell. I'm certain he's sending the notes, maybe at her urging, but no more. He may keep trying to scare me for a while, but I know now I'm not in any real danger. Not from him."

As she spoke, Ceci felt the horror of the last weeks slip away. The tension drained from her shoulders. The knots that had taken up permanent residence in her arms and legs untied themselves. Her lungs finally admitted enough air for a deep breath, and she was aware that her heart was no longer pounding and had slowed to some sort of reasonable rate. She leaned her head back against the seat and closed her eyes. Everything felt new and sweet—and she forcefully closed the door on what might or might not be going on between Devon and Alex.

CHAPTER **THIRTY-SEVEN**

The stress relief left Ceci so weak she almost fell asleep in the car. Rousing herself, she asked Brian about the family she was meeting that day.

"Tell me about your mom. You speak of her in such glowing terms I feel a little intimated by her wonderfulness."

"Don't be. She's about the most welcoming person you could ever know."

"What's your best memory of her from when you were a kid?"

"That's something I've never been asked before."

"I'm a reporter. We try to ask provocative questions."

"I guess there are two, and both of them are connected to my father's death," Brian answered, concentrating on the road, not turning to Ceci. "I was with him when he was killed." Ceci gasped. "I don't think I ever told you. I watched him bleed out before anyone arrived to help." His expression was devastated, even two decades after the fact. He spoke swiftly, as if to get through the story as fast as he could.

"When the other car hit us, the door was shattered and a piece of what was basically shrapnel shredded his femoral artery. His blood was spurting everywhere. I tried to stop it, and I was covered with it. He asked me if I was okay and then he passed out. Within a couple of minutes I saw him turn gray and felt the last breath leave his body. His eyes were open. The squad got there fast but he was long gone. After that, everything was a blur for a couple of days. I had a broken wrist, but I didn't feel it. I don't even remember anyone putting a cast on my arm. I completely checked out." Ceci noted the sheen of tears in his eyes and she knew her own face had gone white.

Without warning, Brian maneuvered the car into a roadside rest area and turned off the engine. Noticing Ceci's quizzical look, he said, "I don't talk about that day very much because it's hard for me to think about it. I'll tell you the rest, but I don't want to be behind the wheel right now. Let's get out and walk around a little."

As they exited the car and headed for a nearby picnic table, Ceci put her arm around Brian's waist. He leaned into her, as if his knees were buckling under the weight of the memories.

Seated on the bench, the two were quiet for a few minutes. Ceci was frightened. She'd never seen Brian this way. He seemed to be both remembering and trying to forget at the same time. As he recovered himself, Ceci ventured a question. "You said your mom was helpful. What did she do?"

"At the funeral, I saw a side of her I'd never known before. Mom doesn't get angry very often, but that day she was practically foaming at the mouth. A whole bunch of people were telling me it was up to me to be the man of the house now and take care of my mother. After a few times of hearing that, Mom excused the two of us and dragged me into a hallway far from the viewing room. Her eyes were blazing. I thought she was mad at me."

"Was she?" Ceci asked, bewildered.

"Nope, but she was pissed about six ways at all the people who were telling me I had to take over my father's role. I'll never forget it. She put her hands on my shoulders and said, 'You *will not* be the head of the house, Brian. *I* will be the head of the house and you will be a ten-year-old boy. You will go to school and learn. You will do the dishes when it's your turn. You will play with your friends and be nice to your brother and sister. And you will grow up the way you're supposed to. It's my job to take care of you, not the other way around.' I remember feeling so much better because I was pretty sure I couldn't pay the bills and cut the grass and cook outside and all the other things my dad did." The corners of his mouth almost turned up, but he couldn't manage a real smile.

"I don't know why people do that to kids. I guess they don't know what to say, so they say anything that pops into their brain. Your mom was really smart."

Brian nodded and then went deep inside himself again. His voice became so soft Ceci could barely hear him. "The funeral wasn't the worst part, though. A few months later, I started to circle the drain. I couldn't get past the feeling I should have saved my dad, and I didn't. I felt like I'd committed murder. It was full-blown PTSD, but the diagnosis wasn't very well known yet. The guilt was so intense nobody could reach me. The only way out was to sleep, and I couldn't even do that because of the nightmares. They scared the crap out of me for hours."

"I'm so sorry. I can't imagine having to go through that kind of pain when you're just a child," Ceci said, as she reached up to stroke his face.

"I tried to go back to school, but it didn't work. I stopped seeing my friends. I stayed in my room and worked real hard to forget everything, but the harder I tried, the more vivid the accident became in my mind. My mom finally withdrew me from school and went on the hunt to get me some help.

"When I look back on it, I'm glad I was only ten," he said, his eyes hooded and his face ashen. "If I'd been a teenager, I probably would have self-medicated with drugs, or maybe I would have killed myself. I wanted to, but I was a little unclear on the particulars." He gave Ceci a wan, anemic smile.

"Did you find someone to help you?"

"My mom located a doctor who worked with me on the flashbacks and nightmares. After a few months with him and a short course of medication, I felt a little better, but it was really my mom who dragged me out of the fog."

"How?" Ceci said, reaching for Brian's hand.

"She sat me down one afternoon and told me the guilt she felt had almost killed her. She told me my dad was the love of her life and she had tortured herself after his death. That if she'd gone to the grocery herself instead of sending him, the accident might never have happened because she would have taken a different route."

"She couldn't have known," Ceci said. "Nobody can see the future."

"That's the conclusion she finally came to. She told me the only one person responsible was the idiot who made the decision to get behind the wheel when he was drunk. Once he did so, my dad and I were just in the wrong place at the wrong time, and there was nothing I could have done to save him. She asked me what I expected of myself as a ten-year-old, when even the medics couldn't bring him back. His injuries were too severe and I couldn't continue to beat myself up over a situation I couldn't have fixed at the time and couldn't fix then. It was an honest, grown-up conversation. Kind of surprising to me."

Ceci saw some of the pain leave Brian's face as he spoke. "She said we were both victims of circumstance. She told me she mourned my dad every day, but at the same time, she thanked God I was still alive. That all married couples know that one of them will have to face a spouse's death sometime, but losing a child is the worst thing anyone can experience.

"Somehow, she got through to me. I'd worried for a long time that she blamed me. When I found out she'd blamed herself, it helped me see that neither one of us was responsible for what happened. I got better, but I have a hell of a lot of respect for what the mind can do to the body. I understand it when you get the shakes because I've been so scared I thought it would kill me."

"I'm so ashamed of myself," Ceci said, tears dripping down her cheeks. "You faced a real tragedy when you were a kid. You had legitimate reasons for a whole lot of emotional upheaval. But I've fallen apart over and over again about a few letters, and I've made you deal with my idiotic panic attacks."

"Don't beat yourself up," Brian said, holding her in his arms. "Those letters were a real threat, and the new ones triggered a lot of memories and fear. Even Zach said they were an escalation." He kissed her lightly on the forehead.

"But I feel like such a dork, quivering away about nothing when I think of what you've gone through, not only with your dad, but then all over again with Rachel."

"That was different," Brian said, wiping away her tears with his thumbs. "I didn't feel any guilt about that. Sad, yes. It was one of the worst times of my life and I was spooked. But not guilty. I knew what to do for her. I knew it would never be enough, but I did everything I could to make her feel as loved and comfortable as she could be. Nothing left unsaid or undone. Her death was very peaceful and a release to both of us."

"Still, I should…"

"Stop with the shoulds. People react to different things in different ways. You've gone through a lot in the last year or so and trauma is trauma, whatever causes it."

"But I'm done being such a dainty flower. I love you so much, now more than ever, and I'm going to toughen up and be the person you deserve. And that's that. Now let's go enjoy Christmas."

CHAPTER **THIRTY-EIGHT**

A half-hour out from Sally's house in South Tampa, Brian told Ceci what "enjoying Christmas" meant to the Walker family. "Tonight is a big dinner. Always a beef tenderloin. Ashley, J.J., and I chip in for that, and then my mom makes all kinds of side dishes and we eat a whole lot. Usually, there are some relatives there, but it varies from year to year."

"So Devon mentioned," Ceci said, trying to suppress the cutting tone in her voice.

"Meow," Brian replied. "Then it's presents and midnight church."

"Catholic?"

"Yep."

"I can do Catholic. It's not too much different from what I grew up with. So far, pretty much alike, except we do presents on Christmas morning."

"Ah, but you ain't seen nothin' yet," Brian said, glancing at Ceci. "When we get back from church about one in the morning, we cook, usually for about two hours. We make pounds of stuffing and mashed potatoes to take back to church—and then because Mom hates a messy kitchen, we clean everything up and put it away. After that we sleep a little."

"And then?"

"The last Christmas Mass at Our Lady of Peace is at ten in the morning. After that, around noon, the church has a huge Christmas dinner for anyone who wants to come. It can be homeless people or just folks who are alone and want some company on Christmas Day—and sometimes it's whole families who love having dinner together but don't have enough room to do it at home. We don't ask any questions. It's a true community gathering. The food has to be there by about nine-thirty. We serve, we eat with the guests, and then we clean up. "

"Great. I'm in."

"Oh, and tonight while we're boiling potatoes and chopping celery and onions and stuff, we're also wrapping a couple dozen presents for the kids who show up at the dinner. Toys and clothes and games. We usually leave that to my dad's sister, Aunt Judy. She worked her way through college as a package wrapper at some department store that closed about twenty years ago, but she hasn't lost the knack. Lots of families bring presents, so there's always a big pile of swag under the tree. When the dinner's over about three o'clock, we come home and collapse."

Ceci was excited about what was to come, but wasn't sure she could keep up with this super-energetic family.

"Sleeping sounds like a plan," she said, smiling.

"Just warning you, honey, we won't have one moment alone until day after tomorrow."

"Oh, really?" Ceci said, with a sly glance. "I bet I can make that happen."

"Give it your best shot. Sounds really good to me," Brian said with a no-less-mischievous look.

CHAPTER **THIRTY-NINE**

A s Brian turned the car toward Bayridge Boulevard, Ceci took in the scenery. "This is a very settled-looking area," she said. "So much of Florida feels new. So many condos and developments with pretentious names like The Mews on the Lake."

"Or The Manors at the Swamp," Brian added.

"Or maybe The Villas by the Sinkhole," Ceci snickered.

"You're right," Brian said, laughing at her. "This part of town grew up around the nineteen-twenties. Mom lived down closer to me until five years ago when she came here to manage the medical practice. It's a big multi-specialty clinic and this was a quick commute for her. She bought well during the recession…"

"Like you and Rachel."

"Exactly, although her home wasn't in foreclosure. The older couple who lived there wanted to live closer to their kids in Virginia, and the market was collapsing, so it worked out well. The old folks got out before everything hit rock bottom, and Mom made a good deal for a house that was larger than the one she left."

"This is my first Christmas in Florida," Ceci said, with only a trace of wistfulness. "Last year I went home for a couple of days. When I was there, it was between twenty and thirty degrees all the time, overcast, but some sun and a little snow the day before I got there."

"I think you must have lived with Lee too long. That whole description sounded like a weather report," Brian teased.

"It didn't look like a New England postcard, but it was a semi-white Christmas. I'll have to adjust to wearing shorts in December."

"Maybe slacks," Brian responded. "It's supposed to drop into the high fifties tomorrow. That'll shrink the gonads."

"Oh, please. That's not even sweater weather in Ohio. Your blood is way too thin."

They drove another block and turned into the driveway of a tidy, two-story Colonial house. "This is unexpected," Ceci said. "You could plop this house down in Cincinnati. But what's with all the plastic flamingos wearing Santa hats? I see one in every yard."

"The neighborhood association decided to do it years ago. At night, all the houses have white lights and there's music and it's very elegant. But about nine o'clock, the flamingos light up, too. It's fugly as hell."

"I agree with you. Absolutely fugly," Ceci said.

"Yeah, effin' ugly and the flamingos get a lot of press every year. After January first, though, they *must* be retired or the association will send you nastygrams."

The door to the house flew open and a slim, attractive woman with black hair and blue eyes bounded out the door. "You're here!" she caroled, as she trotted to the car and opened Brian's door. He jumped out and embraced her, lifting her off the ground. "Ceci, this little ball of fire is my mother, Sally."

Ceci was immediately entranced and struck by how much Brian looked like his mother. Though Sally's dark hair was sprinkled here and there with silver and her eyes were a couple of shades lighter than her son's, there was no question of Brian's lineage. He and his mom even sported the same slightly lopsided smile that had so charmed Ceci the day she met him. Sally's nose turned up at the end, though, and she was shorter than Ceci had anticipated. Nonetheless, dressed in definitely-not-Mom jeans, a narrow silver belt, white t-shirt, and little white Keds, Sally easily could have been mistaken for Brian's sister—and if lined up with Ashley, the three of them could have been triplets.

She dashed around the car to hug Ceci, too. "I'm so glad to meet you. Brian talks about you all the time, and I have a very good report from Ashley, too.

"Have you eaten?" she went on, holding Ceci by the waist. "We tend to eat lightly during Christmas Eve day because we're such pigs at dinner, but if you're hungry…"

"Not really," Ceci said.

"Well, at least let's get you settled and have something to drink." She grabbed a couple of suitcases from the open trunk and sped into the house.

"I should have warned you Mom goes a thousand miles an hour. It's hard to keep up," Brian said, shaking his head as he observed his mom's energy and drive.

Sally leaned out the door. "I put you guys in the bedroom next to mine. I'm giving Ashley and Jack the bigger room. She needs more space these days. And J.J. will want to camp out in the den so he can fall asleep with the TV on."

"Well, I'm relieved," Ceci said, as she and Brian walked toward the front door carrying the Christmas packages. "I didn't know how your mom would feel about our sharing a room."

Brian exploded in laughter. "Ceci, I'm over thirty, not thirteen. I don't think she expects chastity after all I've told her about you."

Ceci wished she could have heard those conversations. She understood the reasons for Brian's closeness to his mother, but now that she'd seen the bond in person, she wondered exactly what he'd told her. Her own mother would have been surprised at the combustible nature of Ceci's relationship with Brian and certainly wouldn't have expected them to be having nearly nonstop sex since the firefighters' party, only three weeks after they met. Ceci appreciated Sally's matter-of-fact realism.

•

Inside the house, the Christmas décor was more slapdash than Ceci was used to: ornaments the kids had made fifteen years before; off-center plaid bows; lights that scintillated at the top and bottom of the tree, but faded to nothingness in the middle. Ceci thought of her dad, who placed the tree in the center of the living room bay window and wrapped every branch in lights, from the trunk to the tips. It shimmered, which made the tree the focal point of all the Christmas activity in the house and a destination the neighbors came to see. The Walkers' tree stood inconspicuously in the corner of the small den off the kitchen. "There's no room anywhere else," Brian said. "The living room's not big enough for all of us and a tree."

As Brian and Ceci headed toward their room, they walked down a gallery of family portraits. Grandparents, great-grandparents, and candids of gap-toothed kids—Brian, J.J., and Ashley— fishing, swimming, hiking, selling lemonade, and blowing out birthday candles. As the years progressed, Brian slowly ceded his position as tallest of the children to J.J.

Ceci stopped in front of Sally and Mark's wedding portrait. "Wow," she said, "when your mom came out to the car, I thought you looked exactly like her, but now I see so much of your father in you."

"That's what everyone says. I have her features, but apparently all of my father's mannerisms and expressions."

"It's a nice gene pool."

"Perhaps you'd like to swim in it someday," Brian said, looking at her with a foxy twinkle in his eyes.

Is he saying what I think he is? Ceci thought, excited and disconcerted all at once.

•

By two-thirty Christmas morning, dinner was over, the cooking for the next day was finished, the counters and stove tidied up, the dishes stowed in the refrigerator, and Ceci and Sally were alone in the kitchen, sitting at the table sipping peppermint hot chocolate. Ashley, waddling around in the final two weeks of her pregnancy, had been excused from duty and gone to bed early. Jack had followed soon after. J.J. was asleep in the blue leather recliner in the den, his long legs sticking out from under the light throw that covered him. Aunt Judy had left for home after wrapping a mountain of toys that were packed into laundry baskets for transport. Even Brian had decamped to their bedroom.

"Sally, the dinner was so good," Ceci said, somewhat at a loss about how to initiate a one-to-one conversation. It had been easy when the rest of the family was around. J.J., clearly the family outlier with his pierced eyebrow and the infinity tattoo on the inside of his left wrist, had united with Brian in teasing their mother unmercifully as Ashley looked on, moaning about what her life would be like if she had boys and had to endure the constant pestering her brothers heaped on their mom. Sally seemed to take it all in stride because there was no hint of underlying hostility or sarcasm, just a lot of joy and remembrance of past events.

"I'm glad you liked it. You seemed to fit right in, especially whipping up that extra pie so quickly," Sally said, patting Ceci's hand. "I know we can be a little overwhelming, but you held your own quite well."

"I hope so. My family is small. All the grandparents are gone, and my parents are not very demonstrative. It's just the six of us, including my brother-in-law and the baby."

"I really like J.J.," Ceci went on, her eyes alight. "It was good to meet him and so much fun having lots of relatives around and all the hugging and kissing from both sides of the family. Everyone seems to like each other a lot."

"We do. We've been a tight unit ever since Mark died when the kids were so little," Sally said, swirling a dollop of whipped cream into the dark chocolate in her cup. "I had to create a safety net for them because there was no way I could quit working. There wasn't much money, so I was really lucky to have both of our families nearby. Mark's sister Judy, my sister Nancy, and I banded together for all the kids, so the cousins are very close, too. Sometimes I can't remember where one family ends and the other begins."

"Brian tells me he had a really rough time in the early days and you pulled him through," Ceci said, wondering if she was walking into an area she shouldn't, especially during the holidays, when emotional landmines might be everywhere.

"He *was* a mess," Sally answered, seemingly not bothered by the direction the conversation was taking. "He had a ripping case of survivor guilt. Why had he been spared when his dad wasn't? And because he was still alive, what was the purpose of his life? Those are pretty tough existential questions when you're a child. Heck, they're even hard when you're an adult."

She took a sip of hot chocolate. "He was depressed. It was such a deep blackness it scared me to death. I think concentrating on him and the younger kids kept me from sinking too far into despair myself. Brian was so traumatized he needed me to help him get out of that swamp. Of course, I fell apart about twelve years later when J.J. left the nest, but being Mom *and* Dad to the kids kept me busy in the first few years."

"Why the delayed reaction?" Ceci asked, the words out of her mouth before she could think about whether they were appropriate. "I'm sorry," she said. "You don't have to answer. It's the reporter in me. 'Why' is always a major question."

"I don't mind," Sally responded. "Of course I was miserable when Mark died, but I was distracted all day every day with dozens of details. Field trip permissions to sign, making sure the kids were on the bus, getting to work on time. Endless tasks, and learning about the things Mark used to do: cutting the grass, fixing broken plumbing, washing windows. I could barely breathe. Then I went back to school myself. I worked in a one-person medical practice, but it was pretty clear big medical systems were the wave of the future, so I studied management and finance. I didn't get another degree, but I took everything I needed to be ready to be part of a bigger practice." She crossed to the microwave and reheated the cocoa for ten seconds.

"I joined a widows' support group, but it wasn't very helpful," Sally continued, coming back to the table. "Most of the women were at least twenty years older than I was and had been married for a long time, and most of their husbands had been sick. There wasn't anyone whose husband had died suddenly and violently. I remember one of them talking about the 'peculiar freedom' of not having to think about anyone but herself. Her kids were grown up and now she didn't have to consider anyone's wishes but her own. She was really struggling with it, but I certainly didn't have any freedom like that. It walloped me hard when J.J. left to go to school in Georgia, though. Then I understood what that poor woman meant. I felt useless…and kind of selfish."

"Whatever you felt then, I'd say you did a wonderful job with your children," Ceci answered. "They all seem to be crazy about each other and I've never known anyone as…I guess the word would be self-possessed…as Brian is."

Sally glanced away, her features darkening almost imperceptibly. "He is. Most of the time. But he tends toward depression. He was down the rabbit hole for quite a while after Rachel died. I'm so glad he's passed all the psychological tests for the fire service. He couldn't have done it three years ago, certainly."

"Wouldn't that be normal, though?" Ceci asked, her brows knit in ambivalence and wondering why Brian had neglected to tell her about the second depression. "To grieve your spouse, especially when they were married such a short time? Is it really depression? Or just feeling sad?"

"Sure, but there's a line between mourning and depression. He could barely get out of bed. He didn't eat. He lost fifteen pounds in a month. The department finally let him take a leave of absence to get himself back together again enough to work. It did the trick, and now he's ready for the next step."

Sally stared directly into Ceci's eyes, and Ceci sensed a warning in her look. It filled her with trepidation. "The thing about Brian is he doesn't deal well with loss. He's had two big ones that flattened him. I know it's the one thing that worries him about the chief's exam. The chief remembers Brian's depression. He's done really well for the last couple of years, but he's scared his leave of absence might be in the back of the chief's mind."

Ceci's heart fluttered. Brian had told her how Rachel's death affected him and he had felt alive again only when he met Ceci. As much in love as they were, what would happen if Brian lost her? Or even thought he was going to? Would he nosedive again and miss the opportunity to earn his way into the fire service? Could she live with that? On the other hand, was she really responsible for his mental health? It felt like a heavy burden. And what of her work? Was she supposed to sacrifice her dreams to keep him on an even keel?

She reflected on the history he and his mother had shared with her: withdrawal from school as a child and a leave of absence from work as an adult. Her certainty about announcing the Augusta possibility wavered and crashed. This was not the time. She would have to wait until after his interview, even though it was only two days before her trip north.

Ceci yawned, more from nervousness than fatigue. She washed out her cup and hugged Sally. "We probably ought to get some sleep," she said. "From what Brian's told me, tomorrow is a busy day."

•

After washing her face and brushing her teeth as quietly as possible, Ceci slid into bed wearing little more than a smile.

"Hi, baby," Brian said. "You don't have to tiptoe. I'm awake. I've been waiting for you." He drew his hand across her breasts.

"Brian," she said, *sotto voce*. "In your mother's house, with her in the next room?"

"She isn't there yet. She always takes a shower at night, and I hear water running. We have time for a quickie." His voice was irresistibly seductive.

"But quiet," Ceci said. "I don't want your mom to step out of the shower and hear us. I know you share a lot with her, but I'd rather keep this to ourselves."

Brian snorted. "Okay. Deep silence. And Merry Christmas," he whispered as he entered her.

CHAPTER **FORTY**

On Christmas Eve, Devon sat in her living room, staring into the embers of the small fire she'd built to ward off an unexpected chill in the air. She remembered last Christmas, a day she'd spent with Brian. He'd been on duty Christmas Eve, but Christmas Day was all theirs and they'd high-tailed it for Tampa, where in a day-long flurry she'd reconnected with Sally and Brian's siblings, and met the rest of his family, including some aunts and assorted cousins. It had been a perfect day, and the family had embraced her. She'd felt at home and even loved, as everyone had thought she was Brian's girlfriend and seemed happy he'd found someone. She smiled all day as she played the role. It had been a few years since she and Brian had had an intimate relationship, but as she moved easily among the group she wondered if her natural magnetism and the family's obvious liking for her would be enough to rekindle his interest. They'd come back Christmas night, though, and there had been no hint of a renewed sex life.

Now there was Ceci. And Devon was alone. Lonelier than she'd ever been in her life. She thought maybe she should get a dog. At least it would be company on nights like these when a miserable solitude inhabited every corner of her home and her life.

A thought occurred to her. She reached for her laptop and searched for a particular phone number—one that would give her some answers.

CHAPTER **FORTY-ONE**

At six o'clock the next morning, Ceci lay in bed feeling the warmth of Brian's body next to hers. She drowsed, listening to him breathe and thinking about the many years she had wakened early on Christmas Day, holding herself in check until her parents knocked on her door at seven, telling her it was okay to go downstairs and dive into the presents Santa had brought.

A naïve child, Ceci held on to the notion of Santa Claus far longer than her peers. No matter how many times she heard the truth from others, she loved the idea of Santa so much she had wept in her closet for an hour when she finally gave up the myth of magical wishes come true. It was nice of her parents to give her what she wanted, she thought, but somehow "Santa is the spirit of loving and giving," as her mother said, didn't stack up as well as the idea of a jolly old elf—and as an animal lover, Ceci found it almost as difficult to dispense with the fantastic flying reindeer, her favorite being Blitzen, rather than that Johnny-come-lately Rudolph.

By six-thirty, Ceci slipped out of bed, careful not to wake Brian. She stood a few minutes by the side of the bed, studying his face. Most people looked different in sleep, she thought. There usually was a certain slackening of the features. Not the case with Brian. He was still, his cheeks taut over the bones of his face. I'd like to look at his face for the rest of my life, Ceci thought. And the body. His shoulders and upper body were strongly muscled, but not bulked up from hours in the gym. More like one of the nude Greek statues she'd studied in her required Art Appreciation class in college. Below the waist he looked like those statues, too. She smiled at the thought. She considered sliding back under the covers, but decided to let Brian sleep. They still had a big day in front of them.

Shimmying into clean underwear and the shorts and shirt she'd worn the previous evening, she tiptoed to the porch where she sat in a straight-back chair, her feet on the ground. Paying focused attention to each sense in turn, she became aware of the sweetness of the florals that surrounded the house, the cacophony of the birds awakening, the breeze rustling in the palms, and finally the pinks and blues that announced the nascent dawn. After a few moments, she began a morning meditation.

Always interested in meditation, she was nonetheless only an occasional practitioner. However, the events of the previous few weeks had driven her back to exploring the techniques as she tried to rid herself of the anger, fear, and frustration engulfing her. For the next few moments, she concentrated on the flow of her breath, feeling it move through her body. She noted the energy of the earth rising from her feet, which gave her a sense of peace on this unusual Christmas morning.

Her eyes closed, she felt the air stir and was surprised to find J.J. at her side. "Merry Christmas," he whispered. "May I join you?" So tall and thin he barely cast a shadow, he sat down next to her in a half-lotus position.

"Sure," Ceci answered. J.J. closed his eyes and the two of them sat side by side in silence. As Ceci once again became aware of her breath, she also noted that after a few moments, she and J.J. were breathing in unison. Somehow the synchronization of breath with someone she had met only the night before but for whom Brian felt such obvious affection created a sense of intimacy she hadn't expected.

As she took a final cleansing breath and stretched, J.J. too opened his eyes. She smiled at him. "I didn't know you meditated," she said.

"It beats booze, which was my drug of choice for several years," he said. "I'm a recovering alcoholic. Haven't had a drink in years, but that doesn't mean I don't want to. Centering myself every morning helps."

Ceci's eyes widened. "I had no idea. Brian never said a word."

"I think he figures it's my story to tell, and I appreciate his not blabbing. I know a lot of guys who'd be happy to give you all the details about their screw-up little brother."

"It looks like you're on top of things now," Ceci said, turning a calm, direct gaze on J.J.

"Most of the time I am," he answered with a shy smile. "But as you may have noticed, I'm different from the rest of the gang here. I don't look like them and they're all outgoing as hell. I can play along for a while, but I'm basically an introvert. It's why I'm in computers. It's quiet, and I don't have to deal with too many people. I feel okay talking with you, though."

Feeling complimented, Ceci continued the conversation. "You and Brian didn't have much trouble ganging up on your mom. You were as loud as he was."

"Oh, that," J.J. said, laughing. "Mom can give as good as she gets. She's the strongest woman I know."

"Brian says she saved him after your dad's accident."

"And then he saved me," J.J. replied.

Ceci settled in because she could feel J.J. was true to his word. He trusted her, and he was going to let her in to a part of his life she sensed he didn't share with many others.

"I didn't fall apart right after Dad died," he said. "I was only six, and I wasn't in the car like Brian. I remember when he came home from the hospital he still had blood caked under his fingernails. Mom washed his hair later that day, and the water turned bright red. She drained the sink as fast as she could, but I know he got a look at it and the blood stains on her hands. He and Mom were both hysterical and sobbing. It scared the hell out of me, even though I wasn't exactly sure why."

Ceci grimaced at the thought of a little boy witnessing such a terrifying scene and turned her full attention to J.J. "You said you didn't fall apart right then. So what happened later?"

"You sure you want to hear? I don't usually dump my whole life story on people almost the minute I meet them, but you're different." A slight flush came to his cheeks.

"Really? How?"

"I watched you last night, and you listen. You make eye contact. You wait for people to finish what they're saying instead of looking like you're trying to think of what to say next."

"That's nice of you to say, J.J., but I'm afraid listening is primarily an occupational trait. If you're in news, you'd better be able to listen. Sources don't open up unless they know you're concentrating on what they have to say and they can trust you."

"Dad's death hit me in high school," J.J. plunged on. "I played baseball, and every game I'd see all those dads in the stands cheering for their boys. Mom came as often as she could, but it wasn't the same. Of course, I was a big stud and didn't talk to anyone about it, so it got worse and I got angrier. I think Mom knew it was about missing my dad. She'd try to get me to open up, but I wouldn't. I turned into a real prick with her, punching holes in the walls and stuff."

"I think you're being too hard on yourself," Ceci said, placing her hand on his forearm. "Most teenagers are pricks to their parents, with less reason than you had."

"I think Mom might agree with you to a point, but I went pretty far beyond that point. When I was about sixteen, I started experimenting with some light herbal refreshment to take the edge off, but then I went to a party and found out I liked booze a whole lot better than pot. I didn't get the munchies. I wasn't sleepy. It loosened me up. Brought me out of my shell and made me more gregarious. I enjoyed myself, which was a rare thing.

"Liquor makes some people mean," he went on, "but it didn't have that effect on me. It certainly lowered my inhibitions. My girlfriend's, too. She got pregnant when we were seventeen."

"You have a child?" Ceci said, her eyes popping open.

"No. Jenny said she'd had a miscarriage, but I never believed it. Her parents hated me, and I'm pretty sure they forced her to terminate the pregnancy. No way were they going to let us get married, which is what we wanted.

"It was the lowest point in my life. I'm sure it was for her, too, but they wouldn't let me talk to her about it. They didn't let me talk to her at all. The pregnancy happened in late summer, and when the school year began again, her parents packed her off to boarding school. I never saw her again. I loved Jenny in that pure first-love way. I still think of her sometimes, but I have no idea where she is."

"I can see it still hurts," Ceci said softly. "You probably could find her through a Google search or maybe on Facebook."

"I tried. Even the alumni page of her boarding school, but I came up empty. She's probably married by now. I don't think getting in touch with her would end well, so I'm not going to try. I just wonder about her."

He was lost to Ceci for a moment, staring into the middle distance. "So there I was. Girlfriend gone. Baby gone. Dad gone. A mom I was fighting with all the time. I drank as much vodka I could find. I was drunk every day and hardly ever went to school. I finally flunked out."

"You said Brian helped you."

J.J. chuckled sheepishly. "Let's say he made me see the light. He was working by then and one night, the squad run was for me. I was driving myself home from a party, lost control, and took out a parked car and a mailbox. I was banged up a little bit, but no injuries. The drunk tank was an adventure, but the next day was worse."

"Why?" Ceci asked, bewildered.

"The next day, Brian came home, yanked me out of bed, and threw me against the wall. He said I was the dumbest shit he'd ever known, and if I wanted to drink myself to death, that was my problem. But if I ever drove drunk again, he'd make sure I got jail time. He kept yelling at me, 'You're not going to do to some other family what that fucker did to ours! He walked away without a scratch, too.' He was furious in a way I'd never seen before."

A rueful smile played around J.J.'s mouth. "He told me I was an alcoholic and while I'd been sleeping it off, he and Mom had made a plan. If I wanted to go on drinking, that was my choice, but I wouldn't be living at home. If I started AA that day and continued to go and got sober, Mom would let me stay. If I refused, he'd help me pack and take me to the homeless shelter. He said I was through abusing Mom and being a capital-A asshole. He gave me sixty seconds to make up my mind."

"Wow! Not too much wiggle room there."

"I'll never forget my mom," J.J. said, with a grin. "She looked at the two of us and said, 'So this is how guys do it? Here I've been talking and talking, trying to get to the bottom of your problem, and all I really had to do was slap you around?' Brian and I burst out laughing. He found a meeting for me that afternoon, and I got a great sponsor. I went back to school the next year and then on to college, where I fell off the wagon more often than I like to talk about. I called Brian the last time it happened, and he came to see me. It was a hard conversation, but after that I found a meeting in town and started going again, and it stuck. I've been clean and sober for six years."

"God, J.J.," Ceci breathed. "I'm stunned you and I are close to the same age and you've been through so much. I've messed up a lot recently. Lost my job and all, but nothing as difficult as what you've dealt with. I can understand why you're grateful to Brian. I am, too. He's pretty much of a rock."

"He is, but he needs protection, too. I'm happy to meet you because he talks about you constantly. He hasn't done that since Rachel died. She was a great girl. I wanted to see about you. Turns out you're a great girl, too. Like her."

"I'm like Rachel?" Ceci asked. "Brian's never said so." Ceci felt a momentary shiver. If Brian also thought she was like Rachel, was she only the substitute for the wife he had so loved and lost? She didn't think so, but J.J.'s words gave her pause.

"I don't mean you're like her. Rachel was great in her own way and you're great in your way. You have a better sense of humor and you're upfront about things. She was quieter and more introspective. She was pretty and so are you. He's lucky. A couple of the other girls…"

"Devon?" Ceci asked, since she didn't know the names of any of the others.

J.J. scoffed. "Looks good, but a big phony."

"Thanks," Ceci said, leaning in to give him a little peck on the cheek.

"Brian wants to marry you, you know."

"*What?*" Ceci's eyebrows shot up as she drew back from J.J. "He hasn't told me that."

"Maybe not, but he does. I was surprised the little Christmas present he gave you was earrings instead of an engagement ring."

"Oh, J.J., I'm not sure I'm ready for that. My last engagement didn't work out so well. I adore Brian, but adoring somebody isn't enough for a marriage. You have to know each other well. We don't yet. We haven't been through anything hard. We'd don't know how we'd react to a crisis. We've already had some unpleasant moments. Maybe we'd tear each other apart."

"I doubt it. Neither one of you looks like the type."

"That's the point, J.J. It's not about how we *look*. It's about how we *are*. Having my engagement break up taught me some things. Alex was a real bad guy, but I was blind to anything I didn't want to see. I was in love with Alex, but I was more in love with being in love."

"I think you'd better be prepared for the marriage discussion. I'm sure the subject's going to come up before too long." He turned his head. "Ah, I hear people stirring and I haven't put the coffee on yet. We'll need to get the cars loaded pretty soon."

Her mind reeling, Ceci followed J.J. into the kitchen, where they found Ashley begging off going to church because she was having contractions. Sally was uncharacteristically agitated, Jack looked as if he'd like to flee the scene, and Brian was asking questions.

"Are they regular?"

"No, and they aren't the same length either. One will be like twenty seconds and then next one will be forty."

"Do you get them when you stand up?"

Ashley looked surprised at the question. "Yeah. I had one when I got out of bed. I had another one when I stood up from putting on my make-up."

"I've delivered a few, Ash," Brian was saying, "and I'd guess these are Braxton-Hicks. Sort of practice contractions. I'd be surprised if the baby came today."

CHAPTER **FORTY-TWO**

When the family arrived home from serving the Christmas lunch, Jack was helping Ashley into their car. "The contractions are every three minutes now," he said, the color gone from his face, "and they're regular and they hurt. I don't think we're going to make it home, so our doctor said to go across the bay and he'd call a colleague there."

"I'll come along if you want me to," Brian offered.

Jack looked as if he'd collapse from relief. "I'd like that a lot," he said.

"I'll drive," Brian said. "You concentrate on Ash. We'll be at the hospital in fifteen minutes. Ceci, will you follow me in? We'll leave Jack's car, and we can come home together after the baby's born." He placed the keys in her hand, giving it a squeeze as he released them.

Speeding across the bridge following Brian, and with Sally and J.J. trailing behind in his car, Ceci flashed on J.J.'s words. Since her break-up with Alex, marriage had been far from her mind, but now she considered it. The more she heard about Brian from his friends and family, and the more time she spent with him, the more convinced she became he was—as Peggy had said—a genuinely good guy. He'd seen her at her worst and cared for her anyway. She loved his family. But getting married would tie her to the Key and effectively end her career unless something opened in the area. It's easier to get a job when you have one, she thought. Maybe I should look around and find *something* until there's a newsroom job available. Chris offered me a job. I could do that for a while and wait for a media job close by. Of course, there's no guarantee I'd get it, and the longer I stay out of the business, the harder it will be to get back in. Besides, Brian hasn't asked me to marry him. Maybe J.J. misunderstood and the whole issue is moot.

She turned into the hospital parking lot. I'm not going to worry about this now, she decided. I'm going to think about Ashley and the baby.

CHAPTER **FORTY-THREE**

"That was quite a trip," Brian said, as Ceci met him at Labor and Delivery. "Her water broke when she got into the car and the contractions dropped from three minutes to two. She was doing some heavy-duty hollering. I think we're probably looking at about an hour at the most."

Ninety minutes later, the whole family was gathered at Ashley's bedside staring into the face of Elaine Hyde Brannon, who was held skin-to-skin in her mother's arms. Ashley, though clearly exhausted, was radiant. "Seven pounds, nine ounces," Jack announced to the family, with the dazed look common to new dads, "and twenty inches long." He bent to kiss his daughter on the forehead. As the baby opened her eyes, Ceci exclaimed, "Look at that color. They're certainly the Walker eyes."

"Actually," Sally said, "those come from my side of the family. The Hydes."

Ceci had an unexpected, incongruous thought. She suspected Devon would have known Sally's birth name and would have said exactly the right thing. She pushed the idea out of her mind. I'm here and she's not, she told herself.

J.J. stoked his sister's head, grinning. "Ash," he said, "apparently a quick delivery agrees with you. You didn't even have time to get your hair messed up."

Ashley smiled back. "You think I didn't ask for a comb? You know me better than that."

"I can't believe I'm a grandma," Sally said, gazing at the baby in wonderment. "She looks exactly like you did, Ashley, right down to the spiky blonde hair." Tears misted her eyes. "I wish Mark were here to see this," she said. "Twenty years and all of a sudden I miss him as much as I did the day he died."

Brian put his arm around Sally. "He'd be so excited," he said. "Ashley always had him wrapped around her finger, and I think this little sweetheart would have the same powers. Could I hold her, Ash?"

As he cradled the baby, Ceci wondered if he thought about Rachel and the child they lost. He didn't appear to be nostalgic, though, and she marveled at his confidence in handling his niece. She saw none of the timidity so common in men confronted with a newborn.

"Merry Christmas, Lainie," he said, conferring the nickname by which she'd always be known, "and welcome to the world."

He'll be a wonderful father, Ceci thought. If he does ask me to marry him, he ticks off all the boxes in the ideal husband category: smart, kind, caring, ambitious, responsible, passionate, and family-oriented. Handing the baby to his mother, he turned and gave Ceci his most heart-stopping smile. She knew right then the marriage question was definitely coming, and she knew when: right after he was selected as the Key's newest firefighter. Almost exactly the time she'd be leaving for Maine. She felt sick.

"Ash, you look great, hair and all," Brian remarked, "but I think we should hit the road and let you get some rest. They don't call it labor for nothing, and they'll kick you out of here tomorrow. Then you won't sleep for months."

•

"You know, Brian," Ceci said on the way home, "you may not have taken over as head of the household when you were ten, but you seem to be the leader of your family now. And J.J. told me you were about twenty-three when you took charge of him. I think you've been the man of the house for a long time."

"Never thought of it that way." He turned to her. "Do you like my family?" he asked, and Ceci sensed there was a lot riding on her answer.

"I love them. I couldn't believe how many different political opinions you guys have, but nobody was yelling at anybody else. My mom and dad are wonderful and agree on almost everything but politics, and around election days, the conversations are...I guess you'd call them spirited. He always asks Mom how she voted and she always says it's called a secret ballot for a reason.

"The Christmas lunch was amazing. I never expected four hundred people."

"This is the fifth year for it and it keeps growing."

"J.J. surprised me. He told me he was an introvert, but he looked pretty gregarious to me. I noticed he gave the most attention to the people who looked the loneliest."

"He's sensitive to them because he's always felt he was on the outside looking in. He's doing better now. Coming out of his shell a little more."

"And I must say Ashley certainly knows how to top off a Christmas celebration."

"She sure does. That child is going to lead Jack around by the nose. And she'll always think Christmas carols are all about her." He smiled.

"And Santa brings her birthday presents. It can be hard sharing your birthday with Jesus, though.

"I had a nice talk with your mom, too," Ceci went on, not wanting to disclose too much of the conversation. "She's so pretty and smart I'm surprised she hasn't remarried."

Brian's forehead furrowed. "We've hoped she would. In the beginning, she didn't want to, but a few years after my dad died, she poked her head up and surveyed the landscape. She found out men her age weren't too interested in women in their early forties with three children. They were looking for thirty- or even twenty-somethings with bikini bodies and no kids."

"What a waste," Ceci sighed. "Sometimes men don't get it."

Brian placed his hand on her knee. "I think she's interested in someone now, but it's early days. He's a cardiologist. They've been to a few movies and had dinner a couple of times. He's divorced, though, and the ex is a problem. I don't know if my mom feels like taking that on."

"Still…"

"I know, but it has to be right for her. She always says there's more than one way to live a life."

That's true, Ceci thought, but it's hard to decide what's the right way at the right time. "Her relationship with my dad was special," Brian continued, "and I don't think she'll settle for something less. Different maybe. Not less."

They arrived at Sally's house, noticing a dirty-brown Nissan that sped away as they approached the driveway. "I know that car," Brian said, "but I can't remember from where."

CHAPTER **FORTY-FOUR**

Ashley, Jack, and Lainie came home the next day. Because Lainie had made her appearance early—and away from home—nothing was prepared. Ceci and Brian fought their way through crowds of Christmas returners at Target and scooped up diapers, onesies, a couple of receiving blankets, a pack and play to be left at Sally's, and a car seat. After standing in line for an hour to pay for the purchases, it was back to the hospital to return the loaner car seat. The baby was fussy unless she was being held, so everyone pitched in for that duty. No one slept, and Ceci could barely keep her eyes open as she and Brian packed the car later that day.

After an almost-silent drive home, they unloaded the luggage and Ceci dragged upstairs to grab a quick shower. As she emerged wrapped in a bath sheet, she heard her cell phone pinging. "Bri, will you see who it is? I'll call them back."

She heard his footsteps on the stairs. He handed her the phone, his eyes ablaze. He sounded as if he'd been gargling broken glass. "It was a text from some station in Maine. They want to know if they can move your interview from the fifth to the sixth. They've arranged for your rental car. You can pick it up at the airport."

Ceci's hands flew to her mouth. "Brian..." Her stomach clenched and she felt unstable on her feet. Her legs weak, she sank down on the bed she hadn't made before they left for Tampa. Her fingers twitched.

"When were you going to tell me about this? Or were you just planning to disappear?"

"Of course not. I was going to tell you."

"When? After you took the job?"

"Will you please sit down and let me explain?" Ceci pleaded. "You look like you're going to crush the phone, and things really aren't so bad."

Brian took his place in a plaid wing chair as far from Ceci as possible, sitting upright and tense, while she perched on the edge of the bed.

"Explain to me why things aren't so bad," Brian said, leaning forward, sarcasm coating every syllable.

"First of all, this trip is exploratory. They haven't offered me a job, and if they did, I don't know if I'd take it. A Maine winter is not something that appeals to me. But I have to examine possibilities, Brian. We talked about it the very first time you came to dinner. I've looked for jobs here. There aren't any. There really aren't. I have to work. It's not like I'm independently wealthy."

Brian turned to her. "But why would you hide it from me?"

"I agonized over that. I talked to Lee and Annah about when it would be the best time to tell you."

"Let me understand," Brian said, each word clipped. "You talked to your best girlfriend and to someone I've met once about a decision that has a huge impact on our lives, but it didn't occur to you to talk to *me*? What sage advice did all these people give you?"

"Don't be hateful," Ceci answered, her eyes flashing with sudden anger probably brought on by lack of sleep. "They both advised me to be honest with you. And that's what I'm trying to do. When I first talked to the people in Maine, it was just a phoner. I decided if anything came of it, I'd tell you after Christmas. That would have been yesterday, but we were a little busy. It was the wrong time. But while we were in Tampa, I thought it would be better to wait until after the chief's interview. I thought you'd be upset if I told you I might have to move, and if you didn't do well on the interview, you might blame me."

"That's ridiculous. The chief's interview is on me. If I blow it, that's my problem. I'm a big boy."

Although both of them were testy and on edge, things weren't going as badly as Ceci had feared they might. She looked directly at Brian. "While we were at your mom's, she said something that scared me. She told me you don't handle loss very well and how depressed you'd been after your dad and Rachel. You'd told me some, but she filled in the whole picture. I worried about how you'd be if you thought you were going to lose me, too. Maybe the interview would be a disaster and you wouldn't get what you've worked so hard for."

"*Jesus H. Christ!*" Brian erupted. "Dad and Rachel *died*! Yes, I was depressed. They were gone from the planet. I would never see them again in this life—and I'm not sure I believe in another one. This is different. And now you've brought my mother into it! Excellent."

"I did not bring your mother into anything. She volunteered the information. And what do you mean different? If I don't happen to die you'll be fine? You've been lying? This whole relationship has been sort of a dalliance? You don't love me?"

"Of course I do. You know I do. This isn't the decision I'd want you to make, but you have a career. I have one, too, and I know what it means to love your job."

He stood up, towering over her. "If you go, will it break my heart? Yes. Will I cry? Yes, probably a lot. I might even get depressed. But one thing I've learned from crashing and burning a couple of times is depression eventually ends. I know how to deal with it now. I've had a lot of practice. I'd pick up my life again. It wouldn't the same life, but it's the one I'd have and I'd have to make the most of it. And if I get through the interview, I'm going to be happy. That should take some of the edge off if you have to move."

Ceci stood to face him. "J.J. told me you wanted to marry me, and now it sounds as if you'll be just dandy if I take off for Maine."

"Did Ashley say anything while she was busy having the baby? You seem to have polled my family."

"Oh, crap, Brian," Ceci said, her usual direct gaze full of anger. In spite of her fury, she kept her tone low and measured to stop any further escalation. "I didn't do anything like that. We were talking about you, which would be normal the first time I met your family, and J.J. offered up some information. I didn't go digging for it. You can ask him—and your mom—if you don't believe me."

Brian exhaled forcefully and his expression softened. He took her hand, drawing her next to him. "The fact is I do want to marry you and have a million kids and live with you forever. That can't be a surprise. But I don't want you to resent me for trying to guilt you into staying. I'm not going to be a millstone around your neck if you'd rather move on."

"It's not that I'd rather! I may not have a choice." Tears threatened, but Ceci choked them back, looking straight ahead. "What do you want me to do?"

"I don't have an answer. I know I can't give up what I've been working toward for six years. I'm greedy, I guess. I want you with me, and I want my job."

"Oh, God, Brian. I know in the great scheme of things, your job is probably more important than mine. But I think what I do is useful—and you're right. I love it. People have a right to know the news about where they live. I'm a good reporter. I've broken some important stories. I want to do more. I want to stay with you, too, but there aren't any opportunities for me here. I have to look somewhere else."

Her eyes filled and overflowed. "Maybe this thing in Maine won't work out. I hope it doesn't and we get a reprieve. But I have to make a living. If I want to stay in this business, which I do, I have to keep looking. And where I land may be even farther away."

Brian's face was a mask of profound sadness. "Then I'm going to lose you," he said. "I don't see a way around it." His hands shook as he touched her face and kissed her gently, tangling his fingers in her hair.

"I won't accept that, Brian," Ceci answered, pulling away. "I'm going to figure it out. Go to work, and when I talk to you next, I'll have the solution. I swear it." She smiled as if she could guarantee the result, but she was lying. She had no idea what to do, except to drop the towel and invite Brian into her arms for make-up sex. Shaded by a fear of loss, it was more intense, more satisfying, and more emotional than ever before, ending in tears for them both.

•

After Brian left, Ceci tried to sleep, without success. As she alternately kicked her sheets off and then pulled them up to her shoulders, she remembered her conversation with Annah, who had followed Hector all the way across Canada and back again. But Annah had a portable skill, she thought. She could set up a studio anywhere. In spite of that, she'd been very unhappy for a couple of years after giving up the fellowship. Ceci thought about her mom, who'd devoted her whole life to her family and didn't feel she'd given up a thing. But I'll have to, Ceci murmured. And Lee, who was going great guns in the career department, but had no man in her life—and didn't care. Everyone she knew had made choices, but Ceci felt all of hers were impossible. Give up the man she loved or the job she loved because there was no way to have both.

Just before she gave into despair, she shot upright in bed. *Producing!* she thought, excitement shaking her awake. In college she'd served a year-long internship working with the producer of an early morning local news program. She discovered a talent for writing quickly, accurately, and grammatically, and she enjoyed editing scripts as elements of a story changed over the course of a day or a week. She loved researching the investigative work the station did. Although some of her coworkers groaned at the need to constantly update web content that supported and sometimes teased the on-air stories, Ceci took it as a challenge and did it well. Her mentor said she had a good journalistic eye and encouraged her to take on more duties as the year progressed.

When she left college, the lure of on-air work was too strong to resist and she moved to the other side of the camera. But I could become a producer, she thought. I know I could. I have experience. I know how a newscast goes together. I know how to stack a show and how to handle breaking news. I know how to manage on-air "personalities" because I've been one. This is perfect.

Ceci leapt from her bed and dashed to her computer. Opening the TV job boards, she found twenty-six production positions in Florida, most of them on the east coast, which made them impossible, but four producer positions were within twenty miles of Brian's house. I could do that for a little while, she thought, and I can move up to an executive producer position quickly. Lots of producers are young, and they move from station to station to advance their careers. I plan to stay, so I'm promotable. This can absolutely work.

In spite of her excitement, however, doubt crept into her mind. I love being on the air, she thought. I love chasing a story and putting it together. I love following it to see if it leads to something bigger. I know I won't get the same kick from producing. I can be good at it, but it's not the same thrill. Should I do it? Producing is definitely better, though, if we decide to have a family. I can't be running down alleys chasing unwilling interview subjects if I'm eight months pregnant. And I do want a family. There is a tradeoff. There always is.

A smile crept over her face. "The tradeoff is Brian," she said to herself, "and that's no contest."

In the early morning, she texted Brian: *I promised and I'm about to deliver. Text me back when you can.*

Brian's returning text showed up immediately: *What happened? Call me. I want to tell you in person.*

Her cell rang.

The words poured out. "Brian, I've been up all night. I've already updated my résumé and answered all four ads. I know I can do this. And I remembered I also worked the assignment desk while I was interning. I'd have to get up to speed on that again, but once I do, they'll get a three-fer. I can make this happen." She twirled around the living room, embraced by delight. "It's going to be okay, Bri. I'll call Augusta Monday. I'm not going!"

His relief and happiness echoed hers, but then she heard the horn signaling an emergency at the firehouse. "Gotta go now," he said, "but thank you, honey. Thank you for everything. I love you so much I can hardly speak."

Ceci crashed on the chaise on the lanai, depleted from fatigue and emotional turmoil. She stayed there, resting and drifting until the sun was directly overhead.

When she woke, she found the note shoved under the door.

YOU DON'T LEARN, DO YOU? IF YOU VALUE
HIS LIFE, YOU'LL STAY AWAY FROM HIM,
STARTING TODAY.

•

Enough was enough. Gathering up the letter, she pulled on white shorts, a green polo shirt, and running shoes, in case I have to get away fast, she thought. She pulled her hair into a rough ponytail and except for brushing her teeth, dispensed with her whole facial routine. No make-up because anger had flushed her cheeks. You look fine enough for this idiot, she thought.

Then, with equal parts agitation and resolve, she strode down the Key to Cowrie Shoals, the condominium community where Alex had set up shop apparently for the fun of terrorizing her.

The temperature had jumped ten degrees from the day before, the wind was nonexistent, and the humidity already enervating. Though the distance between Ceci's condo and Cowrie Shoals was only about a half-mile, her skin became gummy with perspiration as she approached the imposing, Italianate high-rise.

Of course he has to have the penthouse, Ceci thought, jabbing at the bell. Why would anyone want to live in a cocoon like this at the beach? I bet he can't even hear the Gulf or the birds or smell the surf or anything else even faintly natural up here. Phony beach house, phony guy.

"Claire," Alex said, opening the door without an inkling of the rancor that had characterized the previous couple of weeks. "I'm surprised to see you here. Is everything all right?" His face was placid and his manner inviting, as if she were a valued client with a carload of money to invest.

"I want you to stop sending me this garbage," she said, holding out the note, her voice icy. "It doesn't scare me anymore, but I'm sick to death of it. You're wasting your time. Threatening me doesn't make me want to rush home to your welcoming arms."

Taking the note from her hands, he stared at it in amazement. "You think *I* sent this? I don't even know what it's about. Who's mad at you? What did you do?" He scrutinized the careful printing again. "Wait a minute. Isn't this like the threats you got in Indiana?"

"*Exactly* like them, and you're the only person on this whole Key who knows all the details and who could recreate them flawlessly. And, by the way, they started coming right after you came to the Key, and they stopped whenever you went back to Orlando."

Alex continued to examine the note. His befuddlement seemed genuine, and the certainty Ceci had felt on the way to Tampa began to leach out of her bones.

"Claire, this is bad stuff, and I wouldn't do it. I'll admit I was out of line and jealous the last two times I saw you, but this isn't my style." For an instant, Ceci caught a glimpse of the man she'd been engaged to, the person who'd seen her through the early days of panic. The thought he might be innocent made her feel woozy and ill at ease. She blanched and her knees went weak.

"Sit down, Claire," Alex said, propelling her to a recliner in the corner of the room. "You look like six miles of bad road. I don't know who's doing this, but I can tell you it isn't me. Have you been to the police?"

"Of course."

"What do they think?"

Still uncertain about direction the conversation was taking, Ceci decided not to disclose to Alex he'd been under informal surveillance. "They don't know. They've ruled out one person, but it could be anybody. They caught the nut case in Indianapolis, so he's not the one."

"This guy you're dating...Brian? You can't have been with him very long. Are you sure about him?"

Ceci threw Alex her most triumphant smile. "Yes, I'm sure. Don't even go there."

"I can't help you, then. I'm asking you not to suspect me, though. I'm sorry this is happening to you, but I'm not the one doing it."

"I'm afraid I believe you," Ceci answered. "And that makes things worse."

CHAPTER **FORTY-FIVE**

By late afternoon, Ceci, though edgy, was resting again, trying to make up the deficit from Christmas. When she stirred, it was already dark. She turned on some lights and surveyed the kitchen. Sally hadn't sent any leftovers home from Tampa—and the cupboard looked almost bare. She finally decided on tomato soup and a turkey sandwich. As she turned on the burner to heat the soup, the doorbell rang. Looking through the peephole, she saw Devon carrying a beautifully wrapped Christmas package.

Oh, no, she thought. Of the people she didn't want to see right now, Devon was at the top of the list.

"I didn't know whether you were back or not," Devon said, as Ceci opened the door. "How was Cincinnati?" Devon said, smiling, but with a knowing tone that put Ceci on the defensive immediately.

"Fine. Too short," Ceci said, unaccountably nervous and wanting Devon out of the condo as soon as possible. Devon seemed in no hurry to leave, though, and extended her gift to Ceci.

"This is awfully nice of you," Ceci said.

"It's nothing. Just some wine I know Brian likes. You can use it to toast the New Year or something."

"How thoughtful. Let me turn off the stove and we can chat." She didn't want to, but her mother's lessons about civility and hospitality had kicked into high gear. After all, I've stolen Brian, she thought. The least I can do is be gracious to someone who's making an effort to be polite.

"How was your family?" Devon asked.

Once again, Ceci shaded the truth, because somehow she knew Devon was aware of her deception. "They were okay. My dad's recovering from a bad bout of bronchitis. That's why I went there instead of everyone coming here."

"What a shame. I would have loved to meet them." The words were right, but the way she said them was full of acid. Ceci became even more agitated. She worked to control her outward appearance as her stomach dipped.

"I'm sure they would have liked that, too." I don't know how long I can keep this up, Ceci thought. She knows I'm lying. I don't know how she knows, but she does.

"Oh, this *is* a nice wine," she said, opening the package. "Thank you so much."

Entering the kitchen to place the bottle in the wine rack, Ceci felt an impact to the back of her head, as if she'd fallen from a height. She staggered to the kitchen island as the second blow landed above her left ear. She collapsed to the floor.

●

When semi-consciousness returned, Ceci found herself slumped in a chair, her hands behind her and both her feet and hands bound with duct tape. Her mouth was taped shut. Nausea from the concussion roiled in her stomach. The thought of choking to death if she vomited dominated her fuzzy thoughts. She swallowed down the feeling of sickness.

As her eyesight cleared somewhat, Devon came into partial focus. She sat across the room from Ceci as if she were a welcome visitor. She held one of Ceci's throw pillows on her lap. "Ah, you're awake," she said. "We need to have a little chat. I'll take the tape off your mouth if you promise not to scream. If you do, I'll have to shoot you in the head, and I don't want to." She lifted the pillow from her lap, displaying a Smith and Wesson .38 Bodyguard with silencer. Ceci recognized it as what she'd carried in Indiana without the silencer. She nodded.

"I want you to suffer as much as possible, and a bullet in the brain would be over too quickly." Ceci gasped under the tape, but no sound escaped.

"No noise?" Devon said.

Ceci shook her head slowly. Devon crossed the room and ripped the tape with as much force as she could muster. Ceci winced as the thin skin of her lips was stripped. Her head pounding, she struggled to remember an interview she'd once done with a hostage negotiator.

Listen, she thought. I have to listen to her. This could be a long night, she thought, but I have to get out of here alive. God, my head hurts.

"How was your trip to Tampa?" Devon said, derisively. "And don't try to say you weren't there."

"I shouldn't have lied to you," Ceci replied. "I knew you were hurting over Brian, even though you did a good job of concealing it. I thought telling you would rub salt in the wound. I didn't want to do that, Dev, so I made Brian lie and I backed him up. I'm so sorry. How did you figure it out?" Keep her talking, she thought.

"I called Cincinnati. I said I was a friend from Orlando wanting to wish you a merry Christmas. Took about six calls to get the right Myers family, but when I did, your mom said you weren't there and she wasn't expecting you. She sounded confused. I didn't have anything else to do on Christmas, so I drove to Tampa to see if you were with him, you lying strumpet. What a wonderful word... strumpet. I'm so glad you taught it to me. It's so much more genteel than whore, which is what you are."

"We never saw you there. How did you find us?"

"My parents have an old Nissan my father adores. It's a souvenir of something. I don't know what. He keeps it in the garage here under a tarp. I think Brian might have seen it, but only once. I parked down the street from Sally's house and darned if you two didn't show up."

Ceci could smell her own sweat, running now in rivulets down the inside of her shirt. She kept the conversation going, even as she felt the blood congealing behind her ear from Devon's second assault. Her eyes blurred again, and her head felt like an overripe cantaloupe. "Brian mentioned he'd seen that car before, but he couldn't recall where."

"He doesn't recall a lot, apparently, when it comes to me. But with you, he remembers every perfect detail. God, you should have heard him the night he came to break up with me. Ceci, Ceci, Ceci. It made me sick. It was all I could do to carry on the conversation. I wanted to hit him right in the face. I pulled it off, though, and got lots of information from him. I used him just the way he'd used me."

The word *empathize* swam through Ceci's muddled awareness. Calm her down if you can. Use her name. "I'm sorry, Devon. I know it hurts. I was miserable when it happened to me, and I didn't want to do it to you."

"You know it hurts? I doubt it. You break up with Alex and a few weeks later you're here and already sleeping with Brian. I don't think you got hurt so much. Not like I did. I think you're a bitch who takes what you want when you want it."

Ah, Ceci thought. She *is* Alex's new friend, the one who told him where to find me. But somehow it didn't matter. She was drenched in fatigue. Her head drooped.

She felt chilly steel lifting her chin. "Oh, no. No drifting off." Devon removed the gun from Ceci's throat. "I want you to be awake for this. You *are* going to die, and he's going to find you dead. It's going to be slow and Brian won't be able to help you."

Lie, Ceci thought. Lie right now. "Devon, Brian wouldn't help me anyway," she said, her words slightly slurred. "We broke up last night. We had a huge fight."

"Don't feed me that. Do you think I'm a moron?" Devon shoved the gun into Ceci's face again.

"It's true. He found out I was going to take a job in Maine. You can see the text from them on my phone. He found it and he was so pissed. He wanted me to stay here, but I can't, and he won't move where I'm going. He totally blew. It's over."

"Where's your phone?"

"In the kitchen next to the stove." Ceci indicated the direction with her head, which was a mistake. The throbbing intensified. Thank God I didn't text them back, she thought. I called them—and seeing the return call will make her believe it.

"Interesting," Devon said, distracted as she went through the messages from Maine. "Unfortunately, you forgot about the later ones." Ceci's heart sank. She had directed Devon straight to the texts about delivering on a promise.

"Looks like you made up pretty quick." Devon's lip curled in distaste. "Together. Apart. Doesn't matter. He's in love with you, and I don't want your leftovers after he tries for months to work it out. I'd rather have him grieve for a while with no chance of your popping up again and ruining everything. Then he'll turn to me, just like he did after Rachel. You sit still now. I have some work to do."

Devon disappeared into the condo's attached garage, returning with a stepstool. As she dismantled the kitchen and living room smoke detectors, she explained her plan to Ceci. "If I do this right, the sprinklers won't go off because there won't be fire. Just a nice, slow cloud of toxic smoke to choke the life out of you. Not much heat at all. But you'll hurt and then you'll die, and I like the idea. I read all about how to do it on the web. It's such a great source of information. I wish I could stay around to watch it, but by the time you're past the point of no return, I'll be long gone. But I'll come back when it's time for Brian to start picking up the pieces. I'll win." She sneered at Ceci, her eyes dancing with hatred.

Please let me pass out now, Ceci prayed. Suffocation had always been one of her biggest fears. The thought of it made her lose control of her bladder.

"Really, Ceci, Brian wouldn't find peeing your pants very attractive. But it pleases me a great deal you're so scared." Devon laughed with unalloyed delight.

Ask questions, Ceci thought. Delay this as long as you can. Make time for a miracle. "It *is* you who's been sending the letters, right?"

Devon's expression was dismissive. "Of course, you nitwit. Who else could it have been?"

The room spun. "I thought it was Alex," Ceci said, keeping her voice as conversational as possible, trying to simulate a friendly exchange.

"Alex was easy," Devon scoffed, as she carried the stepstool to the kitchen. "Brian had already told me a lot about how you were stalked, and anything I didn't know I pried out of Alex. Didn't take too much work. He thought he was manipulating me, but I had him right where I wanted him all the time. He's dumb as a bag of rocks. What did you see in him?"

"When I look back on it, not much. I was deceived."

"You must be incredibly naïve, then. He's a fool. All flash."

"Did you know when he'd be out of town so you could send the letters at the right time?" Ceci wiggled her wrists, trying to lessen the strength of the duct tape.

"Sure. He told me everything. We met for lunch several times, and I'm a very, very good listener. I knew it would be simple to make him look guilty if I timed everything right. He's the ideal fall guy. Believe me, they'll blame him for this."

For a moment, as Devon settled into the armchair opposite Ceci, she seemed to relax. Her tone was less venomous. Hope flared but was soon extinguished when Ceci realized Devon was simply enjoying her superior position. She was proud of what she'd done. She smiled.

"How did you know I was at Brian's house the night of the

thunderstorm?" How many more questions can I dredge up, Ceci thought, before this concussion takes away my ability to think and talk?

"Dumb luck," Devon laughed. "I saw his car at the big intersection at the square. He was headed to the mainland, and I noticed you were with him. I came through the light to go east and followed you, about three car lengths behind. I saw you turn on to his street, so I waited and I watched him leave without you. Then I followed him back and he went to your place."

She stopped, recalling the incident. "That confused me, so I went back to the mainland a couple of hours later and everything was the same. I figured you were alone, and when the storm blew up and the power failed, I had to take a shot. It was too perfect not to. I knew it would freak you out. How did 'he' know where you were?"

"What about Mandy?" Ceci said, realizing it might not be the best tack to pursue. Devon might see it as a challenge. "If you kill me and get caught, Patton will take her. You'll never see her again. I saved her for you. Why are you doing this?"

Surprising to Ceci, Devon's voice caught. "Patton says I'm not well, you know. It's why he keeps trying to get custody of Mandy. I'm tired of fighting him...and everything else. Every day seems so hard. Maybe she'd be better off with him, after all. He does love her, even if he doesn't love me anymore. If I'm going to lose her eventually anyway, so why not let him have her and get rid of you at the same time? You deserve it. I love Brian more than anything in this world. He and Mandy and I could have been a perfect family. *Perfect.* That's dead, though, so you may as well be, too.

"And now I've had quite enough conversation," she said, turning cold and businesslike. "I have to finish what I came to do, and I think I'll shut you up while I get it done." Pulling the roll of duct tape from her beach bag, she waved it in front of Ceci's face. "I remember how you liked this bag. I thought it would be a nice touch to use it to carry all the things I need to get you out of my life."

She cut the tape and closed Ceci's mouth again. Ceci fought, trying to scream before Devon applied the tape, but she was too weak. The sound she produced was barely a squeak. "It's time for you to take your last look at the world, because your time is up."

Ceci's mind darted to Christmas, when she and Brian had their first glimpse of Lainie. The beginning and the end, she thought. A tumult of memories, jumbled by her head injury, crowded her awareness. Her mom stroking her head when Ceci had the flu. Her dad driving her to her dance lessons. Learning to ride her bike. She and Gigi hanging by their knees on the limb of the oak tree. Passing the AP English test with a five. The senior prom with Anthony. The friends she'd made at stations around the country. And for what? So I can die at thirty? Brian, come help me before I'm gone.

"This would be so much easier if you had a gas stove, but I'm prepared," Devon said, as she methodically shut the door to the lanai, lowered the shade, and packed towels into the slider. She muttered as she worked, pulling down additional shades and making sure no windows were open upstairs or down. She talked to herself, rambling on about Patton and Mandy, Brian and Ceci, her boss, and some people Ceci didn't know.

Ceci continued to fight against her restraints, but her strength waned quickly. Devon moved around the apartment, painstakingly removing her fingerprints from Ceci's phone, the stepstool, the banisters, and the chair where Ceci was confined. She packed up her bag and set it by the door. "I'm taking the wine back," she said, turning back to the kitchen. "Perhaps Brian and I will drink a toast to your memory.

"Okay, Ceci," Devon whispered. "Here we go." She opened a box of wooden matches, lit one after the other and placed them between the sofa cushions, far away from where Ceci was sitting. "This kind of furniture produces lots of gases, especially carbon monoxide and cyanide, and they'll smother you before they kill you. You can't get away. Just a few breaths should do it. It ignites fast, but burns slowly, and if it does flare, it might burn you, but you won't know it. You'll already be dead. The last face you see will be mine, not Brian's. Too bad."

Devon opened the door. "See you soon," she trilled, as if she were taking leave of a dear friend after a brief holiday visit. "Thanks so much for the present."

CHAPTER **FORTY-SIX**

C eci felt fresh air on her face. She heard Matt's voice, quiet and controlled, and bits of conversation. "Carbon monoxide poisoning. Probably cyanide, too, so get the kit for that. Forty over palp. Her heart rate...I'm going to tube her right now...step away, Brian. I need to get this done." Ceci sank into unconsciousness again as the endotracheal tube was placed in her throat.

"She has soot at the outlet of the nostrils and a significant head injury, too." Ceci didn't recognize the voice. "We'll get an arterial blood gas and see where we are. She's not burned. Smoke inhalation for sure, but we don't how much or how severe it is. She comes around a little now and then, but she's mostly out."

Another voice she didn't know wormed its way into what was left of Ceci's consciousness. It was gentle and soothing and reduced her anxiety almost immediately. "My name is Iris," she said. "You're at St. Raphael's Medical Center. They brought you here from St. Luke's on the Key. You're badly hurt, but there's every hope for recovery. The doctors and nurses here will take very good care of you, and in just a few days you'll be on your way home. Recovery will take some time, but you're going to get well."

"Hmm," the first voice said. "Her vitals look a little better, but I want her in the hyperbaric chamber as soon as possible." Ceci felt herself being moved and loaded into something. She was surrounded by vivid color, but she couldn't stay awake. The night closed in.

•

As Ceci lay in the ICU, Zach's voice rose through the mist. "I know, Brian. I know. Alex was there, but he's also the one who broke down the door when the dogs were going crazy. The Allenbys called 9-1-1 when they saw the tiniest bit of smoke coming from a back window. Alex dragged her out and started CPR...No, I don't know why he was there and neither do you. I'll question him. That's my job. You stay the hell away from him. I mean it. Don't you go near him again. I'll lock you up myself if you get in the way of my investigation."

It wasn't Alex, Ceci thought. I wish I could tell them it wasn't Alex. The pain in her throat was excruciating. She passed out again.

CHAPTER **FORTY-SEVEN**

Her eyes too swollen to open, Ceci felt rather than saw light. She tried to blink, but she couldn't. She heard her mother's voice, tentative and trembling. "Ceci?" She felt her mother's tender hand on her forehead and reached for it.

"Brian, get the nurse," her mother said. "Right away."

The next few moments were a flurry. She heard the nurse and doctor discussing her awakening, her mother weeping with her head on the bedrail, and her dad saying, "Thank you, God," again and again. But over them all she heard Brian. "Hi, honey. Welcome back." She wasn't sure what he was talking about, but she tossed her head, trying to dislodge whatever was in her throat. "Don't do that, baby. You won't have the tube down too much longer. I promise. I know it's uncomfortable. The nurse is going to give you something for the pain. Go back to sleep if you can."

She sank once more into oblivion, but her sleep was restless, haunted by nightmares she couldn't understand.

•

Later, Ceci was more alert, but still confused and unable to speak because of the searing of her airway. She heard a voice that sounded like Sally's alternating with Brian's.

"Brian, you've been here nonstop since the accident. You have to rest. In two days, you have the interview. Ceci would want you to do it. You know she would."

Yes, Ceci thought, in a moment of clarity. Yes, Sally's right. Do the interview. Please, Brian. She moved her hand to her mouth.

"You want to say something, honey?"

Ceci nodded only once because it still hurt to move her head.

Brian handed her a notepad and a pencil. She scribbled on the pad.

"I'm sorry, Ceci. I can't figure out what it says."

Ceci whispered the best she could, trying to form words around the tube. The effort was exhausting.

"Did you say 'do it'?"

Ceci nodded once.

"Yes?" Brian asked.

She reached for his hand and squeezed it once.

"Once for yes?"

She squeezed his hand again.

"I told you," Sally said. "She's young and strong. She'll come through this and she'll be devastated if you don't at least try. She wants it for you."

"Is it what you want, Ceci?"

She pressed his hand once.

"That's what I'll do, then. But it's not for a couple of days. I'm going to stay right here with you tonight. It's New Year's Eve, and we're going to start our first year together." Although it hurt, Ceci tried to smile.

CHAPTER **FORTY-EIGHT**

Ceci's eyes were slits, but open. Consciousness and memory were returning. The tube in her throat had been removed and she was on nasal oxygen only. Speech was still nearly impossible, though.

With surprise, she heard Lee's voice and was overwhelmed to see her standing by the bed, looking much the worse for wear, her typical eye make-up smudged and her lipstick long gone. "Hey, girlfriend, you're doing better today," Lee said.

"How would you know?" Ceci whispered.

"You big dope, I was here with you early last night while Brian grabbed a little sleep. I held your hand for an hour. Sorry my healing powers aren't so memorable."

Ceci sighed, grateful for Lee's presence. She took her friend's hand and held it to her cheek. "Working now," she mouthed. "Thank you for coming."

Lee's voice sounded strangled. "Where else would I be, sweetie? Too many good memories to let you slip away. We have considerably more hell to raise."

Ceci could hear Brian was on the phone with J.J. "Seems more alert today," he said. "And that bastard Buchanan is in custody. He's cooling his ass in jail right now, and Zach is working on him. His story isn't very plausible, and he had means, motive, and opportunity. I think it's a lock. He's going away for a long, long time."

Ceci removed her hand from Lee's and tugged at Brian's shirt. "Alex?" she wrote on her pad. Brian broke off the conversation with J.J. and turned to Ceci.

"Alex was at your apartment the night of the fire. He was lurking around outside but when we got there, he acted like he was trying to save you instead of kill you. He was giving you CPR."

Ceci closed her eyes and concentrated hard. She tried to assemble the pieces of memories that had been jarred loose by two hits to the head and breathing what the doctors referred to as "products of combustion." Coherent thinking was almost impossible, but something didn't feel right.

A fragmented thought rose like a bubble to the surface. The dogs barking incessantly. Alex yelling her name and finally bursting through the door with Hector. Sirens.

She tapped the bed to get Brian's attention. "Alex saved me," she wrote.

Brian's face registered shock and disbelief as did Lee's when Brian showed her the pad. "That's what he says, too. He says you went to see him a few days ago, very upset about the last note. Is it true?"

Ceci squeezed Brian's hand once. "He said even though he'd been nasty to you, he didn't send the letters you were ranting about. He got worried and cased the condo a couple of times when I wasn't there to make sure you were okay. When he heard Thelma and Louise barking outside your door, he found Hector and Annah there, trying to get in, but their key wouldn't work."

Ceci wrote, "Changed locks."

"Alex says he and Hector broke in the door."

"Remember that," she wrote, her handwriting spidery with fatigue. "Felt breeze."

"Hector corroborates his story, but Alex isn't off the hook. When the dogs started carrying on after he left you for dead, he might have realized his plan wasn't going to work. So he covered himself. He said he saw someone leaving the condo about ten minutes before. Is that right? Did you have a visitor?"

Ceci struggled to remember. "Don't know," she wrote, and tossed the pad onto the bed in frustration.

"Do you remember anything else, honey? If Alex didn't do this, do you know who did?" Brian leaned in close.

"No." Drained from the effort of trying to recall details and writing what she could, she dropped the pen.

"It's okay, Ceci. We'll figure it out."

Exerting herself to the limit, she picked up the pen again. On the pad she scrawled, "Camera."

•

Ceci stirred from sleep as she heard Brian, Zach, and Lee speaking softly by the door of her room. "Camera?" Zach said, peering at the piece of paper with Ceci's quivery writing on it.

"I don't know what it could mean," Brian answered. "She has a big concussion as well as the smoke inhalation. I don't know if she's dreaming, remembering, or hallucinating."

Zach's voice was full of excitement. "It's none of those things. I know exactly what she means. I'm going over to the condo, and I'll be back as soon as I can."

•

True to his word, Zach returned to the hospital a couple of hours later, almost crowing with satisfaction. Ceci was in and out of awareness, but she heard snatches of conversation that began to release full and terrifying memories.

"*Devon?*" Brian said, incredulous.

"Yep. The camera shots are pretty clear. She disabled all the smoke alarms. Obviously she knew about the security system since she talked about it in one of the notes, but she missed the camera. It's tiny and buried in the bookcase in the living room. We could see almost everything she did and hear what she said. She's a real sick ticket, Brian. Ceci's lucky. She did a great job of delaying things, but Devon wasn't messing around. This was murder one stuff."

"What was she upset about?"

"You're kidding, right?" Zach said, disbelief in his voice. "You can't figure it out? It was all about you. She thinks Ceci stole you from her."

"God," Brian whispered. "Ceci always told me Devon still had feelings for me, but I thought Dev understood about her and me." He rubbed his eyes as Zach patted him awkwardly on the shoulder. "Ceci damn near died and it's all because of me."

"Well, men can be stupid where women are concerned. But we'll find her and this will all be in the rearview mirror within a few days."

Ceci trembled uncontrollably as memories overpowered her. She pounded on the bed rails and grabbed the pad of paper. "Where?" she wrote.

"Where is she?" Brian said, crossing the room to hold her in a firm, comforting embrace. "Do you know yet, Zach?"

"There's no sign of life at her house. Her car is gone. We're checking the airport. You know her. Any ideas?"

"No, but her ex-husband might. His name's Patton Carter. His family lives in South Carolina. Their daughter is there, too." Turning to Ceci again, he said, "Don't worry. She's gone."

I'll be long gone. Ceci heard as if from far away.

"She can't hurt you," Brian continued. "There's security outside the door, and somebody will be with you every minute. Your mom or your dad or my mom. J.J.'s coming down and Gigi's on her way, too. Of course, Lee's still here." Ceci attempted a smile. "I'll make sure everyone has a picture of Devon. She won't get near you. Even if she's around. Never again. You're safe."

Zach sighed. "Now the chief and I have to try to talk Buchanan out of a lawsuit. I'm not looking forward to it. I hate it when I'm wrong."

CHAPTER **FORTY-NINE**

Ceci awakened to find Alex standing by her bed, his hand covering hers. "Hi," he said quietly. "I'm glad to see you. You look a lot better than I thought you would."

"Your turn," Ceci rasped.

"For what?"

"To look like six miles of bad road," Ceci said, struggling to get enough air behind her words. "I'm sorry you were in the lock-up."

"I'm just glad you're okay," Alex said, and Ceci was struck by the sincerity she heard in his voice.

"Thanks, Alex," she said. "For everything. I'm sorry I accused you. It all fit. Devon's twisted, but she's smart, too."

"And I'm sorry I led her to you. I never would have done it if I'd known. I was pretty pissed at the way you responded to me when I came here, but I wouldn't put your life in danger. I know I'm a self-absorbed kind of guy...maybe a little egocentric..." Ceci giggled softly and then winced... "but I did and I do care about you."

"Whatever you felt, you got me out of there and started to bring me back to life." Ceci tried to clear her throat and picked up her writing pad. "I'm very, very grateful to you," she wrote. "I'm glad I lived to clear you. She wanted you to take the fall for her."

Alex patted her hand. "I know. And she damn near got her way. Hard to believe someone could be so devious." He turned his face away from Ceci. "I want to apologize for Nicolette, too," he said. "It was wrong. I hope we can be friends again someday."

"We'll get there," Ceci scrawled.

"Grab some more sleep now, Ceci. You still have some getting well to do."

He called me Ceci, she thought, as she lowered the head of the bed a few degrees. He's never done that before. It's nice.

•

"I don't know, honey," Brian said, his eyes droopy with fatigue as he kicked back in the reclining chair he'd slept in since Ceci had been released from ICU. "I think it went really well."

"What kinds of things did he ask?" Ceci choked out.

"It was kind of weird. The interview is when the chief asks some background questions. I was prepared to answer them, but since he already knows me so well, it was kind of hard for him to dig up something he was unfamiliar with. And I'd practiced my brains out."

"When?" Ceci murmured. "Ashley said you were practicing, but I never saw it. It worried me that you were spending so much time with me when the interview was coming up."

"I practiced with the guys I work with. They know the questions. They know the chief. They tossed me everything they could think of. They told me to be confident, not cocky. To be sure my résumé was perfect. All kinds of stuff. They really picked me apart."

His face clouded. "The only thing that might have tripped me up was the depression thing. I think I answered it well because I really am okay. And Alex."

Ceci sat up straight. "What about Alex?"

"I was on the squad run the night you got hurt."

"I know. I could hear you," Ceci said, her voice fading again.

"When I saw Alex giving you CPR, I wanted to kill him since I thought he set the fire in the first place. Rick kind of had to hold me back from him while Matt was working on you. The chief didn't like it when he heard about it. He understood it, but he didn't like it. I think I did well enough on the other stuff to overcome it. As I say, he's known me since I was a kid, and he knows this is what I live for. We'll see."

After all this, Ceci thought, I still might be the reason he doesn't get the job. Damn Devon!

"Alex came by," Ceci wrote on her pad, giving up any more attempts at speech.

"I sent him."

"Why?" she scribbled.

"The guy was a wreck. We actually had a long talk, and I think he had a couple of come-to-Jesus moments in the slammer. Now we know he was a victim, too, but he was really sorry about…what's her name? The one he left you for?"

"Nicolette," Ceci wrote. "He told me that, too."

"Yeah. He's mad he let you go. I sympathize, but he loses. I win." He flashed the smile that always made her knees turn to jelly, but then she remembered Devon had said the identical words. *I win.* She quivered, but refused the memory.

"Enough about him," Ceci wrote. "When will you know?"

"The other two candidates interview today. I should find out by the sixth."

"The day I was supposed to be in Maine," Ceci wrote. "Glad I'm here."

"Me, too. I want you right here when I get the news, no matter which way it goes."

"Want to be here. Love you."

"I love you, too," Brian said.

"Go to sleep," Ceci whispered.

Brian fell asleep almost immediately, with his head on the bed. Ceci rested her hand on his hair and fell into the slumber that comes when questions are answered and stress is gone.

CHAPTER **FIFTY**

"We'll spring you out of here in a couple of hours," Ceci's doctor said.

"Can't wait," Ceci croaked, making a wry face at the sound of her own voice. "But, Dr. Abbott, there's one thing I want to do before I leave. I want to meet Iris. She was in the ER when I was brought in. She talked to me. She told me where I was and to relax. That you were all going to take care of me. She had the kindest voice I've ever heard. Do you know if she's on duty now?"

The doctor looked perturbed. "Ceci, there's nobody on the emergency room staff named Iris. Nobody."

"But she talked to me. I couldn't see her, but she talked to me and I saw bright colors."

"I can't explain that."

"She was there."

Dr. Abbott looked around as if to see that no one could overhear her. "I'm going to tell you something I don't understand and probably shouldn't talk about. You're the fourth person in the last couple of years to tell me about Iris—and all I can say is there's no Iris. But you are at St. Raphael's. He's the archangel of healing. Maybe he sends Iris to help. I don't know. What I do know is in Greek mythology, she's supposed to be the messenger of the gods and has something to do with rainbows. Everyone I've talked to about this has mentioned bright colors. Unexplainable things happen sometimes. That's all I can say. You can call them miracles if you want. I would. I certainly wasn't sure you were going to survive, but you did. So maybe God, Raphael, and Iris were all working together.

"Now I want to talk about you," the doctor said, becoming all business once again. "The hoarseness you're experiencing should get better on its own, but it it persists, there's speech therapy and even surgery, if we have to."

"I'd rather skip that," Ceci said, smiling with only slight discomfort.

The doctor continued with discharge instructions and then paused. "I wish I could tell you more about what you really want to know, but I can't. I don't know anything about Iris, but if she came to help God or Raphael or just showed up on her own, accept that with gratitude and say thank you."

Ceci leaned back against her chair trying to digest Dr. Abbott's message, but she found it almost unbelievable. "I will—every day." Tears came to her eyes.

•

"Miss Myers, may I come in?" A man with the buzz cut men use to cover the fact they're balding appeared at the door. He was wearing a well-cut suit and wingtips. Behind roundish glasses, his nondescript blue-green eyes were clouded.

"Are you a reporter?" Ceci had had enough of the wall-to-wall coverage of her situation: "Former anchor at sister station fights for life after arson fire." "Hero newswoman felled in attempted murder. Person of interest disappears." Lots of video of the smoke-damaged condo and file footage of Ceci's rescue of Mandy. She was happy her friends Annah and Hector, Lee, Matt, and even Alex had had little to say for public consumption, and the doctors' briefings had been just that—brief.

"No," the man chuckled. "Not a reporter. I'm Patton Carter."

Startled, Ceci sat straight up in her chair, which caused a bout of coughing. "Come in. I'm astonished to see you." He was older than she expected, shorter and less attractive. Based on Devon's striking looks, her description of his popularity with the ladies, and Patton's aristocratic-sounding name, she'd expected a preppy Adonis.

"Not too much conversation on her end," the doctor warned Patton as she left the room.

"I promise." Patton pulled up another chair and seated himself opposite Ceci, looking at her intently. "I only wanted to tell you how incredibly sorry I am. You saved my child's life and Devon did this to you. It seems strange for me to come now. I should have looked you up after you dragged Mandy out of the Gulf, but Devon was adamant I stay away."

Patton sighed, his face lined and sad. "She's been…mentally ill for a long time. She was diagnosed with borderline personality disorder years ago and obviously it's become something much more. When she first met you, she couldn't say enough good things about you, but when you got mixed up with Brian, she veered in the opposite direction."

He shifted in his chair, wiping a bead of sweat from his hairline. "That's the way it is with this disorder. People who have it either idealize others or they despise them. Everything is perfect or it's garbage. And they often turn on a dime. Then they go for the jugular. But they don't usually try to kill people."

Ceci remembered Devon's voice: *Brian and I would have had the perfect family. Perfect.*

"I put up with it for a long time," Patton said, sighing. "She'd get some therapy and then she'd hate the therapist. We'd have to start over. She'd fuss over Mandy and then rage at her for minor discipline infractions. Our friends disappeared, because Dev was always accusing one of them of betraying her. The neighborhood kids didn't come over to play because she was so irrational about their families. I finally couldn't take it anymore and I bailed. I tried to take Mandy with me, but the judge sided with Devon. She can put on a good show when it's important."

"Was she always this way?" Ceci asking, laryngitis cracking and deepening her voice.

"She was mercurial, but not like this, of course. She seemed to get better when she moved back here. It was her home and I think she felt more secure. She was doing a great job at work and she'd made some friends. Your coming disturbed that. I never expected her to be violent, though. Inappropriate and hard to deal with, but not dangerous. Her doctor says this is a psychotic break."

"Do you know where she is? It scares me to think she might be around."

"I'm not sure, but I think she might be in Portugal. Her parents are the constant in her life and she might have wanted their comfort. The police here and in Charleston are on the hunt, and I think they'll find her there. Portugal extradites to the United States, so if they locate her, they'll probably send her back." Ceci stiffened. "She won't be free. She can't hurt you again."

Patton stood up, extending his hand. "I'm going back to Charleston to take care of Mandy. No more boarding school. It's the end of term, and I can put her into the local public school easily. It served its purpose keeping her away from her mother's illness, but she needs stability now. My family and I can provide it. Of course, Devon hated my folks, but they're good people and they love their granddaughter and she loves them, although Devon tried hard to convince her they were evil. Mandy's alive because of you, and I'll take good care of her. That's a promise. I'd like to keep in touch, if it's okay with you."

"Of course. I do have a vested interest in Mandy, and Devon even told me you were a good father. I'm sure she'll get through this with you and your family to help her. She's a smart, level-headed kid."

Within a few minutes, Brian entered the room with Ceci's wheelchair and her discharge papers. "Signed and sealed," he said. His megawatt smile seemed to light up the whole area. "Come on, honey. I'm taking you home."

A look of concern passed across Ceci's face.

"No, baby. Not back there. We're going to my home. *Our* home." Ceci remembered what Lee had suggested: *Move in with him.* It appeared that was what was going to happen—and she hadn't even had to ask. "There are a whole lot of people waiting for you there."

CHAPTER **FIFTY-ONE**

Ceci stood in the bride's room of the candlelit Key Chapel with her father as she waited to see Brian for the first time that day. Hunched down, Lee and Ashley straightened Ceci's hem one more time, as Mandy, in her first long dress, checked Ceci's veil. Ceci peeked out the window as Brian's firefighter brothers and sisters streamed into the tiny church on a perfect May evening. She exhaled with relief when she saw Gigi barreling up in her car, late as always. Nearly as beautiful as her sister, Gigi was tall, with a peaches-and-cream complexion, blue eyes, and vibrant red hair intensified by judicious use of L'Oréal's Light Cherry Auburn. Ceci grinned as Gigi hustled up the walk and slammed open the door to the bride's room.

"I wondered if you were ever going to post," Ceci said, with a familiar sense of consternation where Gigi was concerned. "These two have been here for an hour."

Gigi blew a gentle raspberry in Ceci's direction and turned to the other two bridesmaids and Mandy. "You're such overachievers," she chuckled. "Ceci, you know I've always been the dramatic one, recent events excepted, of course. I'm here now, and you look totally amazing, sis. Glowing. There's probably a word for it," she said, with the knowing look that passes only between sisters.

"Really? At this moment, I can't imagine what it would be." But there is, she thought. It's just not time to say it yet.

"Thank God. A first," Lee said sarcastically, as the whole group laughed out loud.

Her hands trembling a bit with excitement rather than anxiety, Ceci fiddled with the bodice of her strapless watered-silk column dress. A simple, waist-length Alençon lace Madonna veil topped her hair, which she wore pulled away from her face, its waves tumbling down to her shoulders. "These heels are killing me. Should have worn my running shoes." Her voice was still husky and might always be, but Brian found it appealing and sexy.

"No pain, no gain. Let's go get you married. Come on, Mandy, you lead off."

Ceci breathed in the intoxicating scent of roses and freesia—the same flowers Brian had sent her the morning after he'd said he loved her and that now made up her wedding bouquet. As she entered the chapel behind Mandy, Ashley, Lee, and Gigi, she was aware of new friends from her current station, where she produced the noon and evening news, some old friends from Orlando, and even her news director from Alabama. She was shocked to see Alex in the last row. He hadn't answered his invitation, so she'd assumed he'd be absent. He looked pensive and regretful. She caught a glimpse of Patton proudly watching Mandy and peripherally noticed Kimberly, smiling broadly, and all of Brian's family, including J.J., who stood beside his brother. She winked at her soon-to-be-brother-in-law Jack, who had Lainie balanced upright on his shoulder. But accompanying her dad down the aisle, only one face was clearly in focus: Brian's.

And she was again, as before, and as she always would be—ensorcelled—and carrying a wonderful secret she'd share with him as soon as they were alone.

DISCUSSION **QUESTIONS**

1. Have you ever fallen in love at first sight—or soon thereafter?

2. Have you ever known someone who had to make a choice between love and career? Which was chosen?

3. Why do you think Minnie and Kimberly are so different, even though they are mother and daughter? Why was Ceci closer to Minnie? And even to Annah?

4. Do Ceci's panic attacks feel real to you?

5. What did you think of Brian's family?

6. How will Ceci balance her life in the future? Might she change careers?

7. Who do you think Iris is?

ABOUT **THE AUTHOR**

Emily Wynne Stewart is a writer of fiction in a variety of genres, including beach and holiday reads and mainstream women's fiction.

As Gretchen S. Hirsch, she has had a long career as a nonfiction writer, with topics ranging from time management to the social-emotional needs of gifted children to football to business books related to communication, business English, difficult conversations, and wealth management.

She is also owner of Midwest Book Doctors, where she offers editorial assistance for fiction and nonfiction writers seeking representation or publication. She had spoken at professional meetings and writers conferences on time management for writers, effective communication, and developing a writing brand.

She looks forward to introducing you to the characters that populate her newest book, *Saving Ceci*, which proves that writing is writing, whether fiction or nonfiction and jumping between disciplines is possible.

Visit Emily and Gretchen online at www.GretchenSHirsch.com.